PENGUIN BOOKS

FOR REAL THIS TIME

FOR REAL THIS TIME

BETH REEKLES

PENGUIN BOOKS

PENGUIN BOOKS

UK | USA | Canada | Ireland | Australia
India | New Zealand | South Africa

Penguin Books is part of the Penguin Random House group of companies
whose addresses can be found at global.penguinrandomhouse.com

www.penguin.co.uk
www.puffin.co.uk
www.ladybird.co.uk

First published 2026

003

Text copyright © Beth Reekles, 2026

The moral right of the author has been asserted

The brands mentioned in this book are trademarks belonging to third parties

Penguin Random House values and supports copyright.
Copyright fuels creativity, encourages diverse voices, promotes freedom
of expression and supports a vibrant culture. Thank you for purchasing
an authorized edition of this book and for respecting intellectual property
laws by not reproducing, scanning or distributing any part of it by any
means without permission. You are supporting authors and enabling
Penguin Random House to continue to publish books for everyone.
No part of this book may be used or reproduced in any manner for the
purpose of training artificial intelligence technologies or systems. In accordance
with Article 4(3) of the DSM Directive 2019/790, Penguin Random House
expressly reserves this work from the text and data mining exception.

Set in 11/17pt Palatino LT Std
Typeset by Six Red Marbles UK, Thetford, Norfolk
Printed and bound in Great Britain by Clays Ltd, Elcograf S.p.A.

The authorized representative in the EEA is Penguin Random House Ireland,
Morrison Chambers, 32 Nassau Street, Dublin D02 YH68

A CIP catalogue record for this book is available from the British Library

ISBN: 978–0–241–71290–0

All correspondence to:
Penguin Books
Penguin Random House Children's
One Embassy Gardens, 8 Viaduct Gardens, London SW11 7BW

Penguin Random House is committed to a
sustainable future for our business, our readers
and our planet. This book is made from Forest
Stewardship Council® certified paper.

*For The hivE (née Gobble Gals, née Cactus Updates),
my very own D&D crew. Here's to the Svens!
Roll for awesome, stay originaL, love you always.*

*And once again, for my fellow weird kids who know an
escape into fandom is always there for you. So's this book.*

CHAPTER 1

My heart is pounding and my mouth feels dry.

This is it. It's happening. I'm *actually* going to do it.

We're stood together in the narrow corridor. The lights are low out here and the hum of the party in the next room feels distant, muted. Like it's just the two of us.

He leans in closer with a smile that's a borderline smirk on his handsome face, and caresses my jaw with his hand.

My breath catches. I can't believe it's finally about to happen, after all this time.

After months of flirting back and forth, going from tentative acquaintances, to friends, to now *this* . . .

The air is charged, electric, and my whole body is alight with it. If he leans in any closer, he'll be able to feel me trembling. The nerves, the excitement, the anticipation – it's all exactly as I imagined it.

He brushes my hair back from my face. It came loose from my braids when I was dancing.

'You're so beautiful,' he tells me, his voice low.

A thousand and one responses jumble together on the tip of my tongue, but my throat is too thick for me to speak. Nodding is all I feel capable of right now.

Then, in slow motion, he closes the last scrap of distance between us, his strong hand tilting my chin up. His body is hot against mine and when I press a palm flat against his chest I can feel his heart beating every bit as wildly –

And that's when I slip a dagger from the folds of my dress and stab him neatly between the ribs.

Hot, sticky blood cascades over my fingers as he stumbles back. 'What the –!'

As I look into his vivid green eyes they turn entirely to black. His face seems to shimmer and his huge wings flicker out of existence as the mystical façade begins to fall away. He staggers once, twice, drops to his knees and fumbles at his belt for the blades that were confiscated on our way into the ball.

'*Traitor*,' I hiss, as he collapses at my feet.

I lift the skirts of my ball gown to make sure I don't get blood on my pretty dress, and run deeper into the castle to find the rest of my adventuring party.

*

There's a cacophony of noise: shocked exclamations, stunned stammering and cries of outrage from the people at my table. We draw a few looks making such a commotion at a cafe on a Sunday afternoon, but my friends are too riled up to notice.

Jake throws his dice desperately, hoping to save his character from imminent death, but to no avail. He buries his face in his hands with a groan and, next to him, Max pats his shoulder in commiseration.

'Don't comfort him!' shouts Cerys, looking like she's going to lunge across the table to slap Max's hand away. She upsets an empty glass and mutters a quick apology before sitting back down. She settles for jabbing a finger towards Jake instead. 'You're a traitor! A shifter in our own ranks, a spy! And to think we trusted you! I gave you my *scrying opal* –'

Jake lifts his head with a sheepish smile and shrugs. 'I couldn't have you finding me out, could I?'

'And to think I was *rooting* for yours and Anissa's characters to get together, ugh!'

I'm about to gush about how proud *I* am of double-bluffing by going along with that subplot, when Max adds, 'Seriously! I thought you were going to have to *actually* kiss for a second there.'

Jake snorts and, though the idea of kissing my very platonic friend is genuinely laughable, my stomach swoops uncomfortably – as if *me* kissing *anyone* is so funny to them.

'HAHAHA!' I blurt. 'TOTALLY. CAN YOU IMAGINE?'

Cerys gives me an odd look but the boys have already moved on, and she falls into the rhythm of their conversation, bickering about all the times that Lord Syxos – Jake's character in our tabletop role-playing game – had pulled the wool over their eyes. My own character, Mida, a sorceress and former palace servant turned rebel spy, had clocked him from the start but, since I'm the gamemaster, I decided it was way more fun to wait for the perfect moment to pull the big reveal – for maximum effect.

Which, judging by the reactions around me, was *exactly* the right decision.

I take a sip of my coffee and find it's gone cold; I got too caught up in the gameplay, and Mida and Lord Syxos's fauxmance.

Although to be fair, it's easy for me to get lost in anything related to *Of Wrath and Rune*. It's been my favourite fantasy series for seven years and counting, with more books in the works and the latest season of the TV show about to start filming. It's even got its own Dungeons and Dragonsesque role-playing game, which Jake and I persuaded the others to play now our first year of sixth-form college is over and summer's finally here.

Being gamemaster is basically a dream for me. I get to flex my deep-cut knowledge of OWAR lore, craft exciting adventures for us to embark on, develop new characters to fit seamlessly into this fantasy universe – *and* I have friends to do it all with.

I'm still getting used to that last part. This is the first time I've ever really had friends.

It's surreal to realize just how drastically being part of the OWAR fandom has changed my life. But it's amazing, being surrounded by people I probably wouldn't have ever called friends if not for our mutual love of the books and the show. I'm no longer the weirdo outcast at college, the chronic loner nobody cared to really get to know.

Jake leans back in his seat with a sigh and says, 'Fair play, Anissa, you really pulled that off. I was dead convinced I'd be able to use Mida as a hostage to blackmail the others.'

'Now you're just dead,' I say, and everyone laughs. A little bubble of warmth rises in my chest at the sound.

'At least now we don't have to do all that pretend flirting.' He chuckles, pulling a face. 'It was getting kind of weird, right?'

And just like that, the bubble bursts, my heart plummets, and my smile freezes. I think I say something blithe in agreement, but my head is clamouring: *Wait, why was it weird? Did I mess it up? Was it that obvious I have no idea how to flirt, did I make a complete idiot of myself?*

Max imitates my character in a breathy, exaggerated voice: *'Oh, but my lord, you already have half my heart, what can I do but pledge you the rest?'* He raises a thick, dark eyebrow at Cerys and says playfully, 'I think if you spoke to me like that in real life, I'd have to break up with you.'

'A total ick,' she agrees, giggling, but she must catch something on my face because she quickly grabs my hand to squeeze. 'But it totally worked in the gameplay! It felt so on-brand for the world of OWAR!'

I turn my weak smile on her, not so sure I'm convinced.

If it's this obvious to my closest friends what a complete amateur I am when it comes to romance, how am I ever going to pull it off in the real world, when it matters?

I'm a little relieved I killed off Lord Syxos, if I'm honest. Not just because I had to play a double-bluff in character, or because the fake flirting was making me feel a bit sweaty, but because I find it so easy to get caught up in sweeping, epic romances when it comes to fiction. In real life? It's another story.

And as much as I love this fandom, it would've been really sad if my first kiss had all been part of some fantasy.

CHAPTER 2

The thing about always having been the weird kid at school, is that as much as you've spent years watching everyone else be normal from afar, it's still difficult to do it IRL.

Like, how many fire emojis are you supposed to react to your friends' fit checks with before it creeps them out? If you share a story about yourself to try and relate, is it building connection or just annoying them because you're supposed to be talking about *them*? Where is the line between being too much and not enough, and how the hell do *they* all seem to find it so easy?

How *are* you supposed to flirt with a boy? I don't even know what it feels like to fancy one, let alone act on it. For all the romance fanfics and books I bury my head in, the idea of doing it in real life (and probably – okay, DEFINITELY – humiliating myself) makes me shudder.

Especially now I know I can't even pull it off inside the fantasy world of our tabletop role-play game. Ugh. *Roll for romance? Critical fail, Anissa . . .*

Determined to not make things any weirder than I apparently already have, I shake all that off and tell Jake, 'I'm sorry. I know you put a lot of work into Lord Syxos.'

He shrugs it off, as unbothered as ever. 'Ah, it's okay – I always knew being a traitor in your midst was a risky choice. I've got a backup character ready to go,' he adds brightly, eyes lighting up. 'I'm going to be a chaos goblin. Well – the character's an orc cleric, not an *actual* goblin, but you know what I mean. I did consider being the *real* Lord Syxos, imprisoned in the palace due to his divided loyalties, but –'

'Ooh, I like that idea! I can definitely work it into the story.' And just like that, my head is already buzzing with ideas for the next part of our campaign. *If Lord Syxos has been taken prisoner, we should head to the dungeons to rescue him, and inevitably get caught up in a battle with the prince's guards . . .*

The rush of excitement I get makes me feel giddy. There's just *so much* to love when it comes to OWAR: the visceral world building, the immersive story, the layers of lore. But the best part is the characters, and Jake's suggestion gives me the perfect excuse to add my favourite into our game; I've been dying to find a way to bring him in.

Prince Kai Osterion. A young man born with corrupted magick, he's quiet, aloof, overlooked by his ruthless family and treated warily by everyone around him, but duty-bound to his position.

I'm fully aware he's a niche favourite character to have. His chapters in the books mainly serve as a gateway to the rest of the palace and his visions are basically a plot device to show us what's happening across the realm, or to act as foreshadowing. And with the TV show a few storylines behind the books, he's only *just* gotten cast in it as a proper role for the upcoming series. (Rude, I've been ROBBED of Kai content for too long.)

But Kai's pain as an outcast, his conflict between who he is and who he could have – *should have* – been, his struggle to be accepted and fit in at court . . . I get it. It feels like seeing parts of my soul laid bare in a way I couldn't explain on my own.

OWAR is important to me – but characters like Kai? He makes me feel a bit less alone. This entire fandom does.

My thought spiral is interrupted by the others packing up their things – I hadn't even noticed we were ready to go, or how long we'd been here.

This happens sometimes. Loads of my school reports have accused me of 'daydreaming too much in class', although my grades were always good enough for me not to get in any *real* trouble for it.

Since Cerys brought me into her group of friends at college and I met Max and Jake, I've been trying to make a conscious effort not to let my head get away from me, but it still catches me off guard no matter how hard I try.

Cerys is busy gathering up the miniature figurines she painstakingly painted for us; Jake stops recording the session on his phone (he keeps saying he wants to turn it into a podcast, but he's still down a 'how to' rabbit hole on that); and Max folds up his map and rule book – he's the one keeping us all honest during gameplay.

I scramble to grab the character sheets I made, shoving them unceremoniously into my bag. Cerys places a hand on Max's arm, saying something too soft for me to catch, and he smiles and nods before kissing her cheek. Cerys blushes, smiling.

They're an unbearably sweet couple. The kind of epic, love-can-overcome-anything stuff like I read about. It's almost unfair that they exist in real life like this – they're such couple goals.

Even the story of how they got together is like

something out of a romcom. Love triangles and yearning and a classic mistaken-identity trope . . . *Ugh, I want that.*

Even if it feels wildly out of reach.

I avert my eyes, feeling like I'm staring too much. Jake, on the other hand, oblivious as ever, leans in to interrupt their moment. 'You're giving me a lift home, right?'

'Yeah, course,' says Max. Then he adds sharply, 'But you're still not coming to the cinema with us. It's *date night*, remember?'

'I wouldn't dare!'

Cerys coughs to cover her laugh, and I try (and fail) to smother a giggle against my hand. Jake has such golden retriever energy. Sometimes he gets so carried away by his eagerness to hang out with his best friends that he doesn't notice they're trying to, you know, leave so they can snog in private.

While Max claps Jake on the shoulder to chivvy him along, Cerys gives me a hug. 'Are you sure Max can't give you a lift home, too?'

'No, that's alright! Really. I've already bought a return bus ticket anyway.' I live on the other side of town to the boys, and I don't want to put them out. Like Jake, I'm also not great at understanding social cues – years of being an outcast means I often feel like

I'm overstaying my welcome. Cerys has told me plenty of times that's not the case, but I'm sure she's mostly just being polite.

'Okay. Well, I'll see you tomorrow, bright and early? First day of work experience!' She squeals, giving me one last squeeze, and I force myself to smile back.

Yay, work experience. A big scary new situation where I have to impress people, whoo!

Cerys's dad knows someone who works for a local TV studio, and he managed to blag us an internship in the art department for the summer. Cerys fell in love with set design when she first watched OWAR and, since we're both studying art for A level, she roped me into this job, too. She was vague about which show we'd be working on, though I'm kind of hoping it's *Doctor Who* – they film tons in Cardiff.

I'd wanted to say no, but it was tricky when she made it sound like such a done deal. Plus, Cerys was so excited about it, and I was *clearly* supposed to share the sentiment . . .

What would Mida do? Well, no question how my role-play character would tackle this – she'd dive right in, feet first, and forge ahead. She'd be spinning it into something *good*, relishing a challenge.

So far, the only 'good' spin I've got is that it means Cerys *has* to spend time with me this summer, and won't forget all about me without college keeping us in each other's orbit. The rest of the girls are away, so it's not like there's even a stacked social calendar of plans they feel obliged to invite me along to.

'It's going to be *so* amazing,' Cerys gushes. I don't think she can hear the gears whirring in my head, and I'm obviously doing a great job of masking my insecurities because she just keeps beaming at me. 'This could be the making of us, Nis! Tomorrow, work experience – next stop, Hollywood!'

'So cool,' I manage to say, feeling a bit ill.

I wish I had her self-assurance. I'm not sure what I want to study at uni yet, or even *if* I want to go, but Cerys has waxed lyrical about how good this placement would be for our futures, and my parents said the same thing. It was hard to argue with that. Besides, it's only for a couple of weeks until the end of summer.

So I promise to see her bright and early tomorrow, do a last sweep of our table to make sure no dice got left behind, then make my way to the bus stop.

What would Mida do? She'd be planning a killer outfit, forming plans and backup plans. I'd be drafting bits of dialogue for her, feeling her confidence expand my own chest.

But my thoughts turn instead to Prince Kai. His imposter syndrome is feeling a lot more relatable than

Mida's boldness right now. And just like that, my fingers are itching to write something and I'm opening up a new note on my phone, unable to wait until I'm home at my laptop, and do what I do best: emotional catharsis to numb myself to scary feelings via fanfiction through the eyes of Kai Osterion.

It might be a nerdy escape from real life, but in times like this, it's my lifeline.

CHAPTER 3

Red Wings Studios consists of a bunch of huge, off-white warehouses that seem to spring up out of nowhere. It's pretty nondescript, except for a dragon emblem and the studio name printed on one building at the front. The car park is tiny, too, with just a couple of men in high-vis vests milling about, not paying Cerys's blue Vauxhall Corsa much attention.

I smooth my sweaty palms over my trousers. They're my old school uniform ones and the smartest thing I own to create a professional-looking outfit for my first day; Cerys insisted we had to make a good impression.

Well, what she actually said was, 'My FUTURE is on the line!' So, same difference.

I pull down the sun visor to give myself a once-over: without my usual smudge of kohl eyeliner, my hazel eyes look less piercing, less *me*. Or less the 'me' I try to be these days, anyway . . . My shoulder-length dark hair is straightened to within an inch of its life, but otherwise I still look like me – brown skin, button nose, gap in between my front two teeth. Just a polished, bland version.

I look like the person I tried to be at school so that I might fit in better, so people wouldn't avoid me and laugh behind my back. (Spoiler alert: it never worked.)

Cerys, also in her old school trousers and with her blonde hair in a slicked-back bun, was unusually nervy on the drive here, her knuckles white around the steering wheel – although, granted, she's only just got her licence, so that could be a factor, too . . .

But once we're out of the car, she turns to me with her hands braced against the roof. Her thin face looks paler than usual as she says, 'Okay, so I may have told you a *teensy* white lie.'

A knot immediately forms in my stomach. 'About what?'

'We haven't exactly secured the work experience placement . . . *yet*.'

And then the whole story comes spilling out, so fast I can barely follow it. Her dad's connection doesn't even work at this studio anymore. They only *mentioned* that some TV show was setting up to film here after their original location was forced to close; it was all very hush-hush but Cerys's dad thought she would be interested. Thus began her hare-brained scheme to work on some major TV set.

'But it's okay! I have a plan,' she declares, hands grasping my arms to placate me before I can even ask what show it is. It was easy to tell myself to go along with this when Cerys was excited, but now her nerves are only amping up my own and I can't help it when an incredulous laugh bursts out of me.

'Cerys! Your last *plan* was to become the perfect OWAR fangirl and ergo Jake's dream girlfriend, until you discovered you'd been flirting up a storm on Discord and fallen in love with *Max*, not Jake.'

Cerys squirms. 'Yes, but it all worked out in the end, didn't it? Anyway, this one is way better, I promise! Step one: we look like smart, sensible, creative young women, not crazed fangirls. *Check*. Step two: we ask them nicely to give us work experience because we are dedicated art students, *and not crazed fangirls*.'

'Okay ... Except you've tracked down this show's new top-secret filming location, which is kind of giving –'

'We'll just glaze over that bit.'

'Shouldn't we have CVs or something?'

'Way ahead of you!' She fishes some papers out

of her bag to brandish at me. 'If anyone asks, you volunteer to help with rescue dogs. I stretched the truth about Harley just a *teensy* bit. She might be your pet but she *was* a rescue, after all. And you do pick up her poo.'

'I'm really not sure about this, Cer–'

'It'll help you figure out if you want to do art at uni!' Her eyes are wide and round and pleading, now, and I grimace – not because of her attempt to convince me, but because the pressure of uni feels too real.

Then she takes a deep breath and pulls out the big guns, quoting her favourite character from OWAR – Lady Adanna di Silver – when she has a serious heart-to-heart with her devoted bodyguard Devon in season four.

'You are always by my side. And I know I'm asking a lot from you but, truly, I cannot do this without you. So I must ask you once more, my dearest Dev – er, Anissa. Will you come with me?'

Goddammit. She really knows how to hit a girl in the feels.

I sigh, and Cerys's face lights up, already knowing she's won.

I respond with another quote, one of her favourite lines from the series. 'Until the end.'

*

The studio's front doors look so tiny against the massive scale of the building, and the reception inside is ... disappointingly nondescript. Undeterred, Cerys goes right up to the man at the desk.

'Hello!' she chirps. 'Sorry to disturb you. We're here to see Danielle Poulter, Lead Set Designer. We're responding to an open call for assistants?' While her posture is all cool confidence, Cerys's voice ticks up slightly at the end as she starts to lose her nerve. I narrow my eyes at her – the name sounds familiar, but I can't place it ... A faint blush creeps up Cerys's cheeks but the receptionist seems too distracted by his screen to notice she is totally bluffing.

'Hmm ... I can't find anything in the schedule about that for today ... Sorry, ladies, it's all been a bit chaotic here, lots of stuff falling through the cracks.' He grabs the landline and dials anyway, and my heart is beating so fast I think I might be sick. 'Hi, Lisa, is Danielle around? I've got a couple of young women here asking about – oh, right, okay. Will do!'

He puts the phone down and tells us, 'If you can just sign in, Lisa's going to be over to collect you in a mo.'

A guest book is pushed towards us and then he busies himself untangling lanyards and passes. I pause before following Cerys's lead, signing myself in, deciding I can't very well let her do this all on her own.

Mida would *never* abandon one of her own mid-scheme.

Just then a door bursts open to reveal a frazzled-looking woman with frizzy hair who pins us both with a look. Lisa – I'm assuming – is wearing two pairs of glasses (one on her face, the other up on top of her head), has three headsets draped around her neck and a whole separate earpiece clipped over one heavily-pierced ear. Her jeans are ripped and stained, and there's chalk on her black T-shirt and some bright blue tape stuck to her boot.

In hindsight, our school uniforms were not the vibe.

'Come on then, you two, no time to waste! We've been run off our feet all morning as it is.'

She's already marching off, and we trip after her down a series of impossibly high-ceilinged corridors that look as bland as the reception area. The flooring becomes laminate instead of carpet, the walls plain greyish-white plaster, and the temperature drops.

Cerys whispers, 'I'm starting to think this might be a bad idea. Do you think we'll get in actual trouble?'

I think back to our OWAR role-playing game; I'd have definitely rolled a deception check already. But what would Mida say, a spy in the depths of the enemy's palace?

'It's not *our* fault they didn't ask more questions,' I tell Cerys firmly. 'They can hardly arrest us for trespassing when they *invited* us in.'

She squeezes my clammy hand in reply, just as Lisa takes us through a door that opens into a cavernous room that seems to stretch on for ages. It looks part office, part storage room and part . . . tavern?

Wait. What is this?

There are three fake walls against a bright blue backdrop, with real windows, a bar, several round tables scattered with stools and chairs, and a large cardboard box of tankards. One wall of the tavern is still under construction, surrounded by people in hard hats with spirit levels and drills. Miscellaneous pieces of wood and furniture are strewn across the room, and there's a massive table nearby covered in diagrams. On one stretch of wall, sketches of a tavern are pinned up. There are close-ups, Post-its covered in scribbles, and wider views from different angles, and . . .

I see a distinct antler motif that makes my brain screech to a halt.

WAIT. This can't be . . . ?

Cerys didn't actually . . . ?

I snatch at her arm, my eyes practically falling out of my head. 'Tell me this isn't –?'

'Please,' she hisses, 'be cool!'

Holy shit. We're on the actual set of *Of Wrath and Rune.*

I gawk at the tavern-in-progress, imagination running wild. Is it run by rebels out near the Gilded Glade, a place for the heroes to gather and plan their next move? It's surely too rough-and-ready to be anywhere in the Capitol. I can totally imagine the Moonwalker with his long, pale blonde hair and his dark cloak, one hand on a mug of ale and another on the hilt of his dagger, and grizzled Rogdan reclined with his feet on a table, drunk and singing folk songs. I'm already thinking about the number of fanfictions I could write, turning a fleeting moment of eye contact across the bar between the brooding Moonwalker and righteous Lady Adanna di Silver into tens of thousands of words of delicious, slow-burn romance . . .

Probably with a 'there's only one bed' trope and the pillow wall they build between them that inevitably will be crossed in the night. A classic.

I can't breathe, I'm so excited to see it up close like this. It's magical. Surreal. Brilliant! Eyes wide, my jaw hits the floor and I don't bother to pick it up; my whole body is practically *vibrating* with the need to run over and inspect it all up close. I'm bouncing on the balls of my feet like I *might* just actually do that.

Cerys nudges me, cringing. '*Please*, Nis!'

The unspoken *tone it down* feels like a gut punch back to reality, where we've snuck into a TV studio to get work experience. Where this *matters* to Cerys – for her love of OWAR, sure, but for her big dreams for the future, too.

And silly, too-in-her-head me, is going to spoil it all.

Lucky for Cerys, I've had years of practice at closing off that socially unacceptable part of me, and I bottle it all up just in time for Lisa to finally stop near the table of diagrams and turn to us.

She pushes her glasses on top of her head where they join the other pair in her wild curls. 'You're a lot younger than I was expecting ...' She blinks a few times, as if only just seeing us properly for the first time. 'Oh God, I'm all for a little bit of padding on your CV, but come on, girls! This is ridiculous. You can't be more than eighteen!'

'Er, we aren't,' I say. There's no point lying now.

Cerys reaches into a smart black leather handbag she's obviously borrowed from her mum and hands over the CVs she made for us. 'We're art students from a local college. We, um, we thought –'

'That you'd just swan in here and get hired on the spot?' Lisa scoffs, but takes the CVs anyway. She grabs a pair of glasses and rams them on to her nose. Her eyes dart rapidly back and forth and then settle briefly on me; I regret not bothering to ask Cerys *exactly* what she put on my CV.

Is she about to call security to frogmarch us out? *Can* we get in actual trouble for this?

What if I'm, like, blacklisted from being able to watch OWAR ever again?

Finally, Lisa sighs. 'Listen, girls, I appreciate your moxie but I really don't have time for this. We're already short-staffed: moving production from Leeds to Cardiff meant we lost a lot of local talent and we're still scrambling to fix that, on top of going ahead with filming as normal. Executives and their damn schedules –' One of her headsets crackles with noise, and she mutes it. 'Let me guess – you're *huge* fans of the show.'

'I wouldn't say we *aren't* fans . . .' Cerys offers.

'Right. Sure. But we're already behind, and neither of you have any industry experience –'

'But –' Cerys starts.

'We could –' I try.

'Alright, Lise? How's it looking? Bloody hell, this isn't too shabby, is it!' booms a voice out of nowhere. It's jarringly familiar but even after I turn around to look, it takes me several seconds to process. It's Daxys! Greater Fae warrior and ex-palace guard who fights with the good guys! Well – I guess, *technically*, it's Brayden Brown, the actor who plays him.

He's perfectly cast: six-and-a-half feet tall, barrel-chested with a buzz cut and huge muscles, he pulls off 'intimidating strongman' fantastically. But he's beloved by the fandom for being really cool and nice IRL too, always making time for Q&As and posting funny videos.

Right now he stands about three feet away – *three feet away! From us! Actual real-life Daxys!* – with his hands on his hips and a broad smile on his face that makes his eyes crinkle at the corners. He's not in costume, just athletic gear with a towel slung over one shoulder.

I did technically meet him at Comic Con a few weeks ago. Me, Jake, Cerys, Max and our college friend Chloe all went. Chloe was there for her Twitch channel but the rest of us all had OWAR cosplay on, and we got a group photo with Daxys. The whole interaction cost us fifty quid and only lasted a few minutes. It's a blur, now I think back to it. I vaguely remember him greeting Max by name, having met him before at previous cons, and then stumbling out afterwards with Jake clinging to me and gushing about how brilliant he is.

A muscle twitches in Lisa's cheek, but then she softens. 'Brayden, hi. Hasn't Danielle been clear enough about you *not* making a nuisance of yourself?'

'Just thought I'd see if you needed any help . . .'

Lisa shakes her head. 'She's not here, so you can

take that little schoolboy crush elsewhere. I'm up to my eyeballs in it as it is, without babysitting you as well.'

'Oh yeah? More newbies to onboard?' He turns to us, then, smile at the ready, does a small double-take. 'Hang on, don't I –?'

'Work experience chancers,' Lisa says quickly, trying to step between us. She looks back at us warily, like we're going to throw ourselves at Brayden's feet begging for a selfie or an autograph. To be fair, I am close. 'I'm dealing with it.'

'No, I know you guys, don't I?' He frowns, and my mouth is dry and all I can think is a single, screaming thought: *THERE IS NO WAY DAXYS REMEMBERS US FROM COMIC CON OMG OMG OMG!!!!* Jake is literally never going to recover when I tell him.

Cerys, luckily, is coherent enough for the both of us. 'Er, yeah. Comic Con in London, and the Cardiff one last October. My boyfriend is Max, the guy with the great Moonwalker cosplay?'

'Moonwalker Max! Yes!' Brayden snaps his fingers, grinning, and then turns to me. 'You were wearing those sick antlers for a Téiglin cosplay! And you guys have that friend, the tall fella with the glasses and cool poster collection.'

'That's him! I mean, us! I mean, yes!' I blurt.

Jake is officially going to *die*.

'You're here for work experience, then?' he asks, causing Lisa to groan.

'C'mon Brayden, you *know* we don't do work experience placements.' She glances at us briefly. 'It's not personal. Someone stole props for resale when we filmed season four, and someone else leaked storylines. Speaking of which, *someone's* clearly leaked our new filming location . . .'

'Aw, go on, Lise. I can vouch for these two. Plus, you should see the Téiglin antlers they made. Like they came right off set!'

Cerys flushes with pride; she made them as part of our art coursework. I only borrowed them for my costume. With a sudden burst of confidence, suddenly *wanting* this – for Cerys's sake more than mine – I say, 'It'd just be for a few weeks for the summer holidays, until we go back to college. Please? I promise, we're hard workers and *really* reliable. And we already know so much about the show . . .'

All three of Lisa's headsets start going off at once and she caves, throwing up her hands. 'Fine! Fine. We need all the help we can get seeing as those girls from *Doctor Who* haven't shown up. I'll have someone take you both to HR to fill out the paperwork. If this backfires, Brayden, it's on your head, d'you hear me? And I'll make sure all of production knows that. *Including* Danielle.'

He crosses his heart, then stage whispers to us, 'Don't let me down then, girls, eh? You heard the boss.'

While Brayden wanders over to the tavern set to get a better look, Lisa beckons someone over to ferry us down another set of corridors. Cerys and I link our arms together as we're told in a bored, rapid-fire monotone about protocol and NDAs.

'The boys are never going to believe this,' Cerys breathes.

'If anybody could pull this off, it'd be you,' I reply.

'No – it'd be *us*.'

CHAPTER 4

The first couple of days on set are a whirlwind of instructions and trying hard not to get lost. People talk about things like call sheets and night shoots, choreography practice, meetings with executive producers and the writers' room. It feels like something straight out of a movie.

I guess it practically is.

Lisa had us email her a portfolio of our artwork so she could decide where best to place us. Cerys has the edge over me: her passion really shines through her OWAR fanart, so she gets placed with the design team, handed some sketches and put to work painting scenery.

I'm helping with set dressing, which turns out to involve unpacking the cardboard box of tankards. They're lightweight and cheap but cleverly painted to look authentically aged, and they need to be placed very precisely around the tavern to give it a lived-in feel.

Cerys gives me a sympathetic grimace when we're both sent on an afternoon tea run. 'I'm sorry, Nis. I feel like I dragged you into this and they've got you organizing the kitchen cupboards.'

'Are you kidding? I LOVE it!'

I do – apparently the tavern *is* going to be a pivotal new location in series six for the heroes, just like I'd imagined. Obviously it's cool to feel like I'm getting an inside scoop – but more than that, it makes me feel like a real, genuine *part* of this world. It's as if I'm bringing my fanfictions or our TTRPG campaign to life.

It's so easy to immerse myself in the *feeling* of the scenes to come, to picture the characters I know so well in this space – bickering, bantering, healing wounds and building relationships . . .

I'm already obsessed, and dreading September when this all has to end.

The tavern set is like a living, breathing thing and it's a thrill to take it from concept to reality. I'm so overwhelmed that I get to be part of it, so grateful to Cerys for pushing me into this, that I know for a fact: this job is going to be the best thing to ever happen to me.

*

Jake, as predicted, is in absolute anguish.

'I'm in literal *anguish*, Anissa,' he tells me over FaceTime as I try and fail to tidy up my room. Mostly, I'm just rearranging stuff into different piles I'll put away *properly* later. 'I can't believe you wouldn't think to ask me, your *best* friend, the biggest OWAR fan you know, to do work experience with you.'

I point out the flaws in that statement in order. 'One, that's mighty bold of you to assume you're my best friend, when I know for a fact I'm not yours.'

'You are!' he insists. Then he adds, 'You're solidly in my top three best friends, and I love you all equally.'

'Mm-hmm. Two, I think you'll find that *I'm* the biggest OWAR fan *you* know ... And three: explain how you were going to work in set design or the art department when you can't draw to save your life?'

He grumbles melodramatically, but soon enough ends up talking about his celebrity crush Brayden Brown again, because of course he does. Jake's still moony-eyed about the fact Brayden remembered him, and called him 'tall'.

'We probably won't even see much of him,' I interject, giving up on the concept of tidying my room to flop down on my bed. 'Or any of the actors, really. It's all behind-the-scenes stuff so far. We're probably not even allowed to talk to them.'

'Dream with me, Anissa! Go on, who'd be top of your list? To meet, I mean.'

I open my mouth but pause – because I know the name on my lips is *not* one Jake is going to expect.

Kai, obviously.

So far, we've only got scraps of scenes in the season five trailer to go off, but the guy playing him, Callum Denver, seems promising so far, and my online fandom friends seem to agree he's well cast. I'd be more excited to see him performing the role than hanging out with the actor himself, but I can't wait to see if he *does* live up to the hype I've built around the character.

I don't think I could bear it if he ruins Kai for me.

'Top three, then,' Jake suggests, mistaking my hesitation.

'Um, I guess Lady Adanna and the Moonwalker. It'd be cool to see if they have as much chemistry off-screen.'

Luckily for me, Jake gets too distracted fantasizing about what he'd do in my shoes to ever ask for my third. He's too busy joking, 'The neurospicy curse of decision paralysis!' before listing his dreams of meeting basically the entire cast.

By the time we say goodnight and hang up, I draw my curtains against the summer sunset, bathing my room in a peachy glow that feels like being wrapped in cotton wool. Then I drag my laptop towards me to click idly around all the tabs I've got open.

Cerys and I agreed not to tell anyone that we got the work experience on set. Well, we agreed not to tell anyone *except* for the boys. And our families, obviously, since we've had to bring home some documents for them to co-sign as we're legally minors ... And then Cerys told the girls from college, because she said they're not in the fandom anyway so they wouldn't really care.

But from now on we're going to have to be so careful not to do anything that'll get us removed from set. Lisa reminded us we can't sneak selfies with cast members in the background, and they're on high alert for any storyline leaks. Plus, if we get fired, it might damage Cerys' chances of working in the industry in the future. I don't want to be responsible for that.

Anyway, we're not telling anyone else. Especially not our online OWAR friends.

Speaking of, I haven't checked Discord lately ...

The group Cerys initially introduced me to is just for local OWAR fans. There are dozens of other ones out there, though, and I even found a server dedicated to my favourite character. He has his own subreddit, too. There's not always a lot going on in there since there's limited new content about Kai and not a lot of dedicated fans like me – but tonight, the tab is alive with notifications.

I dive in greedily, and lose myself in my online community.

OWAR Discord Kai-rry On My Wayward Son

General

@therunestar
I'm SOBBING, the studio they film OWAR at has officially gone under? Like, *weeks* ago, and we're only just finding out? What does this MEAN? They're supposed to start filming s6 any day now!!!

@rubytherapscallion
source?

@osterionprincess1
I saw some rumours on TikTok they're moving filming to Scotland

@osterionprincess2
I HOPE SO!!

@rubytherapscallion
OP2, you live in Manchester.

@osterionprincess2
EXACTLY

@therunestar
Guys seriously I'm really worried, what if OWAR is shutting down filming altogether?! Like they've only JUST cast Callum Denver to play Kai and now he's already talking about auditioning for other roles... It was all in his Reddit AMA the other day

@wrathfulqueen93
sure there's a good explanation?! plus they've basically ignored Kai's existence so far in the show so maybe his role's still really minor

@osterionprincess1
literally OBSESSED with anything Callum Denver does at this point tbh, it all feels like more of an insight into Kai and how he'll be as him!!!

@osterionprincess1
did NOT love that AMA though ... hate to say it, but does anyone else think he came off kind of rude?

@therunestar
I'll literally never forgive him if he gives Kai a crap reputation by being some kind of Hollywood diva lol

@rubytherapscallion
omg no I thought he was hilarious, love his sense of humour – felt like he was playing into his character!

@osterionprincess2
That's how I read it too!

@ladyanissadishipper
hey I'm just catching up on all this ... somehow missed the reddit ama?! can someone drop me the link pls? sure the studio thing is nothing to worry about ...

r/TheOfficialOWAR

u/TheOfficialOWAR   3 days ago

Ask Me Anything with Callum Denver! (Prince Kai Osterion)

Hey everyone, Callum aka Kai here – that magickal OWAR prince you all love to hate. Not as moody as the Moonwalker, but trying to be. Please don't ask for spoilers for s5, production have a trained sniper ready if I try to spill the beans. (Kidding. Mostly.) AMA. – C

u/runewarrior012
How does it feel playing a character nobody cares about?

> **u/TheOfficialOWAR**
> Harsh, dude. Rune Warrior coming in hot with a death blow. – C

u/justadaxysstancalledstan
Can we expect a bigger role from you/Kai in the new seasons!?

> **u/TheOfficialOWAR**
> Perhaps. – C

u/whackygoblin_
Do you know how Kai's story ends? The whole character arc? In a previous AMA with key actors they mentioned they met with the authors to discuss things like that. (I know the authors are still anonymous but ARE they a cast member?! Can you tell us?!) Hope they're setting you up to be the next big villain!

u/TheOfficialOWAR
'Key' actors being a key word there. But also, may I remind you about the sniper – my lips are sealed. Always nice to hear fans want me to be a villain, though. – C

u/eldritchlad
What do you think about the headcanon that Kai is ND-coded???

u/TheOfficialOWAR
That's exactly how I understood his character, too. I had a coach who's worked with characters this nuanced before. We really tried to incorporate the idea that his corrupted magick is representative of his specific neurodiversity and keep his character authentic to both the fans, and the writers' intentions. Hopefully I've done it justice. – C

u/eldritchlad
I'M SURE YOU HAVE!!!! I got diagnosed a while ago (autism and ADHD) and relate so hard to a lot of Kai's scenes. (The constant overstimulation he gets with his visions? How he has to recover from them afterwards kind of like you have to after a meltdown? Everyone around him acting like he just needs to 'get a grip' and never understanding HOW his magick affects him bc it's sooo easy for those who don't have magick? Mood, lol.) Anyway, it's really helped me process some stuff. Honestly can't thank you enough for taking that on board!

u/TheOfficialOWAR
That means a lot. Thanks, Eldritch Lad. – C x

u/daisymaeflowers
Saw on your IG story that you're auditioning for some new roles, exciting! Hope you get that Bridgerton one! Are you taking a step back from OWAR?

u/TheOfficialOWAR
Wow, stalker. My manager took those posts down within about twenty minutes. Good sleuthing work, Daisy Mae. – C

u/TheOfficialOWAR
Things are in the works, though. Potentially. But I'm not going anywhere when it comes to OWAR. I've only just started, after all – C x

u/rubytherapscallion
Hope you know how much we are OBSESSED with your character Callum????

u/TheOfficialOWAR
Is that a question??????? – C

CHAPTER 5

'What happened to everybody working from home on Fridays?' Cerys grumbles, then winces. 'Ew, God, I sound like my *mum*.'

The traffic on our way to the studio is so horrendous that Cerys has to turn down the radio and lean all the way forward in her seat to concentrate better. Which at least means she doesn't mind that I'm not in a chatty mood, my brain still full of the AMA I read last night.

How is this Callum Denver guy ever going to portray sweet, misunderstood, complicated Kai if he's that shallow and dismissive? Although I don't exactly blame him for being a *little* bit curt in his AMA responses – they walked a line of deadpan humour and seriously annoyed – because some of those people were *mean*. (Worse still, they were mean about *Kai*.)

I guess I can relate to people assuming they know everything about you based off what they see. There was a rumour at my old school that I was an *actual* witch, just because I wear an evil-eye bracelet my nan gave me. I had no end of people dodging me in hallways, picking me last in PE, coughing *freak* under their breath when they passed me in the corridor. They saw a quiet girl who didn't have friends and liked books, and they made a lot of snap judgements.

It's a bit sad, really, that even someone who's a bit of a celebrity can't escape that.

I can't explain why, but I'm suddenly possessed by the overwhelming urge to find out more about this actor. I think I'm terrified he won't actually do Kai justice, but it feels like if I can convince myself I know Callum well enough, I'll know if I can trust him with the role.

Which, sure, *my* opinion won't make a difference to the fact he's already been hired – and even filmed a whole season so far. But hey, fandoms and the internet can be an unstoppable force when they want to be . . .

I shudder, remembering the viral images of Sonic the Hedgehog's teeth.

Anyway, it's what Mida would do. She's a spy, so she'd find out everything she could about an interloper. Know thy enemy, and all that.

For the first time ever, I call up Callum Denver's Instagram. Everything I've seen about him so far has been second-hand, decanted into Discord by other people. His first pinned post is stills from the recent season five promo, including one of him looking right down the barrel of the camera. That one's been doing the rounds *a lot* in the Kai fan forums and it's been a big hit already; he looks the part at least. Then there's a red-carpet event he attended in London a few weeks ago, a brand deal promoting cashmere socks . . .

So, you know: super relatable stuff.

I look for a long while at that last photo. It shows a stocky teenage boy sat sideways in a plush green leather armchair in some fancy library. His legs are dangling over the arm with his socked feet on display, his brown hair stylishly tousled, and a wide and friendly smile on his face. It's hard to reconcile *this* boy with the one being sort of snarky in that AMA.

It's also funny seeing him with brown hair. The Osterions are ginger; he must dye his for the show. He looks so far removed from that season five promo I've seen reposted a million times over, he's almost unrecognizable.

Scrolling further back, I find his whole feed is polished, sanitized. Callum's earliest post is only dated about two years ago, and the only ones that look *real* – like maybe Callum himself posted them instead of some social media manager or whatever – are unexpectedly bookish. Like a carousel of a special edition *Lord of the Rings* set he found, or Reels of classics and sci-fi novels he recommends . . .

I click on a recent post of him holding Ali Hazelwood's *Check & Mate* in front of his face, his designer sunglasses peeking over the top of the book. The caption simply reads *Got the beach and a good book to match!* – yet it's exploded with thousands of comments.

Most of them are sparkly-heart emojis, or things like 'It's giving book boyfriend!'

My own fingers are moving across the keyboard before I can stop myself, leaving a comment of my own. Wanting to be part of something, of *this*, to pretend I might be seen by this star and feel all the more worthy for it.

That's what a *normal* teenage girl would do, right? That's what everyone else is doing.

OMG LOVED THIS ONE!! Hope you enjoyed it!

Is he giving book boyfriend? I guess so. He's attractive. He looks like he belongs in a Netflix teen romcom. It's no wonder his career is suddenly all kicking off.

But more importantly than that – *is he giving Kai*? I'm less sure. His toothy smile and artfully styled hair looks more akin to Kai's older brother Oscar, the golden child and heir to the throne – a guy with a lavish life who gets everything handed to him.

I click on a recent Reel. It's a small clip from the season five trailer, shouting a release date that's still several weeks away. I've already watched it hundreds of times, dissecting each scene, setting and spoken line, so I don't need the sound on to follow along.

Even without the sound on, Kai's delivery of his single piece of dialogue – '*It would seem there is a traitor in our midst after all*' – is so ruthless and cold that I get goosebumps.

When I try to swipe out of the video I accidentally click the sound on, and the familiar OWAR theme music booms out of my phone loud enough to make both me and Cerys jump.

'Are you watching the season five trailer *again*?'

'Mm-hmm.' I haven't mentioned outright to Cerys just *how* much I love Kai Osterion, but I ramble on, 'I just think this subplot is going to be so cool, with Kai learning how to wield his magick after years of trying to suppress it, and, like, really stepping into his own instead of just being a side character . . .'

(Not that I can relate. It's totally not *exactly* how I felt at my old school, versus having proper friends at last.)

'I would honestly *love* to see him face off against

Roach,' Cerys says, surprising me. 'Like if you consider how much Roach's magick got him into trouble because he never learned to control it, then you have him battle someone like Kai, whose family motto is all about control . . . That would be *such* a cool showdown.'

'Right?!'

I abandon my Instagram scrolling and take a breath, ready to launch into a verbal essay on how the parallels between main character Roach and Prince Kai are *so* underrated, when I stop myself.

Because I suddenly remember the look on Cerys's face on set. It's the same look I used to get all the time at school, and even sometimes from my family. *Tone it down, Anissa, you're being TOO MUCH.*

So I bite my tongue.

Stepping out of the shadows isn't as easy as Kai makes it seem.

CHAPTER 6

The *real* car park everyone uses at Red Wings Studios is hidden behind the main building, with strict security that we bypass by flashing our employee passes, which is a total thrill. You can see the actors' trailers on the other side of the lot, but we're nowhere near enough to bump into any of them.

Today, we find our usual entrance blocked by more security guards who inform us it's a closed set so we'll have to go the long way around, and they point us in the direction of a door all the way at the other end of the colossal studio building.

'We're going to be *so* late,' Cerys puffs as we dash towards the door. 'I don't even know how to get there from this end of the studio! D'you think this is a sackable offence?'

She looks so genuinely worried that I mimic drawing

a sword, and cry, 'Onwards, adventurers! We Rascals wait for no one!'

For a split second, I'm worried Cerys will cringe at this kind of behaviour outside of our TTRPG, but she only giggles and grins at me.

Once we're inside, it's impossible to keep a good sense of left or right when there are no windows, and the paper signs tacked up only say unhelpful things like 'Cave 1' or 'Palace (antechamber)'.

Honestly, you'd think if any TV set had good directions, it'd be one based on a book with *five* separate maps.

We accidentally stumble across a room full of crash mats and weapons where stunt doubles and the choreography teams are rehearsing, and we somehow also find the finance department – who help us get as far as catering, which is all we need to get our bearings back.

Cerys pulls me to a stop. 'We should get some teas to take in with us.'

'What, as like a cover for why we're late?'

'No, as a "please don't fire us, we've brought you tea, aren't we lovely" sort of thing.'

'Oh, good shout!'

But as soon as I take a stride toward the refreshments cart, I walk smack into someone, and the next thing I know there's a crunch of plastic, the scattering of ice cubes, and an 'Oof!'

As we both stand stock still in shock, drenched in iced caramel latte, I look up at the person I just barrelled into.

Someone with auburn-tinted hair, a purple cloak, tall black boots and a stern expression I know all too well, because I've stared at that *exact* expression – this exact person, in this exact outfit – a million times in stills from the season five promos.

I gawp as *Prince Kai* – aka Callum Denver – looks back at me, eyebrow raised, his mouth twisting into a grimace. There's a makeshift bib of white tissues stuffed into his collar, marked slightly with make-up and now liberally splattered with coffee.

Ohmigod, this is the stuff of literal DREAMS.

'Are you –?' he starts to say, and I blurt out, 'You're HIM. Ohmigod. You're Kai – I mean, Callum – I mean, HI. Sorry. I'm such a huge sorry. I'm really fan. I mean –'

Scratch that – it's the stuff of literal *nightmares*.

Now it's his turn to stare uncomprehendingly at me, which is fair, because I am babbling like an idiot.

'HAHAHA! NO! I MEAN! It's just really great to meet me. You! I'm Kai. No, you're Kai, well, you're not Kai, but you *are*, and you know what I mean. I'm coffee about your sorry.'

He keeps staring at me.

'HAHA,' I shout again.

I think I might actually be dead? I think this is hell.

He moves back half a step. He's probably thinking he should run, very fast and very far away from me and yell for security.

Cerys must get that impression, too, because she's tugging at my elbow. 'Oh my God, Nis, please shut up,' she whispers.

'WE WORK HERE,' I tell him, then I clear my throat. 'Actually.'

'Actually,' he repeats, a bit numbly.

'Just for now. For summer.'

'Okay.'

'Right, then.'

He nods.

I nod.

Cerys squeaks, 'Can we get you another coffee? We're really sorry about that.'

'Can you get me another *free* coffee?' he says, and from the corner of my eye I see Cerys's cheeks flame bright pink. Mine are probably doing the same thing. My whole body has probably become a neon pink beacon, in fact.

Bit rude, some distant part of me thinks, *just like in his AMA* ... But I'm too mortified to call him out.

In fairness, he has every right to be rude right now: I've just screamed in his face and doused him in coffee, and – oh, crap, will the costume department hate me for it? Will I get fired for spoiling his clothes? What if they can't film his scenes because of me? What if *I'm* single-handedly responsible for ruining Kai's role in the show?

So I blurt, 'YOUR CLOTHES!' and Cerys winces at my volume. Callum baulks too. 'Let me help!'

I lurch sideways for the little table with stirrers and sugar, grabbing a wedge of paper napkins to thrust towards Callum's damp black shirt, but he reels back and fends me off. His mouth moves into a rigid approximation of a smile.

'Thanks, but I think I can sort that out myself. Wouldn't want you to risk it.'

'HAHA!' I shout again, and Cerys pinches me. She's staring at me hard, and I clamp my mouth shut.

'Sorry,' she tells Callum on my behalf. Which is good, because I apparently am incapable.

I try, though, taking a deep breath first, and I manage not to yell this time – although my voice does come out sounding low-pitched and a bit like some of the character voices I do for our TTRPG campaign. 'I'm just a big Kai fan.'

'Yeah,' he says, with a breathy noise somewhere between a scoff and a chuckle. 'I kind of gathered that. Well, don't let me keep you.'

He gives Cerys another one of those fake, forced-polite smiles and gives us a wide berth as he leaves.

'Wait, what about your coffee?' I call after him.

'I'll survive,' he calls back, and vanishes around a corner.

I am going to pass away. I am going to get fired, and then turn to dust, and then simply pass away from shame. I am never going to be able to watch OWAR again. I am going to have to scrub all trace of myself from the Kai Osterion corner of this fandom. I'll have to change my name, and move to Point Nemo to get as far away from the rest of human civilization as is physically possible.

When I *finally* turn back around, Cerys looks like she also wants the ground to swallow her whole. People are staring at us. Someone has come over to mop up all the spilled coffee, and they give me a sympathetic smile.

Then I meet Cerys's eye, and a laugh sputters out of her. She fights to hide it, and turns away, whispering, 'Please don't even look at me right now, I think I'll die.'

'I'm sorry –'

'If I start laughing, I'm never going to stop,' she squeaks, and a giggle escapes again. She swallows, hard, focusing her gaze on the other side of the room. 'That was the best and worst thing I've ever seen, oh my God. If we get fired, it was *so* worth it.'

CHAPTER 7

By some miracle we don't get sacked because I fangirled helplessly over Prince Kai – I mean, *Callum*.

But by lunchtime, it's become on-set gossip – though at least I'm not named and shamed. My team know it was me, but that's mostly because I spend the day covered in coffee stains and being super skittish, expecting Lisa to yell at me and send me home.

One of my colleagues pats my shoulder kindly. 'Don't worry, honey, we've all been there. I met David Tennant when we did some of the *Doctor Who* specials and I was so star-struck I started talking to him in German. I think I asked him where the library was, and if he liked boats.'

Great. Just when I thought I'd had a chance to reinvent myself, find somewhere I *actually* fit in, I had to go and ruin it. I am, once again, the resident weirdo. I'm too mortified to even explain it wasn't *Callum* who had me so star-struck, but seeing him as *Kai*. Somehow, that seems even worse.

I suddenly can't wait for summer to be over, just to escape this humiliation.

Mum and Dad try to call to tell me about their whale watching trip in Kaikoura, but I decline and send a text saying I'm too busy to talk. I just *know* they'll pick up on how mortified I am, and I want to make them proud by being able to say that work experience is going well, and of course I haven't screwed it all up by being too weird.

By the time Cerys and I finally meet at her car at the end of the day, we can't go anywhere for *ages* because she's laughing too hard, recounting The Worst Two Minutes of My Life in *excruciating* detail.

'Please don't,' I whine. 'I was there, I lived it, once was horrible enough.'

When we finally start the drive home, she says, 'But you didn't do that with Brayden Brown! What *happened?*'

I lean over my knees, covering my face with my hands, and groan.

'Are you *that* into him?' She pauses. 'He is kind of cute. Niche celebrity crush though . . .'

'It's not a crush,' I mumble, not knowing how to begin. 'Sure, Callum's – he's good-looking, I guess. But

I don't fancy *him*. It's more like . . . he's just . . . Kai's my comfort character.'

'Your *what*?'

Right. Sometimes I forget how new to fandom Cerys is. *Of Wrath and Rune* was her first foray into this lovely, nerdy little world. She didn't even know what a coffee shop AU was this time last year.

By contrast, I've been a long-standing lover of these books and the TV show; I wasn't involved in Discord or anything before I met Cerys, but I'd devour fanfics and lurk on Reddit threads.

But that's all I did – lurk. Online, like in real life, I'd only recently found the courage to actually participate, which is part of why I've clung to Kai Osterion so much.

'Comfort character,' I repeat to Cerys. I take a deep breath before explaining, 'It's when you just feel connected to them in some way, or relate to what they're going through. Like how Kai's a bit of an outcast. A wallflower. People judge him, but he's actually really misunderstood . . .' I hesitate, feeling queasy for being so openly vulnerable. It's easy when it's hidden away in layers of storytelling in a fanfic or something. Out loud, in real life, it just makes me clammy. I bite my lip, but now I've started, it's hard to shut up. 'Like how he's branded by everyone around him as awkward and unwanted and just sort of annoyingly *there* all the time –'

Cerys looks stricken. 'But that's not you!'

I give her a flat look, and she pulls a face.

'Well,' she concedes, 'not *anymore*. Maybe that's how you used to be at school and stuff, but you have us now! Me and Jake and Max, and all the girls . . .'

The girls wouldn't even be friends with me if Cerys hadn't forced them to include me. I'm sure they still use their original group chat to talk – the one without me in it. They only invite me to hang out because they don't want to upset Cerys. Without her advocating for me, they'd probably be bitching behind my back and shunning me as a weirdo, too.

They did a bit, actually, at the start of college last year. Not wanting to get into all that, I tell Cerys, 'I just – feel like he *gets* it, you know?'

'And not like, *can get it*,' she replies.

'Right, you get it!' We make eye contact, both giggling. 'It's like how you love romcom movies so much. You keep going back to them because they make you feel good and help you make sense of stuff you're going through. They're just sort of . . . *there* for you. I know that – that sounds silly, but . . .' My voice gets smaller, until it trails off altogether. My hands fidget in my lap, and I gulp.

'Comfort character,' Cerys says, testing the phrase. 'Huh. Totally checks that you'd choose Kai. I see that.' Before I can decide if I should be offended, she tosses me a smile and says, 'Like how you're *both* shaking off that whole wallflower vibe for some more main character energy.'

I smile back, because she's right. It's almost like if *Kai* can come back from being such an outcast, if he can turn into someone confident and in control and sure of themselves, maybe I can too? Maybe they'll even finally give him a romance storyline of his own . . . ?

If I can't have one, I could carry on living vicariously through him at least. The most exciting thing to ever happen in my love life is the almost fake kiss with Jake during our last campaign session. The girls at college might finally be giving me a chance, but *boys* are another matter altogether.

Being shy, awkward and quiet has never exactly endeared me to guys before now – but being loud and excitable and overenthusiastic . . . Well, I was like that with Callum this morning, and look how well THAT turned out.

One day, I'll feel comfortable in my own skin. In who I am. If it can happen for Kai, it can happen for me, too. I *have* to believe that.

Cerys drops me home and promises to see me Sunday for our next round of TTRPG. She's working her actual job at H&M and seeing Max tomorrow, and she cheekily tells me that she'll leave it to me to tell Jake all about my celebrity run-in today.

Once inside, I'm immediately accosted by our rescue dog, Harley, a beast of indeterminable breed and loveable nature, who smothers me in affectionate licks.

Nan calls out from the direction of the kitchen. 'Anissa, love, is that you?'

'Yeah!' I shout back, and cringe at my coffee-stained clothes before making my way through the house to find her. The patio doors are open, and she's sat in the little garden, a cup of tea next to her and a knitting project in her lap. I go over to kiss her soft, wrinkled cheek. Even though it's hot out, Nan's layered in a long, heavy skirt and a woolly cardigan she made herself. Gemstone necklaces glint around her neck, like the ones I often wear.

My parents left last week for a long holiday to New Zealand. It's their twentieth wedding anniversary, and they never really did a honeymoon the first time around because money was too tight. They're even visiting some of Mum's relatives in India on their way back home, making the most of it all. I'm a little disappointed to miss out, but even if we're a tight-knit family, there's no *way* I'm crashing their at-long-last honeymoon. Anyway, I have *loads* of plans with all my new friends for the summer. (Or, you know: *some* plans, which is *loads* more than I used to have.)

And despite the very responsible, boring, albeit easily distracted and chronically late seventeen-year-old I am, I was apparently *not* allowed to stay home alone for the whole summer, so Nan's flown over from Ireland to stay with me for a bit. It's nice, though. We get on really well; we're so much alike, it feels like she gets me on a level my parents don't necessarily.

Nan waves a heavily ringed hand at me. 'Look at the state of you! What happened?'

'Er.' I cough awkwardly. I really don't feel like rehashing it all right now. 'I dropped a drink ...'

She harrumphs and says, 'Hope it wasn't hot.' Then she sets aside her knitting – a purple jumper she's making for me – and beams. 'So, how was your first week at your big fancy job? Are you ready to take Hollywood by storm?'

'Not quite,' I laugh, and sink into the seat next to her. Harley comes bounding over to plop her big head in my lap, looking for ear scritches. Even if I don't want to get into the whole 'I met *the* Prince Kai! And it was AWFUL!' thing, I do find a whole host of feelings bubbling up in my chest now my first week at the studio is over. I let it all come spilling out, unfiltered, and Nan is happy to listen while I process it.

'I do really like it there. The people are nice – even if they're all a bit stressed and overworked, which makes things a bit tense sometimes . . . And I feel like I have all these ideas but I don't know if it's my place to share or speak up. But Lisa seems really happy with all my work so far! And it's so brilliant to see it come to life, I feel so lucky to be part of it . . .'

Nan lets me natter away about props and all the different elements of creating a fantasy TV series I'm learning about. By the time the sun's gone down and we've eaten dinner, I'm still breathless with the general overwhelm of it all but much lighter and less mortified.

I can't let one silly, stupid interaction with one actor spoil my time there. I *won't*.

And I'm sure Callum Denver will be fine as Prince Kai. I caught him at a bad time. That's not his fault, I shouldn't judge him on that. I just hope he won't judge *me* on it, either. He's an actor in a widely-loved franchise; he must understand I was a bit overwhelmed?

Anyway, chances are I'll never even see him again. The studios are huge and there's so many sets. Today was just – a really, *really* unfortunate fluke.

OWAR Discord Kai-rry On My Wayward Son
General

@wrathfulqueen93
Loooool did everyone see Callum's insta story today?

@osterionprincess2
No?? Can you screenshot, I've got one of those timer apps locking IG for me rn, I'm trying to digital detox a lil!

@rubytherapscallion
... my dude you've sent me like thirty tiktoks in the last four hours

@osterionprincess2
But no Reels!!!

@wrathfulqueen93
He just reposted this quote that said 'let's normalize talking to people like they're real people, and not the bits and pieces you see on social media'

@therunestar
I thought it was cute!

@rubytherapscallion
lol a subtweet if ever I saw one, wonder who it was about

@wrathfulqueen93
I wondered if it's about an ex or something! He never gave us a clear answer in his Reddit AMA if he's single or not... Could be hinting at a messy breakup?

@rubytherapscallion
it totally had that kinda vibe now you mention it

@osterionprincess1
Probably getting swamped with DMs now he's hitting the big time! Poor guy! I feel for him

@therunestar
Ugh that's so shitty, he deserves MUCH better than some randoms harassing him based off a few branded insta posts! Probably some shitty OWAR fans mad that he's not a natural redhead or something lol

@ladyanissadishipper
I mean, we don't know what happened, or what it was about... it could just be generic and totally not related to anything irl?

@therunestar
Doubt it!!

@rubytherapscallion
yeah lol there's no way

@wrathfulqueen93
I'll be keeping a close eye on other things he shares/posts, if anyone can get to the bottom of it, it's us!

@ladyanissadishipper
alright Sherlock Holmes, calm down, we don't need anyone getting doxed just for being a harmless fan...

GIRLIE POPS 2.0! ✨

Daphne from college
Hi hi hi girlies, happy Friday! How's everybody doing? France is STUNNING but oh my God am I ready for a break from my family, how have I still got three more weeks of this??? WHY did my mum think a full summer away was a good idea? Send me all your gossip, I'm dying out here xxxx

Cerys
Missing you so much Daph!

Chloe with the Twitch channel
Well I'm LOVING summer in London! Still can't believe my auntie put me up and is helping me organize brand deals and stuff, I feel like such a nepo baby lol

Daphne from college
You are the LEAST nepo baby ever, those brands approached YOU remember!! You're just lucky your auntie works in media and can help you out!

Is your dad still kicking off about it?

Chloe with the Twitch channel
Yup. Shocker.

Not to bring the mood down sorry haha

Evie Price from school and also now college
Ugh, can relate

I knew it was a crap idea to come down to Devon to live with my dad and his shiny new family for the summer, HATE IT HERE. @Daphne can I pls come stay with you in France???

Daphne from college
I WOULD LOVE THAT!!!!

Could you actually tho!?

Evie Price from school and also now college
I wish . . . my little brother's having a great time here. I need to stay and make an effort for his sake, promised Mum and all that . . . Plus my dad's affair partner-turned-new wife is PREGNANT, and she keeps expecting us to BOND by going BABY SHOPPING

Cerys
No!!! Oh babe I'm sorry, that sounds grim

Hold for voice note about how work experience is going though!! Am LOVING it! Ft. Anissa drama

Cerys is recording a voice message

Me
Don't you DARE

Nikita from college (Daphne's friend)
Okay, Evie wins Worst Summer Ever

I'm just bored out of my absolute mind missing you all so I can't complain lol

Chloe with the Twitch channel
Wait I thought you guys were all doing brunch tomorrow???

Daphne from college
Yeah what happened to brunch?!

Also am on TENTERHOOKS for this voice note!! Anissa how could you not tell us there was drama!!

Nikita from college (Daphne's friend)
Cerys bailed bc she has to work a shift at H&M (honestly Cer idk how you're doing it all)

And Anissa always bails if Cerys can't make it

CERYS STOP TEXTING ME FFS

@Anissa sorry if that sounded mean. Didn't mean for it to

                                                Me
                                               That's okay!

                              I could still go if you want?

Nikita from college (Daphne's friend)
That's okay

Another time

Me
Totally!

CHAPTER 8

Deeper, deeper, down into the dungeons we go.

The corridors are ice-cold thanks to the layers of dark, ancient magicks that enchant the bowels of the palace; not even the burning torches can chase away the shadows.

There's blood on my skirts from the guards we had to dispatch on our way down here. The Moonwalker strides ahead, cautious and keen-eyed, on the lookout for traps and foes alike. Cailean, our dwarf blacksmith and a skilled fighter, brings up the rear of the party, battleaxe in hand.

We're soon joined by the newest addition to our party: an orc cleric named Wreevo, who speaks in a voice that's somehow both high-pitched and guttural all at once, an old friend of Téiglin and the resistance movement. At any rate, he's far more trustworthy than the imposter Lord Syxos.

We just have to find the real one, and hope we're not too late to save him . . .

'Wait!' squeak-grunts Wreevo. 'I think I hear something!'

Before we can stop him, he runs into a nearby cell where there's a metal glint like armour, and a flash of cobalt the colour of Lord Syxos's cloak – but it's only an old jousting lance with a lady's favour still tied to it.

Wreevo picks it up. 'Do you think I should bring it with us? Could be useful!'

With his clumsy, unpractised hold, he swings the lance about wildly – and in a horrible twist of fate, pushes at the open cell door, locking himself inside.

Behind me, Cailean the dwarf hoots with laughter. The Moonwalker mutters a curse under his breath and storms over, digging out his lockpick tools. 'I knew it was a mistake to bring you with us, orc.'

Jake glares at me across the table, but there's no heat in it. He scoops up his twenty-sided die.

I shrug. 'Sorry, but that's what you get for wanting to show off with the lance and then rolling a one. Critical fail means *critical fail*.'

'You're lucky I've got plus five to break you back out,' Max mutters.

Cerys is still laughing. I'm not even sure if it's in

character or not anymore but I grin, pleased she's having so much fun, and we dive back into the game.

With Wreevo freed quickly, it's not long before we discover our quarry: the real Lord Syxos, imprisoned in a cell, shackled and sickly.

His once-proud voice is feeble. His Greater Fae wings are bound behind him, his clothes torn and stained, and his skin sallow even as he manages a weak smile for us. 'Friends. Oh, friends. My saviours. Thank you. I owe you a deep debt of gratitude.'

The Moonwalker whips out a concealed dagger to hold to his throat and growls, 'Prove it's you, traitor.'

'It is! On my honour, I swear it. The Osterions caught wind of my betrayal of them, thanks to Prince Kai's visions; they sent a decoy in my place to uncover our rebel plot –'

Max whistles appreciatively. 'Damn, that's a good twist! Nice, Anissa!'

I flush. 'I can't take all the credit. Jake helped.'

Jake waves his current set of notes at me, smiling. 'Nah, this is all you.'

Cerys shushes them both irritably. 'Stop interrupting! It was just getting good! Go on, Jake.'

'... So I have spent the last few weeks languishing in this dungeon, kept alive only so they could use my blood to help that shape-shifting imposter take my place. I am only sorry you all fell prey to his evil ways, but you have no idea how glad I am to see you now. I have vital information that could change the course of the resistance movement.'

'Like what?' Cailean asks eagerly.

'The Eldritch Crown,' says Lord Syxos, his weary voice the strongest we have heard it yet. 'It is here, in the palace vaults, kept hidden all this time by the Osterions. If we can liberate it, we can use it to heal the realm and overthrow their evil rule once and for all.'

The Moonwalker sucks in a sharp breath, and Cailean gasps loudly.

Wreevo cries, 'Then we must find it!'

I slide a piece of paper over to Max, who's positively fizzing over a campaign storyline that's yet to unfold in the books and the show, shrouded in mystery and fan theories.

In the actual *Of Wrath and Rune* series, after their quest to find the long-lost Eldritch King turns out to be a trap, the heroes turn their focus to seeking the source of the king's power to restore peace to the realm – his crown.

A crown stolen long ago by the Osterions.

Max picks up the paper. It's a new character sheet, with some instructions and a few lines of speech to prompt him.

His eyes blow wide, but he gulps, runs his hands through his long black hair, and gets into character.

From the shadowy dungeon hallway behind us, a voice says, 'Well, well. What do we have here? Jailbreakers? Rebels? That simply won't do.'

We all turn in unison to see the youngest Osterion prince, Kai, in his purple cloak and with a sword at his belt, flanked by no less than a dozen guards.

He snaps his fingers, and the guards lurch into action.

'And that's where we'll leave off today,' I say, unable to keep the maniacal masterminding grin off my face while the others shout in protest, not even caring about the attention we're drawing at the cafe.

'Bloody *Prince Kai!*' cries Jake, jaw hanging open. 'I did NOT see that coming! And an ambush from his guards? I'm starting to regret not playing a fighter again . . .'

'*I'm* starting to regret talking us out of taking a short rest to regain some health points,' Max mutters. I can already hear his brain whirling to begin strategizing. He goes to give me the character sheet for Kai, but I tell him to hang on to it.

'I'll have some new prompts ready for you for next time. Do you mind playing him? I thought . . . I thought he might be a cool twist, especially with all the fan theories about how his family might force him to take the Eldritch Crown . . .'

'Are you kidding?' Max grins. 'It's genius! I just hope I can do him – well, *you*, our gamemaster – justice.'

'Have you had this planned for very long?' Cerys asks oh so casually, and my cheeks start to burn under her scrutiny.

'A while . . .'

I know what she's thinking, but it's genuinely nothing to do with the other day. The memory of Callum Denver's unimpressed frown while we were both drenched in iced coffee swims in front of my eyes, but I shove it aside. One less-than-ideal interaction with the *actor* is no reason to turn my back on a character that's always been there for me.

And it could be fun to see what kind of dynamic Kai and my character Mida could have! Maybe she'll understand he's a victim of circumstance and, from her time in the palace as a servant, she'll *know* Kai's not as fearsome as he likes to portray . . .

She could fix him.

While I'm spinning out different romantic subplots in my head, the others are in their own worlds too: Jake is already totally distracted, grinning down at a string of texts on his phone instead of worrying about saving the audio recording of our session – I think he's lost interest in his idea of turning this into a podcast. The tips of his cheeks are stained pink and his blue eyes alight behind his glasses. Meanwhile, Max has linked his fingers through Cerys's, and he lifts them up to kiss her knuckles with a tender look.

It's something straight out of a fanfic, the way they look at each other like they're the only two people in the world. And *who* is Jake messaging to blush like that? The way he types, deletes and retypes a response makes me think he must be flirting.

There's a pang in my stomach, and I look down at the pile of dice on top of Prince Kai's character sheet. There's a certain kind of irony in being surrounded by close friends and feeling lonelier and more on the outside than ever.

[Wallflower](#) by [ladydishipper](#)
Prince Kai Osterion, One Shot, Canon, s3 ballroom scene, fated magick, Kai Osterion visions, mentions of Prince Oscar Osterion

The House of Osterion are throwing a ball. The Moonwalker and Lady Adanna aren't the only people sneaking about in the shadows that night.

Words: 471   Chapters: 1/1   Hits: 12

The party unfurled below in a whirlwind of pearl-encrusted ball gowns and chiffon skirts. Noblemen whisked their dance partners about elegantly. Palace guards lined the walls in formal livery, the Greater Fae soldiers tucking their wings back neatly. Kai's parents oversaw the entire spectacle with benevolent smiles that surely everyone knew must be fake.

In the centre of it all, his brother Oscar was holding court. Guests hung off his every word, tittering prettily and simpering their endless stream of empty pleasantries. Oscar's laugh carried through the entire ballroom, echoing off the ancient columns and the shimmering glass dome in the centre of the high ceiling.

Kai winced at the sound.

It clashed with the buzz of noise inside his head, the mess of visions his corrupted magick kept him from fully mastering. Distracted, some of it filtered to the front of his mind – a flash of a brunette elfin woman in a green dress talking to his brother in some private room; a guard's bloodied body and the edge of a black cloak disappearing around a corner; shattered glass sparkling like diamonds on the floor.

Kai pushed them all away and took a swig of his drink. Champagne he *probably* shouldn't be drinking, really, but nobody had stopped him when he swiped the glass off a passing tray and made his escape up to the gallery, where he could observe the party in relative peace – and avoid all the people who pretended *they* weren't avoiding *him*.

Quiet was hard to come by with the visions. He could rarely unmuddle them enough to trust them. For all he knew, that woman in green was flirting with his brother, not threatening him. The broken glass – well, he'd just hope that was nothing to do with him. The absolute *last* thing he wanted to do was make a scene by knocking someone's drink over – he hated attention and the inevitable gossip.

And as for the dead guard – that wasn't necessarily *tonight*. It could be any time. Any miscellaneous hallway in this massive, stolen palace.

Anyway – what fun was a party, without a little scandal and murder?

It would hardly be an Osterion ball without one.

Really, he should be down there, part of it all. His parents kept insisting that it was his duty as prince to represent the family – and, as their youngest son, that it would *do him some good*, to get involved, to participate.

He didn't see the advantage, personally.

No, as long as people looked at him warily like he might cause them to burst into flames at any moment, or whispered '*freak*' as soon as his back was turned, he'd much prefer to stay on the fringes of things like this.

A wallflower.

Foolishly, secretly, hoping that maybe – just maybe – someday that might all change for the better.

r/TheOfficialOWAR

u/TheOfficialOWAR   7 days ago

Ask Me Anything with Callum Denver! (Prince Kai Osterion) . . .

u/fantasyfandomfaerie4
How does it feel going from minor roles to being cast on a critically acclaimed show with a cult following and blowing up on socials? Your BuzzFeed interview last month was awesome btw. Loved that video you did with the cast from that Amazon movie, too. Your face when The Rock popped up to prank you all was hilarious!

> ### u/TheOfficialOWAR
> It's new, that's for sure. Still processing tbh. – C

u/fantasyfandomfaerie4
Must be cool seeing fan edits and thirst traps of yourself!

> ### u/TheOfficialOWAR
> Yeah, must be. – C

u/runewarrior012
Who needs decent acting skills when you can be a clout chaser with a good Hollywood surgeon. You're not fooling anybody with that 'glow up'

> ### u/TheOfficialOWAR
> God forbid I have (checks notes) a regular ol' teenage growth spurt or my acne clears up. Shoutout Neutrogena #notspon. Kindly suggest you bully someone your own age, dickweed. – C

u/TheOfficialOWAR
Please know that we are in no way affiliated with Neutrogena, and do not endorse use of profanity or trolling. Any users who abuse our AMA guests will be reported and banned from this subreddit. Kind regards, The OWAR Team.

u/owarfanforumuk_admin
Are you single?

> **u/TheOfficialOWAR**
> I did assume we'd be getting questions about the show. – C

u/owarfanforumuk_admin
Are you though?

u/daisymaeflowers
Ooh, any showmance gossip you can share with us from behind the scenes?

u/magickalmalady
Have you ever been in love?

> **u/TheOfficialOWAR**
> No. – C

GIRLIE POPS 2.0! ✨

Daphne from college
Sorry but I am still absolutely SCREAMING over the whole coffee drama

@Anissa cannot BELIEVE you shouted in his face like that omgggg

Nikita from college (Daphne's friend)
Wish I'd been there lol, it sounded HILARIOUS

Chloe with the Twitch channel
Noooooo omg I'm absolutely dying for you babe, like, HOW are you going to show your face tomorrow?!

Evie Price from school and also now college
I'd have to take the L and abandon ship

Cerys
Oh come on guys, you're making me feel guilty for telling you now! @Anissa it wasn't that bad, I promise

Nikita from college (Daphne's friend)
She's just saying that bc she doesn't want you to quit so she has to go on her own lol

Me
You're just saying that bc you don't want me to quit so you have to go by yourself

Daphne from college
Haha jinx you two!

Seriously though, didn't mean to make you feel crappy about it Anissa . . . more like, omg can't believe that happened, thoughts and prayers for tomorrow! We're here if you need us! xxxx

Chloe with the Twitch channel
Yes please let us know how it goes!!

Evie Price from school and now also college
You probably won't even see him again! Cerys said the set's so big, even you two haven't seen each other some days and you work in the same department!

Nikita from college (Daphne's friend)
Good luck acting like a normal person lol

DAPHNE STOP TEXTING ME

THAT WASN'T EVEN MEAN

Me
Thanks girls, will keep you posted, but you're right, I probably won't even see him again x

CHAPTER 9

On Monday morning, I'm determined to put last week's fiasco behind me – if only because Nan had to come and drag my duvet off me when I couldn't face getting out of bed for the shame of it all.

The girls from college weren't exactly encouraging in the group chat last night, even if they were trying to be. Nikita's comment about 'good luck acting normal' is sticking with me, making my brain feel itchy. It's hard to know if she meant it generally, or as a personal dig because I'm the weird kid from college who infiltrated their cool group. Nikita's always so blunt and unfiltered, I really can never be sure if she's just saying something or trying to be nasty.

It'll be fine, I reassure myself. *I won't even see Callum and if I do, I'll play it cool and laugh it off. Maybe he'll laugh about it too, and then we'll become friends and he'll introduce me to the rest of the cast. I'll become part of the*

OWAR family, on the inside and surrounded by people who share an intense love for this series . . . And they'll discover I like writing and invite me to write scripts for the show!

Ugh. Not bloody likely.

If only because I don't think I have ever 'played it cool' in my entire LIFE. My spiralling imagination is proof enough of that.

Cerys has another shift at H&M this morning and Nan needs the car so I have to take a bus in, but the solo trip gives me time to compose myself like I would on the way to school and college. Pick up all the parts of myself that make me stand out or seem odd and package them away. Turn down my volume, shove aside anything fun I want to talk about, like yesterday's TTRPG session or the one-shot fanfic I wrote, and replace them with small talk like 'Isn't the weather nice?' or 'No I didn't get up to much this weekend . . .' A façade that's as close to 'normal' as I can get.

I get off the bus feeling like someone else is operating my body.

It's probably for the best.

I detour via the canteen on my way in, fingers tapping agitatedly against my thigh as I go. I pass some of the stunt team, a few camera operators and two women from the costume department but it's otherwise eerily quiet this morning. Today's an evening shoot, so that explains it.

But when I get to the tea and coffee cart, there's one person there.

The absolute *last* person, out of the literal hundreds – thousands, maybe! – of people employed on OWAR, that I want to see. Clearly, I've rolled a critical fail on how today is going to go.

Wearing workout gear today instead of his princely get-up, Callum Denver walks into the room from the other side of the studio, and we both stop as soon as we see each other. Facing off like duellists ten(ish) paces apart. His face looks as annoyed as I feel.

Whatever robot has been operating me since the bus seems to have vanished, because sensations come flooding in all at once: hairs prickle along my arms, blood roars in my ears. I'm suddenly hyperaware of the tightness of my shoelaces – and a matching too-tight feeling in my chest.

My hands drop to my side, balling into fists. Callum rolls his eyes, but his need for caffeine seems to win out.

I debate turning around and running away, but that would almost be *more* embarrassing. What if he thinks I'm so star-struck I can't even cope with being near him?

No. I'm determined to prove him wrong after last

week and prove to everyone else, and myself, that I *can* be normal.

'Stalking me now?' he says, when I reach the coffee cart.

'I got here first.'

He scoffs. 'You really didn't.'

'Maybe *you're* stalking me.'

'Why? Any particularly interesting insights on Prince Kai you want to share? Self-insert fanfics, maybe? Comments on my Instagram you're hoping I'll see?'

'Someone thinks highly of themselves,' I snap, cheeks flaming because he's totally caught me. Not that any of my Kai fanfics are self-insert, where people write themselves into the story, making one of the existing characters fall in love with them. I'm almost surprised he even knows what they *are*. Mine are more ... me projecting some of my feelings or experiences on to Kai's character. Which is totally different.

Anyway, he doesn't *know* me.

'Looks like someone can speak in full sentences today,' he drawls. 'Congratulations.'

I flush, and he takes advantage of my silence to order himself an iced Americano.

I bite the inside of my cheek hard, seething. He's stolen my coffee order. But I do note, 'No caramel today?'

'See?' He grins, and it's not the awkward, stiff one he gave Cerys last week. It lifts higher on one side, crinkles the corners of his brown eyes, and flashes some of his movie-star white teeth. It's *cheeky*. 'You *are* stalking me.'

'Am not,' I argue, which only makes him grin a little wider as he turns away. 'I had the misfortune of wearing your coffee all over my clothes on Friday, remember?'

'I'd be hard pressed to forget. I'm surprised you haven't put them on eBay yet.'

'How do you know I didn't? Sounds like you might be the one stalking me.'

He chuffs a laugh and I finally understand what that fanfic term means: sort of a huff of air with a hint of a chuckle to it. While his coffee is being made, the barista asks me, 'And what can I get you, love?'

'Iced Americano,' I say through my teeth. Callum gives another half-laugh, and I add pointedly, 'With *vanilla* syrup, please.'

'Copycat,' he accuses me.

'What are you even *doing* here? Aren't you supposed to be – I don't know, polishing your lines or your teeth or your face or something? Whatever it is you do when you're not filming.'

His expression hardens slightly, but he says, 'Not

that it's *any* of your business, and not that I'm allowed to leak any spoilers –'

'Obviously. I mean, same. They had us sign NDAs.'

'Right.' He rolls his eyes. 'But hypothetically speaking, I might be in with the stunt coordinators to work on a sword-fighting routine.'

'Fun!' I say, too sincerely and enthusiastically, and I'm immediately embarrassed. I'd love to know if they use real, blunted weapons or if they're lightweight props and if it's as much fun as it looks. But those are the questions of a star-struck fangirl, so I tamp them all down and say instead, 'Hypothetically speaking, I mean, that might be fun.'

There's a pause before he murmurs, 'Yeah, actually. It just might be.'

He picks up a straw to fidget with, eyes downcast. I stare at him, then try *not* to stare at him, in my mission to be a Very Normal Person. He's my age and up close, he looks it. There's a softness to his cheeks and his jawline, and some acne visible near his hairline without stage make-up or an Instagram filter to hide it.

I try to imagine what it'd be like if I'd run into Callum at the canteen in college instead, but that plays out just as badly in my head as the reality did last week. He'd *definitely* be a cool kid, probably on a sports team, and I doubt he'd have time for me.

Would we have shared classes together, though? A group project? Would I have been too shy to speak to him, or would he have been nicer to me when his first impression wasn't me screaming in his face? It's almost a shame I'll never know.

I swallow what's left of my pride and say, 'I'm, um, I'm sorry about last week. Especially if I made you uncomfortable. Or . . . not like a person.'

His coffee is ready now, placed on the counter for him to take.

He doesn't take it.

I risk a glance at him and find one of Callum's eyebrows arched. He looks genuinely surprised, but when I open my mouth to say something else – that I was just really unprepared and won't ever do it again – his expression closes off and he shakes his head as he turns away.

'Figures,' he mutters.

'Sorry?'

He snatches up his coffee and begins to stride away and before I can consider what I'm doing, I chase after him to block his path. 'What's *that* supposed to mean?'

'Nothing. Just –' He sighs and clearly has some internal debate before giving me that false, polite smile that's fragile as porcelain. Then he says in a rigid, careful voice, 'I appreciate that you're a fan. The support means a lot to me. I'm exceptionally grateful.'

'It doesn't *sound* like it. Look, you're totally entitled to feel some kind of way about me being weird before, and like, I'm glad you didn't name and shame me on your Insta –'

'I don't know your name,' he points out, and I grit my teeth at the interruption. His eyes flash, which is unnerving up close. It's something I've seen him do as Kai in the season five trailer. He's angry, irritated, close to the edge. Like if I poke him just a bit further . . . his mask might shatter, and leave behind something real underneath.

I shake myself, trying to remember that's more of a Kai thought than a Callum thought. I don't even *know* Callum Denver, as he so kindly pointed out in that Instagram story the gang were discussing on the Kai Discord.

'I understand you're mad at me,' I go on, regardless. 'I'm mad at me, too. But it goes *both* ways, you know. You shouldn't be treated as less than human for being sort-of famous, but you also don't get to treat *me* as less than for being a fan. You can't post publicly, then be mad at people for seeing it, or want to be treated like a normal person, then resent me for trying to do exactly that. I've been on the receiving end of enough disparaging comments throughout my life for just *liking* something, for *caring* or *being interested* – I don't need it from you, too.'

I don't want Callum ruining this show, or Kai, for me. He can't. It's not fair. Cerys is right. This work experience is a once-in-a-lifetime opportunity. I'll never be closer to OWAR than I am now. I refuse to let him take these few precious, magical weeks away from me.

'Sort-of famous,' he echoes, deadpan. He clutches a hand to his chest. 'Ouch.'

'If you don't want fans, you should be less good at what you do,' I quip.

Callum pauses, blinking, and then a laugh bursts out of him so suddenly that I reel backwards. He laughs again, then drags a hand back through his hair, and that cheeky grin returns. (Cheeky? No, I take it back. It's *insufferable*. It's – it's conceited and arrogant and *annoying*, that's what it is.)

'You should really work on your insult game,' he tells me. 'You should've stopped at "sort-of famous".'

I spin on my heel, face hot. My coffee is ready now too. The barista jerks away quickly – clearly having witnessed the whole exchange. I pick up my drink, ready to storm off to my corner of the studios, far away from Callum Denver.

This time, though, he stops *me*.

'What is it?' he calls. 'Your name?'

I pause, just about turning to look over my shoulder. 'Wouldn't you love to know?' Probably so he can get me fired, or track me down on his Instagram and block me. Either. Both.

Instead, he only laughs once more, the sound following me as I duck between some of the wig technicians and try not to spill my own drink.

'Well,' Callum shouts after me. 'Until next time, Fangirl.'

Until *never*, more like.

r/TheOfficialOWAR

u/TheOfficialOWAR   8 days ago

Ask Me Anything with Callum Denver! (Prince Kai Osterion) . . .

u/writingwizardry_eldritchstyle
Did you do much research into the books to play Prince Kai?

> ### u/TheOfficialOWAR
> Kind of tricky when most of his character is used to showcase the other characters . . . Seems like most of the info out there about WHO Kai really is comes from the fandom, and anyone who's willing to actually read between the lines during his scenes. - C

u/justadaxysstancalledstan
Not a question but just to say, big OWAR fan here and LOVING what we've seen of your portrayal of Kai so far in the s5 trailer, can't wait for the full episodes to drop later this year! Glad we've gone from 'forgettable background character who gets recast every season bc who's even going to notice' to him actually having a full role. Will be so cool to see what this does for the plot of the show!

> ### u/TheOfficialOWAR
> Appreciate that. I've really tried to give him some more complexity than just 'guy who has super convenient visions to help his evil royal family sabotage the heroes' plans', which is how most people seem to view him. Hope me and Kai live up to expectations. - C

u/kingroachtheorist1
Kai's a shit character who only got an actual storyline this season because you're out here chasing your fifteen minutes of fame. You should be ashamed

u/TheOfficialOWAR
Wow, should I? I'll make a note. – C

u/fantasyfandomfaerie4
Don't listen to them!! FWIW I think it's awesome you've joined OWAR, you seem like a fab actor!

u/rubytherapscallion
hardcore same, you deserve it Callum!

u/howdyrascals
Guys, he's just a kid, lay off him. Adding Kai to the storyline is purely the showrunner's decision, and if it wasn't Callum, it'd be someone else. Get a grip.

u/whackygoblin_
Petition to keep Callum/Kai *until the end*!

u/runewarrior012
Petition to recast to someone who actually VALUES this show. All those books he posts on Instagram and not a single one of them is OWAR? Talk about a fake fan

u/kingroachtheorist1
agree. plus he's out here doing OTHER shows/films. can't even commit to an annoying, useless character. sucks that they're giving him extra screentime – for what? some thirsty fangirls swooning over a floppy haircut?

u/howdyrascals
Seriously, this is uncalled for. Why are you even here?? I'm contacting the mods. You realize you're bullying a SEVENTEEN-YEAR-OLD?

u/TheOfficialOWAR
Don't talk to me, my haircut, or my haircut's haircut ever again. – C

u/whackygoblin_
deep cut! And they dare call this guy a FAKE FAN? That's some peak niche internet culture right there. If anyone gets it, it's Callum!

u/TheOfficialOWAR
Thanks everyone for participating in the AMA today! Unfortunately we're having to wrap up early, but huge thanks to Callum for spending some time with us this evening. Thanks also to the dedicated fans who engaged respectfully in the conversation! BE YE A RASCAL?! More behind-the-scenes content soon! – The OWAR Team.
#rascals #s5OWAR #ofwrathandrune

CHAPTER 10

'It's Anissa, isn't it?' says a voice behind me.

I jump, dislodging the plate of fake roast ham and sending a few wine goblets tumbling over. Luckily, they're empty.

Unluckily, I turn to find –

Kai, Prince of the House of Osterion. His purple cloak (the family's trademark colour) is pinned at one shoulder with a bronze brooch, his tall boots are polished to a high shine, and there's a sword hanging from a belt at his waist. Deep, bruised shadows mar the skin beneath his eyes. His face looks sunken, gaunt – exhausted.

I do a double-take. He didn't look this terrible on Monday. What's happened in the last two days? It's like he hasn't slept in months.

Duh. The make-up department happened.

'Ka–*Callum*. Hello,' I say stiffly, not sure why

he bothered to approach me at all, and barely managing to not mix up the names. I go back to fixing the feast table, rather than staring awkwardly at him.

The huge dining hall is abuzz, a real hive of activity. There are five banquet tables laid out with heaped platters of (fake) food, with a sixth, smaller table on a raised dais. Two of the chairs are styled like thrones. The floor is made to look – and even sound – like flagstones. There are frescoes set into the walls depicting scenes from *Of Wrath and Rune*'s history as told by the victors – the Osterion family, literally painting themselves as the heroes.

There are also huge lighting and camera rigs, boom mics and trailing wires being taped down for safety everywhere. Stand-ins are milling around, and there are important people in headsets consulting clipboards.

I got roped in today to help add final touches for filming, as some of my team are off sick. It's the first time I've been *properly* on set when it's active like this, but I figured I'd be ushered out of the way – or kept out of the room altogether – long before any of the actors showed up.

'Anissa,' Callum repeats. 'That's right, isn't it?'

My blood goes cold. How did he track down my name? *Why?* Did he ask about me? Am I going to get fired?

Unable to look at him, I carry on sorting out the table and say, 'Now who's stalking who?'

'You're on *my* set,' he points out.

'*You're* early. Aren't actors only supposed to arrive once you're ready for your close-up, or something?'

'I'm only *sort-of* famous, remember?' he points out. 'Nobody cares about my close-up. Or they didn't used to, anyway . . .'

He mutters the last part and then quickly clears his throat as if he didn't mean to say it out loud. I glance back to see him tugging at the ends of his auburn hair, and notice he's blushing. His stage make-up hides it well, but the pink flush creeps down his neck, disappearing beneath the high collar of his costume.

'You look really hot,' I blurt, then make a strangled noise of horror. 'NOT LIKE THAT. I mean – not that you *aren't* . . . HAHA, NO, ACTUALLY –' I'm only in a thin T-shirt and a loose pair of dungarees, and I gesture to them. 'I *mean*, even with the air-con blasting, I'm sweating. So you must be baking. That's . . . *That's* what I meant.'

Ugh, what *is* it about this guy that makes me incapable of shutting up? I always used to be so good at that.

Callum gives me that eyebrow raise followed by a brief flash of the cheeky (correction: *insufferable*) grin, and just about manages to hide his laugh with a cough. 'That's a new one.'

'Sorry, am I supposed to be performing the role of *thirsty fangirl* from your Instagram comments?'

His more serious expression returns, and I almost feel bad about it. He looks a bit uncomfortable, actually – but he *should*. It's his turn to be embarrassed. I've done plenty on that front already.

'You get used to it,' he says at last.

'The costume or the comment section?'

'Both, I suppose.'

There's something so startlingly honest in the reaction that I'm almost tempted to ask – does it bother him, the stuff online? Does it ever get overwhelming?

Does he relate to Kai's current character arc, too? Going from awkwardly on the sidelines with his minor TV and film roles, to seizing his place in the world with both hands and being more in the spotlight at last? The parallels with his current situation can't be lost on him.

Callum clears his throat. 'So you're in Danielle's department, then? Set design.'

'What gave me away?'

'Nepo baby?' he asks, but there's no accusation in his tone, only idle curiosity.

'Only if you count the fact that my friend really impressed Brayden Brown with his cosplay, so Brayden

Brown vouched for me and my friend to do work experience here. A different friend, not the cosplay friend. There's a few of us who . . . um, you didn't ask about all that.'

Callum's head cocks to one side. 'Do you always use his full name?'

'I don't think we're buddy-buddy enough for me to upgrade him to just "Brayden", yet.'

'Ah, right. Working on it?'

'Absolutely not. Doing my best to avoid any and all interactions with actors after last week, thank you.'

'And here I thought I was special,' he deadpans. 'But turns out you're just fangirling over everybody.'

My cheeks turn hot. Something about these interactions – *confrontations* – with Callum make me feel like I'm back at secondary school, constantly embarrassed just for existing.

I tell him, 'I wouldn't worry too much. I'll stay out of your way – you just have to work on staying out of mine. I'm only here for a few weeks anyway, so that shouldn't be too difficult for *either* of us.'

'Are you always this prickly?'

'What can I say?' I give him a sweet, deeply sarcastic smile, and bat my eyelashes for good measure. 'You seem to bring out the best in me.'

Callum laughs again, surprise flickering across

his features like the sound catches *him* off guard, too. A couple of people look over, and I wonder if I can smack a plate of fake boiled potatoes to the floor just so I can duck out of sight for a few minutes. Maybe crawl under the banquet table and just stay there, actually, forever and ever.

At least then I'd get to say I'd (technically) been in OWAR season six.

He says, 'Anyway, shouldn't be too tricky. Tomorrow you'll find set a Callum Denver-free zone, so enjoy it while it lasts.'

'Devastating,' I quip. 'I'm not even here tomorrow. What a waste.'

'Oh! Wait, are you – how old are you?'

'That's a particularly stalker-like question.'

'It's results day,' he says, and suddenly it's not such a weird question at all.

We're the same age. I never really considered that he'd be juggling his job on *Of Wrath and Rune* with college, but it makes sense now he mentions it. It's weird to think about a sort-of famous actor waiting on his AS-level results like the rest of us.

'I'm eighteen in October,' I say.

'An older woman,' he jokes, pointing at himself and adding, 'May.'

'Gemini. Of course.'

'How'd you guess? Or –' His mouth twists into a wry smile. 'Right. You knew that, obviously.'

'It makes a lot of sense now I've met you.'

'Does it?'

I nod, which must look terribly cool and cryptic, but honestly, I'm just sparing him the verbal essay. Nan *loves* zodiacs and birth charts and all that stuff – she does tarot readings for people and reads oracle cards for them, and she's dead superstitious. It's kind of cool, really. At least, I think so. Callum Denver probably doesn't, like the kids at school used to think it wasn't.

'Are you nervous? About your results?' he asks.

'A bit.' And because I seem incapable of keeping my mouth shut around him, I hear myself adding, 'I think I did okay, mostly. I'm just worried about my French oral. I fumbled so much of it. I got too caught up in trying to make sure my grammar was right. Those past participles always trip me up.'

Callum's face turns sympathetic, and he makes another gesture at himself. 'I'm doing German. I know what you mean. Something about doing it one-on-one and the time pressure makes you forget how to talk altogether, doesn't it?'

'I would've thought you'd be a pro at that. Being an actor, I mean.'

He shrugs.

I want to ask what else he's studying. English would be an obvious assumption with the amount of books he posts about . . . but I'm worried he'll think I'm prying, and I genuinely *don't* want to make him feel like I'm turning him into someone who 'only exists in bits and pieces on social media'.

If this is some kind of tentative peace we've reached, I don't want it going up in smoke. I don't want any more angsty reposts subtly shaming me, either.

I'm spared the awkward silence by Lisa shouting to me from across the hall: 'That looks fab, Anissa, thank you! And you were right about switching out the napkins, good call! The purple really pops. Can you dress the other table now, please?'

'Okay!' I call back, a rush of pride making me dizzy. I've been building up the courage to share more ideas lately, trying to make the sets as immersive as I see them in my head when I'm writing or reading about them; it's refreshing to have people not just listen, but *care* about things like that as much as I do. I grab my empty boxes from the props I've unpacked and see Callum is on his phone, already ignoring me. He looks almost like he found himself standing here by accident, like I don't exist to him.

But I obviously *do*, because he went and found out my name, and he asked if I was nervous about results day tomorrow. The thought thrills me more than it should.

'Um, good luck,' I tell him. 'With results, I mean.'

'You, too, Fangirl.'

I hurry off to help at the other banquet table, discarding my cardboard boxes as I go, and trying not to think about the fact he took the time to find out my name.

CHAPTER 11

Oh, thank God for that.

I got As! And one C in my French oral, but that's okay! It doesn't count for a *huge* proportion of my overall grade anyway, and I smashed the rest of them.

I could collapse with relief. I expected good grades, but that's only because I usually do well at exams – and *that's* because I usually don't have much else going on in my life beyond schoolwork and living vicariously through fictional characters.

From the other side of the hall, at the 'A–D' surnames, Nikita screams. I look over in time to spot her bursting into noisy tears.

Cerys is still queuing to get her results and I hesitate a second before hurrying over to Nikita, who's keeled over. I'm not sure how to ask what she got without making it worse, so I settle for putting a hand on her shoulder.

She drags herself back up, her usually immaculately styled chestnut curls now wild about her face, and her typical, beige-toned outfit making her flushed face look practically neon. She's shaking so hard that the paper with her results on is going *flap-flap-flap*.

'All As,' she chokes out, then starts sobbing again. It's the most genuine, raw emotion I've ever seen from her. Her default state is usually a smirk or a scoff – and I should know, we have two classes together. We even sit by each other, but I think that's only out of a begrudging sense of obligation to our mutual friends.

She's probably my least favourite in the whole group, but it's not as if I *dislike* her or anything. We just aren't each other's people, which is fine.

So when she throws herself at me, I'm so alarmed that I don't know what else to do but hug her back and say, 'That's amazing! Well done!'

Cerys comes running over then, telling us in a rush that she got top marks for art and a mix of grades for English, history and media. 'It's okay, though,' she says a bit shakily. 'I can pull them up next year! And they're still good marks! Aren't they?'

'Definitely,' I say, but I still put an arm around her shoulder to give her a comforting squeeze now that Nikita's let go of me. When Cerys asks what I got, I feel sheepish admitting how well I did, but she only beams at me.

'No surprises there! You were always a swot at school, I knew you'd smash it.'

Nikita *must* be feeling out of sorts because she exclaims cheerfully, 'We can be swots together, Nis! I'm gonna go phone my mum and dad. I'll see you guys outside, okay? I can't wait to celebrate!'

Cerys hurries off to collect Evie, Chloe and Daphne's results for them since they're all away. I should probably phone my parents, they're waiting to hear from me, but I'm immediately distracted by some notifications on my phone.

Max and Jake have texted us already – Max also clearing the board with all As, and Jake's ranging from As to Cs to one absolute fail in a maths exam he'll have to resit.

But there's another message on my phone that steals my full attention.

> **Callum Denver** @callumdenver_owar
> How'd the French oral go in the end? Très bien?

Why is Callum Denver sending me an Instagram DM asking about my French results?

How did he even find my . . . *Oh, God*. The comment

I left days ago on his weeks-old photo with an Ali Hazelwood book.

I swipe frantically to my notifications and there it is, glaring up at me: *Callum Denver liked your comment on his post*. That must be how he found out my name – because I was practically stalking his socials. If I cringe any harder, I think my body will turn itself inside out.

What on earth is he doing *messaging* me, though?

Follow-up question: what on earth am *I* doing, messaging him back?

> **Anissa O'Shea** *@thatfangirloverthere*
> Very très bien in fact. Secured myself a respectable C. Just glad I passed tbh

> How'd German go? Sehr wunderbar?

> **Callum Denver** *@callumdenver_owar*
> You betcha. Breezed through with a D

> (I'm going to have to resit. Shit.)

> **Anissa O'Shea** *@thatfangirloverthere*
> ☹ I'm sorry, that is shit

Callum Denver *@callumdenver_owar*
How'd your other results go?

> **Anissa O'Shea** *@thatfangirloverthere*
> Good, yeah! Thanks

Callum Denver *@callumdenver_owar*
... which I guess either means you failed them all, or got REALLY good marks

I'm willing to bet it's the latter?

> **Anissa O'Shea** *@thatfangirloverthere*
> You caught me

Callum Denver *@callumdenver_owar*
Swot

> **Anissa O'Shea** *@thatfangirloverthere*
> Shockingly you're not even the first person to call me that today

> How'd your other ones go?

Callum Denver *@callumdenver_owar*
Decent! No other resits, at least

Weird question but do people, like, know what I study?

I'm never quite sure what's public knowledge and what's not

Feels like you would know, though

> **Anissa O'Shea** *@thatfangirloverthere*
> Swot at your service

> I haven't seen anything about it, your A level choices are apparently a well-kept secret

Callum Denver *@callumdenver_owar*
Huh

Good to know, thanks Fangirl

@callumdenver_owar is typing...

@callumdenver_owar is typing . . .

@callumdenver_owar is typing . . .

Anissa O'Shea *@thatfangirloverthere*
You can count it under my NDA if you want

Like, 'I won't leak OWAR s6 scripts OR what you're studying at college'

Callum Denver *@callumdenver_owar*
Lol I wasn't worried about that

Never mind

Anyway I've done English, history, and film as well

Anissa O'Shea *@thatfangirloverthere*
That's cheating

Bet film's an easy A for an actor

Callum Denver @*callumdenver_owar*
You'd be surprised

Anissa O'Shea @*thatfangirloverthere*
Somehow you are full of surprises

@callumdenver_owar is typing...

@callumdenver_owar is typing...

Callum Denver @*callumdenver_owar*
For a sort-of famous actor you fangirl over?

Anissa O'Shea @*thatfangirloverthere*
No, for a Gemini

A string of skull emojis and a laugh-react spark a fizzy feeling in the pit of my stomach.

'All good, Nis? Are you texting Jake? He's really cut up about that stats exam, poor guy... I haven't had a chance to talk to him properly yet, I've been too busy phoning the girls! I'm sure Max will help him revise for the resit, though. Are they on their way?'

I jump at Cerys's voice, and must look guilty as sin when I scramble to hide my phone.

'Just, um, updating my parents,' I lie.

Why is Callum messaging me?

Why am I messaging back when I'm meant to be ignoring his entire existence lest he ruin my favourite show and comfort character?

Why is it so, *so* hard to keep this giddy little smile off my face?

It's very, deeply, confusing.

CHAPTER 12

There's a party that night, organized by some of Jake's college friends. The boys spring it on us last minute – a casual mention over ice creams down Cardiff Bay that sends us into a frenzy trying to extract details like timing, location and, crucially, if Daphne's latest crush Raf will be there. (Cerys and Nikita are instructed to be on *high* alert for him getting too cosy with other girls while Daphne's away this summer.)

Cerys drops me home so I can get changed. With the time difference to New Zealand, my parents are fast asleep and won't know I'm at a party until it's too late, but I can guarantee they'd be more excited about it than I am. They're just happy I'm 'getting involved' these days. They were so over the moon when I said I couldn't talk to them for long on FaceTime earlier because I was out with everyone, I almost expected them to hang up on me. Although they did stay on the line long enough to tell me, Jake and Max about the Hobbit holes they'd be visiting tomorrow, promising to send lots of pictures.

Now, Nan stands in my doorway, offering unsolicited input on the different party outfits I'm considering and finally giving an approving smile at a purple strappy sundress. It's got a skirt that twirls all the way out if I spin around; I love it.

'And are there going to be *boys* at this party tonight?' she asks.

'All pronouns welcome,' I confirm. A wave of disappointment nudges at me, knowing her comment is pointless – it's not as if *anybody's* ever shown interest in me like that. Much as I might wish otherwise.

'And booze? Because I don't want you minesweeping your way around –'

'What?'

'Drinking any old thing you come across. But if you're going to, I'd rather know so I can make sure you're at least being a bit *sensible* by taking your own –'

Last time Cerys and I went to a party, Mum gave me this very same speech along with a bottle of gin and lemonade – sans the gin. I swallow a laugh, wondering if she prepped Nan for this scenario before going away.

'Jake's older sister is getting us some wine to share,' I admit.

'Just be *sensible*. That's all I'm asking.'

Nan sits on my bed while I finish getting ready, picking out some earrings – like my favourite snake-cuff piece for my left ear, and the dangly one that looks like a dagger – and filling her in on some gossip. Like Daphne's three crushes who are *all* going to be there tonight and who she wants us to keep an eye on; Chloe's brand deal that her auntie just helped her sign; and Nikita *hugging* me earlier and joking that we can be swots together.

Before long, Jake's older sister Ginny is parked outside, and I throw open the door to find Jake beaming and bouncing on the balls of his feet. Harley comes shooting out of the living room to slobber over his hands and steal a few pets.

We say goodbye to Harley and Nan and pile into Ginny's car. Bottles clink around Jake's feet in the passenger footwell. I squash in next to Cerys. She's wearing a bright pink crop top and matching skirt, and Max is on her other side, in jeans and a faded green OWAR tee that reads 'BE YE A RASCAL, ROACH?'

'All aboard the party train!' Ginny shouts and toots the horn once before speeding away.

At some point in the night, the party goes from a sad field full of isolated groups, to a thriving mess of people drunk on summer. (And a bit of alcohol, too.) Music blares from a Bluetooth speaker somebody showed up with. People are dancing, sat playing games like *Never Have I Ever*, laughing with friends and flirting with their crushes. Like Nikita – who started the night very dedicated to keeping an eye on Daphne's crushes, but soon enough ended up snogging one of Raf's friends instead.

Before long, Cerys is also very busy snogging Max.

Jake and I sit leaning against each other for balance, passing a bottle of Ginny's cheap rosé between us while Jake rambles on, jumping from one topic to the next seemingly at random. I don't mind, though; it's comforting, and it sounds like how chaotic *my* brain feels sometimes. A short way off, Cerys is sitting in Max's lap, his face clasped in her hands while his arms are anchored around her lower back. They've barely come up for air in the last twenty minutes.

'They're so cute together,' Jake remarks.

Jake's arm and leg are pressed into mine, but that just feels normal. Unremarkable. I stare down at where our bare knees touch – me in my dress, him in his shorts – and wonder if, with someone else, this would feel *exciting*.

I wonder if someone holding me close like Max is holding Cerys would make me feel the swoon-worthy fireworks I read about. If a kiss with someone I cared for, really truly *liked*, would feel every bit as incandescent as fanfics make it sound.

I want that. I want what they have.

But it's not just that. I want ... to feel just like everybody else. I want to be the kind of teenager who kisses a cute boy at a party, like Cerys and Nikita. I'm so sick of being *me*, sometimes.

It's not as if there's anybody here I fancy, and I'd rather spend my night hanging out with Jake than making an idiot of myself flirting with a boy who doesn't care about me. But still, I feel ... like I'm missing out. Like no matter how hard I keep trying, I'm *still* stuck on the outside looking in.

'I love them so much,' Jake sighs, oblivious to my spinning – and somehow still totally on the same wavelength as me. 'Doesn't it make you wish you had what they have sometimes?'

'More like all the time,' I mutter, but Jake laughs like I don't really mean it. I take the bottle off him, have another swig of wine. It's sweet and sharp all at once, but the taste isn't so bad anymore. There's a pleasant, buzzy feeling in my head and body. I feel warm and loose, less guarded and awkward.

I even got up to dance, earlier. *I* was the one who pulled Cerys and Nikita and the others up to dance!

I started everyone jumping around, singing along to the music! That was fun. Jake was the first to join me, of course. He's rarely got inhibitions about anything – and I rarely have inhibitions around him. It was just nice to feel that way with everybody else, too, for a change.

Just then, I notice Nikita wandering away from a group of people. She clocks Cerys and Max tangled up together and rolls her eyes. Her eyes land on me and Jake, next, and she grimaces as I stare back at her. She was in kind of a mood when the boys showed up down the Bay earlier to hang out with us, and clearly *anything* is better than hanging out with me, because she turns sharply on her heel and stalks off.

I feel like I've messed up, but have no idea why. I just hope she doesn't find some reason to kick me out of the group for whatever *that* was.

Then Jake says, 'Speaking of . . . I'm kind of . . . Well, I think I'm sort of *talking* to someone?' He blurts the last part so fast, the words a little slurred with wine, that it takes me a second to process. Then I whip around so fast I tip him off balance and he goes falling sideways into the grass with a laugh.

'Who? Since when? How did you meet them? Say more. Say *everything*.'

He's blushing. I can tell even in the dark, and his grin is so wide I can see all his teeth.

'His name's Teddy. His brother is one of Ginny's uni flatmates. He'll be starting at Bath next year, too, so he's only a year older than us. I met him when we helped her move out of the student halls at the end of term –'

'Ohmigod. Not the cute guy with the Afro and the freckles that you sent me a voice note about?'

'Yes! Him! And he thought I was a student –'

'Because you were carrying all Ginny's textbooks, and you didn't realize when he asked if you studied music –'

'And I was just like "Yeah, I play the trumpet in the orchestra!" and then he started asking about my favourite composers –'

'And *you* said Lin-Manuel Miranda –'

'Which I stand by. But yes, him. That guy!' Jake says excitedly, his voice climbing. 'Anyway, he ended up finding me on Instagram afterwards . . .'

'Ohmigod I'm *obsessed*.' I am. My eyes are about to fall out of my head. My cheeks hurt from smiling so wide. *That's* who Jake must've been messaging on Sunday at the cafe!

He carries on, 'So we've just been, you know, talking. But he said maybe if I went to visit Gin next term, he might see me around. It's a good sign, right? Do you think that's a good sign?'

Jake's eyes are wide too, but they're pleading, and he bites his lip nervously, looking over towards Cerys and Max. His glasses have a smudge on them that he doesn't seem to notice.

'I think so,' I say, although I am hardly the authority on the topic of boys flirting. Or *anyone* flirting, really. 'Let's see your messages?'

We bend over his phone, passing the wine back and forth and scrolling through the hundreds of messages they've exchanged. I swipe on to Teddy's profile and he really is every bit as good looking as Jake made him out to be. He has light-brown skin and a face full of freckles, and a bright, friendly smile in all his photos.

'You should ask Cerys,' I say at last. 'Or send screenshots to Daphne. They're much better at this than I am . . .'

Granted, Daphne's been stuck in the same flirtationships for ages, and Cerys spent *months* chatting to Max online in an OWAR Discord channel before realizing it wasn't Jake she was flirting with . . . but still. Daphne dates! Cerys has watched every romcom under the sun! I have . . . read more than my fair share of fanfictions.

'Oh come on, Nis. I refuse to believe nobody's sliding into your DMs.' Jake bumps his shoulder to mine playfully, and I bark a laugh.

Sure – just a sort-of famous actor I sort-of insulted, and spilled coffee all over.

Jake's smile softens, more sincere than his usual jokey nature, and we cwtch back up together in silence for a few moments. I wish I had better advice for him. I wish I had *any* advice for him.

What would we do if this was happening in our TTRPG campaign? If our characters were facing down a problem that needed solving and met someone whose intentions were unclear?

Mida would know what to do. She'd have great advice. Something like . . .

'Maybe it's not such a bad idea to meet up with him. You know, casually. It doesn't have to be a whole *thing*. You could go see Ginny, and he just *happens* to be there, too,' I suggest. 'Like he mentioned.'

'D'you think so?'

'It can't hurt. And in the meantime, you can just carry on like you are. If it *does* feel flirty . . . that doesn't have to be a bad thing.'

'Yeah. Yeah! You're so right! Okay.' He beams, and swings his arm around my shoulder, wrapping me up in his body heat. He's sweaty from the summer heat and booze, but I probably am, too. 'You always have the answers, Anissa. You're the best, d'you know that?'

I smile, sinking my head on to his shoulder. And maybe it's just the wine talking, but it's nice to believe him, if only for tonight.

OWAR Discord Kai-rry On My Wayward Son
General

@osterionprincess1
omgomgomg did we all see this article yesterday?

@osterionprincess1 sent a link: *12 Celebrity Teens Who Got Their A-Level Results Today!*

@osterionprincess2
ew why are you up so early it's the summer holidays

@osterionprincess1
Not for those of us with JOBS, 2. Why are you up?!

@osterionprincess2
I haven't been to bed yet lol! Too busy reading that Hades/Persephone retelling you lent me!

@therunestar
Oh my goodness, yes! How cute is that! Up there with a literal pop star sensation and TikTok comedian with twenty mil followers, love this for him!

@rubytherapscallion
would never have guessed he was studying German? idk why he just doesn't strike me as a languages guy?

@osterionprincess2
Well, he did fail that exam apparently lol so maybe he's not much of a languages guy after all!

@wrathfulqueen93
DID YOU SEE AS WELL

@wrathfulqueen93
HE WAS IN THE TRAILER FOR THAT NEW NETFLIX THRILLER

@wrathfulqueen93
WHEN DID HE EVEN HAVE TIME TO FILM THAT?

@wrathfulqueen93
I hope this doesn't mean he's barely in s5 of OWAR, my heart couldn't take the Kai-baiting

@therunestar
Wait @ladyanissadishipper how did your results day go! You never told us!

@rubytherapscallion
hope French went better than Callum's German did lol

@ladyanissadishipper
Haha, just a bit, no resits at least! Got all As otherwise so I'm happy!

@osterionprincess1
That's amazing Anissa!!! Congrats!

@osterionprincess2
proud of you!

@therunestar
WHOOO! We were never in doubt!

CHAPTER 13

I'm in the canteen grabbing lunches for my team and there's a nagging, leaden feeling in the pit of my stomach that I can't quite shake.

It has nothing to do with the hangover I'm carrying around from last night's party.

Or the fact I can't remember which salad dressing Lisa told me to get.

It's because I went to look back at my DMs with Callum this morning, almost convinced I'd made them up, only to find I couldn't access his Instagram at all. I thought maybe he'd deleted his whole profile, but no – just me. He's *blocked* me.

Why would he talk to me, only to block me hours later?

What a weirdo. Maybe his Reddit AMA responses weren't deadpan humour after all, and he wasn't just having an 'off' day whenever I've run into him – he's just genuinely incapable of holding a polite conversation.

I get my answer when he suddenly appears at my shoulder while I'm at an empty lunch table, trying to stack all the takeaway salads and sandwiches to carry back. He startles me so badly I almost upend the whole lot.

'Bloody hell! Where did you come from?' He's dressed in gym gear, so I ask, 'Ooh, are you training for the sword fight again today?'

'Why?' he snaps. 'Going to tell everyone about that, too?'

'What?'

That's when I realize that he hasn't come to chat – he's *seething*. Clenched jaw, furious eyes, his hands balling into fists before he shoves them into his jacket pockets. He glances about furtively, aware how busy the canteen is, and his mouth contorts into another rigid, fake smile before he speaks through gritted teeth.

'What the hell, Anissa! Why would you do that? Did they pay you or something? I just – you could've *told* me, if that was the case. I'm not that much of an exclusive, but it's good to know I am worth selling out.'

'What are you *talking* about?'

'My exam results. My resit! It was all over the internet!'

I baulk, remembering the link @osterionprincess1 sent over Discord this morning. I hadn't thought much of it at the time, but – 'Is that why you blocked me? You think *I* did that?'

His irate silence says it all. He refuses to look at me, choosing to glower at my Jenga tower of lunches instead.

'Who would I even tell?' Aside from the different Discord server I'm part of, and the wider OWAR fandom in general . . .

I course correct. '*Why* would I tell anyone? It didn't seem like you were broadcasting it.'

'No – you did that well enough on your own.'

'Oh my God!' I exclaim, letting the salad bowls fall across the table. A few people look over, and Callum jumps to help me with them before anyone else can. Somehow, that annoys me even more than his accusation. As *if* he's such a decent guy!

I grab the sleeve of his jacket, like I'm about to shake some sense into him. I'm careful to keep my voice low, aware we could easily be overheard. If rumours start to circulate that I sold Callum Denver's exam results to journalists, it would hardly be a leap to assume I'd sell OWAR's season six secrets, too, getting me and Cerys kicked out. 'What is *wrong* with you? I didn't tell anybody!'

He scoffs. A muscle rolls in his jaw. I've seen him do that in scenes he's filmed for Kai when the character's browbeaten and holding back, but I don't know what it means coming from Callum.

I let go of his sleeve.

I can't BELIEVE he's accusing me of this! As if I'd blab about his German oral exam when I had my own results to be thinking about and celebrating! As if *he* was even on my mind at all!

Now *I'm* seething.

'Real mature, blocking me,' I snap. 'You could've just asked, you know. If you thought I was the one leaking it.'

'Who else?'

'I – I don't *know*! But that seems like a you problem.' He's about to protest again, so I cut him off. 'This might shock you, *Your Highness*, but I've got plenty going on in my life that I don't need to spend all my time thinking about *you*. I told you this goes both ways. You don't get to – to dehumanize me for being a fan of OWAR, or whatever.'

So what if *Of Wrath and Rune* is such a huge anchor in my life? If Kai is? Callum most certainly is *not*.

'That's not . . .' he says through gritted teeth, but he trails off, stops himself, never finishes that sentence. Because it is *exactly* what he's doing, and he knows it.

He sees my love of OWAR – of Kai Osterion – as a weapon.

Why does it sting this much? Anger flares hot and bitter in my chest, and something caves in. In that moment, all the parts of me that have loved this fandom – the parts that were chipped away over the years by unthinking, cruel comments from people at school – begin to crumble under the weight of his accusation.

He's taking it away from me. Spoiling it, souring it. Turning it into something poisonous and aching.

My mouth pinches into a line, and it's all I can do not to let this horrible, conceited boy make me cry. I'm sure he'd get a real kick out of poking fun at a sad fangirl, the prick. My hands tremble as I gather the lunches back up.

When I try to plaster on a polite smile, for the sake of anybody else watching, it feels brittle and thin. By some miracle, instead of crying, I do at least manage to glare at him.

He says, 'If you weren't already going to be out of here in a few weeks –'

'Lucky for you, *I will be*.'

'Yeah? Good riddance.' It comes out so petulant I roll my eyes, smirking, which only seems to rile him up even more. Good. He deserves to feel like crap if he's going to talk to me like this.

'Do us both a favour,' I tell him, 'and stay out of my way.'

'Gladly.'

'GOOD.'

'GREAT.'

'*Wunderbar,*' I say, and his mouth twitches. A little louder, as I begin to march off, I add, 'And just so you know, the coffee station is all out of caramel syrup. Sucks to be you.'

'You just worry about your own coffee, Fangirl.'

'Oh, I will!'

Back in Téiglin's forest cottage, where we're working today, I dole out the food and get back to work with renewed fervour. I was so excited for this set earlier. It's in season five, but we only saw a brief teaser of it in the trailer; it's having to be remade totally from scratch now, since production moved, and I could hardly contain myself when we pulled together a thousand tiny touches rife with Easter eggs and nods to the character's backstory. Now, it just feels like . . . like I'm stapling fake vines to a fake moss wall. It doesn't even matter that it's in an antler-shaped pattern, to reflect the character.

I was giddy about this earlier. That feels so far out of reach now.

And in that moment, I decide I hate Callum Denver.

CHAPTER 14

I'm running low on spell slots after this latest battle against the palace guards, and it's risky to use any of my few precious remaining spells in case we come across more guards, traps or foes.

So instead I hit Prince Kai on the head with the butt of my dagger.

I can't *stab* him, can I? That's a bit drastic. And it'll trigger a fight scene. I'm not really sure the rest of the party would defend *me* in that instance ...

'Whoa! I'm still tying him up!' shouts Cailean, who's currently binding the prince's hands behind his back with some extra-durable, dwarf-made rope.

'Errr, Mida? He's only just regaining consciousness,' the Moonwalker adds, which isn't *really* a protest, but he doesn't seem too impressed with my actions.

'Exactly!' I grumble. 'I trust him about as far as I

can throw him – and I've already had to dispatch one traitor at this party. He's too high value a hostage to be worth this risk. But since you've all outvoted me and chosen to take him *prisoner* rather than kill him, this is the next best thing.'

I throw my D20 die a little bit too furiously. I roll a sixteen. It's a hit – barely. Unfortunately, my character Mida is not very physically strong, and the official character sheet for Prince Kai Osterion shows he's actually pretty tough. Ugh.

I roll some more dice and grumble again.

'Only two health points' worth of damage . . .'

Prince Kai, stirring, winces at the blow, though it's barely enough to leave a bruise. He strains against his bonds, to no avail. 'Hardly sporting, to kick a man when he's down, my lady.'

Wreevo chokes out a laugh. 'Ha! A lady! First time you've gotten that from royalty, I'll bet, Mida! You've gone from pouring their wine and emptying their chamber pots to being called "my lady"!'

Anger licks along the top of my spine, squaring my shoulders. I grind out, 'There's plenty more where that came from. I'd hate for him to underestimate anybody here.' Me, in particular.

'Then maybe you should've used the pointy end,' the prince drawls.

Glowering, I make to lift my dagger again.

'No!' the others shout, and the Moonwalker dives forward to catch my arm and restrain me. He levels me with a stern look. 'I don't trust him either, but you're right – he's too high value. We want him captive, not bloodied up and injured. Cool it, Mida.'

Max sits up in his seat, already rattling his dice in his hand. 'And I am going to try and wrestle the dagger off you, which will be . . . What do we think, stealth check while she's distracted? Strength check?'

Much to my chagrin, I roll a measly four on my defence. I lose my dagger to the Moonwalker and have to settle for glowering at Kai. I'm itching to use up a spell slot on this smug, insufferable prince.

Jake smothers a laugh behind his hand, his eyes gleeful. 'Mida's such a badass. Amazing. I did *not* see this coming from her.'

'None of us did,' Cerys echoes, giving me a puzzled look, probably confused by my attitude now she understands that Kai's my comfort character. But she doesn't know about my latest argument with Callum, or the whole Instagram blocking thing. She had told me I seemed a bit quiet in some of our car rides home, but I fobbed her off with excuses about being tired from work.

It's fine. I am TOTALLY fine.

I just thought it might be a *little* bit cathartic to take some of my anger at Callum out on his fictional character in our even more fictional game. But really, I should have anticipated the others wanting to kidnap Prince Kai, for the plot.

Which, like, *yay*. Whoopee. More time with Kai Osterion, when I'm dying of shame.

I did this to myself. Lesson learned, I guess.

Relieved of my dagger, I'm left seething while the prince smirks at me. 'Wonderful. Now that's settled, I suppose it's worth admitting I know exactly why you're here. I foresaw much of this. I suppose you're responsible for the dead spy upstairs, my lady? It didn't look clean enough to be the Moonwalker.'

I scowl in response.

'You'll have to work a lot harder if you expect any kind of help from *me*,' Kai informs us all. 'I am a prince of the noble and royal House of Osterion. You won't get away with this for long.'

'Oh, I don't know,' says the Moonwalker, and his

smile is dangerous. 'The party upstairs has only just gotten started. It'll be a *very* long time before anybody even notices you're missing.'

'Brutal,' mutters Wreevo, while Cailean chokes a laugh.

Even though I should feel a sense of satisfaction at the dig, I have to look away.

The Moonwalker announces, 'We should get a move on. These dungeons are huge, and who knows what kind of traps or protective magicks are in place? We have to find the Crown before sunrise, and before the party is over.'

Wreevo – the largest of our party as a seven-foot-tall orc – easily wrestles the young prince to his feet, and frogmarches him over the dead bodies of the guards we just dispatched and into the dungeon corridor. 'Come then, Your Highness! No time to waste.'

'You'll never find it. And I'll *never* help you.'

Cailean laughs, and spins his hand axe deftly, before helping the real Lord Syxos to his feet to accompany us on this next leg of the quest.

'On your head be it, Prince Kai. On your head be it.'

As we wrap up the session, the others are buzzing – amped up from another fight scene and the excitement of new character dynamics with a cool, interesting hostage.

'I hope you'll find a way to bring Roach in,' Jake tells me. 'That's my favourite theory – that *he's* the one who'll take the Eldritch Crown, and become the next ruler . . .'

I actually prefer the contradicting fan theory that the Osterions seize it first and try to force Kai to wield it, since he's the only one of them with any kind of magick; especially after he's been such a source of exasperation for them . . .

The thought suddenly hits me like a gut punch: I might've been able to explore that plot line and play it out now we've brought Prince Kai along (however unwittingly) for the adventure.

Except apparently all I want to do is make sure everyone knows how much I hate Callum. I mean, Kai.

'Are we still dressing up for the convention next week?' Cerys asks, breaking me out of my reverie. She's looking nervously at all of us. For all her confidence, she's still getting used to showing the fangirl side of herself with things like cosplay. It's weirdly validating – that even she feels the way I do sometimes, like when I'm around the girls from college. Or people in general.

'For sure! I repainted my wings and everything the other night, so my Daxys cosplay will be *perfect*! Who said the ADHD urge to hyperfocus on one task for hours would never come in handy!' Jake beams, laughing while Cerys rolls her eyes at him. Max on the other hand merely nods – as if it was ever in question he'd be in his meticulous Moonwalker cosplay, with the long white-blonde wig, elf ears and black leather armour pieces.

Cerys lets out a sigh of relief. 'Great! I've got to make sure my Lady Adanna di Silver wig is still in good shape . . . What about you, Anissa?'

'I was going to go in character, as Mida, since there's going to be stuff there about the OWAR tabletop role-play game. I saw on Discord loads of other people are doing that, too.'

Cerys's eyes light up. 'Love that! If it's anything like her miniature, you'll look amazing!' She grabs the tiny figure from the dungeon map on the table to thrust towards me: my sorceress with her dark hair in a bun and in a red dress with heavy, draped sleeves and bronze detailing. The dress I ordered off Amazon and got Nan to help me alter is a fair imitation. Cerys has even painted the miniature with a tiny snake-cuff earring.

I only hope I can do Mida justice, in real life.

The con next week in Bristol isn't specific to OWAR, but more of a general fantasy fandom one, focusing on niche series as well as indie authors. There's a romantasy ball afterwards, too, but you have to be eighteen or older to attend that, which sucks. At least we'll still get to enjoy the panels during the day though, and Jake and I plan to attend the one-shot TTRPG that's being run by some other *Of Wrath and Rune* fans.

'You know,' Cerys says brightly, with a sing-song edge that feels conspiratorial, 'I heard they announced a couple of OWAR cast members are going to be attending the con next week, to take part in some panels.'

'Oh yeah?' I smile, gesturing at Jake leaving the cafe just ahead of us. 'How many times do you think he can get Brayden Brown to sign the same poster before it gets weird?'

Cerys giggles, but says, 'And *Callum* will be there.'

'Denver?' As if she means anybody else. She's giving me another *look*, though, so I force myself to shrug. 'So what?'

'Seeing as how he plays your favourite character and all, and he'll probably be there to talk about Prince Kai . . . And,' she says, and *there* it is – what I've been dreading, 'apparently the two of you hang out a bit on set.'

'According to *who*?'

'Just, you know, people. Apparently you're getting quite friendly.'

The sound I make is somewhere between a snort of disbelief and a laugh of outright hilarity. As if we're anything close to *friendly*! I can only guess we've done too good a job of trying to conceal our animosity from eavesdroppers and onlookers.

'He's even got a nickname for you, I heard.'

Fangirl? That feels more like a barb than a nickname. A nickname would imply some degree of affection.

The thought makes me laugh all over again.

CHAPTER 15

For a couple of days, everything is going ... *well*, I think. There's nothing much going on at home and the group chats tick along as normal, with the girls making plans for back-to-college shopping trips and an end-of-summer brunch when they're all home again, and the boys discussing the timetable for the upcoming con.

But most importantly, for a blessed few days, I don't run into Callum on set.

And, since he's blocked me on Instagram, I don't see him on my feed.

I *may* also have muted notifications from the Kai-rry On My Wayward Son Discord, but that's just a small, tiny, insignificant and (probably) temporary measure.

Then mid-morning on Wednesday, everything turns promptly to shit. Filming today is of another palace scene, and I've been called in again to help. The studio is total chaos, with loads of the crew off on holidays this week, technical issues with one of the main cameras and two entirely different call sheets distributed.

Only half the actors are here. Runners are sent scattering in all directions.

Someone nearby lets out a frustrated groan and curses under their breath. I think he's on the production team – he's always involved with the director and actors. I'm not sure what his title is, but I'd bet his job boils down to 'keeping the ship running smoothly'.

'Where's . . .? Oh, bloody *hell* . . .' His head snaps towards me. 'You.'

I startle. 'Um, yes?'

'Grab Denver for me, will you?'

'S-sorry?'

'*Callum*. From his trailer. Don't think anyone went to get him. Here.' With a flourish, he pulls a sheet from his clipboard and presents it to me. 'Just don't get distracted gossiping at the coffee cart again, alright?'

I cringe at the way he says it, as if it's such a regular thing.

I don't *want* to go and fetch Callum. But what else am I supposed to do? Production Guy is already striding away, so I take a breath and dash off in the direction of the trailers at the back of the lot. As I weave my way through them, I want to stop and grab a pic for Jake of all the actors' names on trailer doors, but the urge is swallowed by a sort of blank screaming noise in my head. Why can't I find Callum's name? Have I gone past it already? I feel a bit sick.

It feels like the entire success of this show rests on whether I collect Callum in time.

Which, obviously, is wildly irrational, but Production Guy trusted me, the set is in chaos, what if it *does* all rest on me? I can't focus enough to calm down. This is so much more responsibility than *please arrange these fake tankards adequately*.

By the time I fling myself to a stop at Callum's trailer (I did run right past it the first time, whoops) I'm hugging a stitch in my side and panting for breath. I'm about to pound a hand flat on the door when I hear: 'I told you, I'm not doing it,' says Callum. 'They'll have to find someone else.'

There's a brusque laugh. It's a bit tinny, and I realize it must be coming from a phone or a video call. 'Believe me, mate, they'll have no problem finding someone else. Take some time, yeah? I'll send the contracts through.'

Callum sighs, and it sounds . . . *heavy*.

He starts to say something, but the voice on the phone beats him to it. 'I'm telling you: you could be *it*. Things are taking off way better than we could've predicted. And *this* role would really seal the deal. No more scripts with barely a single line of dialogue, or crappy convention halls . . . So take a look, yeah, and we'll circle back in a couple of days. You owe me some audition tapes, too.'

'About that –'

'Got to go, kid. Don't forget, alright! Sooner the better! Favreau put in a special request for you – that doesn't happen often. Who would've thought he'd be such a big OWAR fan . . .? Right-o, speak soon! Shout me if you've got any questions!'

'Richie –'

Richie, though, has presumably hung up.

There's some frustrated muttering, and in the few seconds of silence, the content of that conversation starts to sink in a little. Audition tapes. *You could be it.* Richie must be Callum's manager or agent. Callum really is taking a step into the limelight. Far beyond 'crappy convention halls', at any rate.

So why doesn't he sound thrilled about it?

Never mind that though, because just then Callum throws open the door of his trailer, and freezes with one foot out the door, staring at me in disbelief. He's in costume – purple cloak, sword belt and all – with his hand stopped halfway through his hair.

'Now you're *eavesdropping* on me?'

I brandish the corrected call sheet. 'No. I'm collecting you.'

'I'm not a Pokémon,' he mutters, scowling, but takes the sheet as I explain quickly – still breathless – about the mix up.

Then I add, 'It seems some people are under the false impression we've had something resembling a friendly conversation.'

'Why?'

'Maybe if you didn't stalk me around set, they wouldn't.'

'I don't –'

'*You've* approached *me* twice. Out of the three times we've talked.' *In person*.

The frown settles deeper into his forehead. Then he grinds out, 'Well, you're here now. So we'll call it even.'

I grumble and wait on the trailer's steps while Callum makes sure he's got everything. He leaves the door ajar, and I can't help but take a glimpse inside. There's a small bed wedged at one end, a chair in front of a tiny vanity that looks like it's being used as a desk. There's a huge stack of scripts on a coffee table, too, surrounded by highlighters and notebooks and a copy of *Of Wrath and Rune* that's thick with coloured sticky tabs.

I crane my neck to get a better look. It looks about as tattered and well-read as *my* copies. Maybe Callum really does care about this role the way I hoped he would . . .?

When he finally joins me outside, I say, 'So do you deface all your books, or just the ones you're filming?'

Something flickers across his face – a series of tiny expressions that shift so fast, I can't catch a single one of them, just the end result, which is decidedly *stormy*. Brow furrowed, mouth set and taut at the edges, jaw clenched on one side, eyes that just *dare* me to push him.

'That's not mine,' he grunts, and stalks away.

'But –'

What did he say in that Reddit AMA? Something about it being tricky to study Kai's character in the books . . . Maybe he *didn't*, after all. Maybe they *made* him use a coach to portray Kai's neurodivergent coding to not upset the fans, and *he* doesn't really care but is just saving face? The thought that he could approach this role so callously hurts so much, makes me feel so silly for how seriously *I* take it, I feel winded.

'Are you coming or not, Fangirl?'

I pull a face at his back before chasing after him. Callum's walking so fast, I have to jog to keep up. The stitch in my side comes back in full force, and I fight to hide the fact I'm wheezing.

Something which, obviously, he doesn't fail to notice. 'Too busy stalking me to hit the gym?'

'Not everyone needs to be fighting fit – *literally* – for their stunts,' I pant.

Callum inclines his head and I notice him bite the inside of his cheek, almost like he regrets the comment. Then, in a surprising plot twist, he slows down and asks me with forced politeness, 'Not really into sports?'

I'm so caught off guard I answer honestly. 'I don't know. I always got picked last for PE and everyone made it clear they didn't want me on their team, so I never got to try much. Hockey always seemed fun, though. And I liked netball in primary school.'

Callum's expression softens with sincerity – some kind of ... sympathy? Understanding? Pity? – that almost floors me. I manage to shake it off with only a small stumble.

As if he needs any more reasons to think I'm a freak. Grade-A Fangirl, OWAR nerd, and a total loser at school. But it doesn't feel like that. It feels like ...

Maybe he's not judging me?

That's new. Not from Callum but from anyone. I'm so used to having to be on the defence; I've spent so long making myself smaller to avoid it, that I'm not really sure how to react to this different attitude now. I've barely gotten used to being myself around Cerys and the others.

We go the rest of the way in silence and when we

arrive on set, order has been restored – there are actors in the room, stand-ins on marks, camera crew at the ready, and everyone else has mostly dispersed. The assistant director spots us with a look of relief, and waves Callum over.

'Thanks, Anissa,' Callum says, a little louder than necessary. 'Appreciate it!'

When nobody chases me out of the room, I debate staying. I've watched a few scenes being filmed and it's always so magical to see the characters come to life and discover new snippets of the story and world I love so much before anyone else. But my eyes light on Callum, who's rolling his eyes at his phone and shoving it ruthlessly out of sight within the folds of his costume, and I make a snap decision to dart out of the room, putting the set firmly behind me. I go to seek out Cerys instead, hoping to clear my head with some mindless chatter about her work, the college girls, her next date with Max. *Anything* but Callum Denver.

We aren't friends. We're barely even acquaintances. And I *won't* let him ruin this experience for me anymore than he already has.

GIRLIE POPS 2.0! ✨✨

Daphne from college
Quick question . . .

How do we feel about boys using the monkey-face emojis? Flirty or cringe?

Nikita from college (Daphne's friend)
Automatic ick, in the bin, cancel him immediately

Chloe with the Twitch channel
Raf seems like a monkey emoji kinda guy tbh

Cerys
No but he really does???

Daphne from college
It's not Raf . . .

Me
Of course Crap Daniel is a monkey emoji man

I'm actually with Nikita on this though, it's not it

Nikita from college (Daphne's friend)
Loooool 'Crap Daniel' that sent me

Accurate tho

IN! THE! BIN!!!!!!!

Evie Price from school and also now college
DAPHNE I THOUGHT WE HAD BINNED HIM OFF!!!??!?!?

Lest we forget, he SNOGGED ANOTHER GIRL at the results day party!!!!!!

Also @Cerys how did date night with Max go?! The picnic?

Cerys
Omg it was SO beyond cute, he made some lush sandwiches and brought my fave chocolates and a fruit platter and it was so so adorable

I forgot to get any pics!! But we watched the sunset and it was just SO lovely

Chloe with the Twitch channel
Max is honestly the sweetest

Me
Cinnamon roll human, protect him at all costs

Daphne from college
Stoppppp that's so cute! I love that! If he wanted to he woulddddd

Nikita from college (Daphne's friend)
And he wouldn't use a single monkey emoji to do it

Me
And not a single monkey emoji in sight

Evie Price from school and also now college
Lol! Jinx you two!

Seriously though, Daph, BLOCK THIS BOY ALREADY

Daphne from college
Okay okay!

CHAPTER 16

The convention's being held in a series of event and conference rooms at a hotel in Bristol. The place is so packed it's hard to move without hitting a set of giant wings or bumping into a foam broadsword strapped across someone's back, or tripping over people sat on the floor taking a break between panels.

The aircon works overtime, but still the place smells of sweat and paint and sickly-sweet candyfloss from a stall hidden somewhere behind the crowds. Throngs of people move between the book hall where authors have signing tables set up, and the other spaces – a hall for actors and voiceover artists; the artists' gallery; the 'creatives centre', which seems to be a catch-all for cosplay, TTRPGs, and vendors selling stuff like badges and crocheted stuffies; and the panel room. The noise is unimaginable.

It's *brilliant*.

Sometimes I feel too much, or not enough, and all kinds of wrong – fumbling my way through and hoping for the best. But THIS is where I belong. These are my people, this is my turf and, dressed up like Mida, I feel braver and bolder than ever.

We lost Cerys and Max ages ago. Cerys ran into one of the girls from the local OWAR Discord who she's friendly with and they ended up going to a little Lady Adanna di Silver cosplay meet-up somewhere upstairs. They strode off arm-in-arm, chattering excitedly in their different costumes for their favourite character, with Max as the Moonwalker trailing along behind them in his dark cloak and pale-blonde wig.

I realize that I can no longer feel Jake close at my back and turn to see him stopped in the middle of the hallway, blushing down at his phone. I roll my eyes and tromp back to grab his arm. It's very cute that he's so wrapped up in his crush on Teddy, but *really?*

'Time and place, Jake!' I have to shout to be heard over the crowds, and I yank him along after me. 'Although Teddy must be special if you're willing to miss a panel with Brayden Brown . . .'

That spurs Jake back into action, though he keeps grinning at me. It's boyish and a bit goofy, his eyes bright. He looks totally love-struck.

It's really sweet.

It's really . . . really . . .

I wish I knew what that felt like.

Jake's too wrapped up in his budding new romance to notice if my face does something wrong, though, and he sighs. 'You're right, Nis. He *is* special. He just said he's started watching OWAR to see what all the fuss was about!'

A laugh bursts out of me. 'Now where have I heard that before? Oh, right. That's exactly what Cerys did when *she* fancied you!'

'I suppose that's a guarantee that he must like me back then, isn't it?'

We make it to the panel room, Jake using his giant Daxys cosplay wings to help us slice through the crowds. It's standing-room only, but the room isn't huge to begin with. We manage to grab a decent spot near the back but right in the middle, so we're directly facing the small stage.

A woman in a plain black tee and jeans with a lanyard around her neck strides onstage holding a microphone, and the audience hushes.

'Welcome, everyone, to this special look behind the scenes of your favourite fantasy world, *Of Wrath and Rune*! Today, very excitingly, we're joined by some of the actors from the show to learn a bit more about what goes into bringing these characters to life.

We'll be joined by fan-favourite Rogdan, aka Mark Hitchcock...' A cheer goes through the room, and Jake whoops next to me. 'The evil Osterion queen, Petra Walker...' That's met by a good-natured booing for a beloved villain. 'Her on-screen son, Callum Denver...' A smaller, distinctly polite round of applause for him, but a couple of enthusiastic whistles from within the crowd.

When Jake said he wanted to see this panel, I'd hesitated – but then I realized it was the perfect opportunity to see if OWAR actually *does* matter to Callum beyond a pay cheque and the boost to his career.

And if it really is just *me* he's so standoffish with. Not that I, you know, CARE, or anything. I'm just... curious.

The moderator finishes by saying, 'And the one and only Brayden Brown!'

The cheers are loudest for him, and I'm not surprised. Even if Daxys isn't everyone's top favourite character, the actor is so involved in the community and fanbase that people adore him. The mood in the room swells as the four actors come on stage and take their seats. Petra Walker looks elegantly chic in a pair of beige trousers and a black blouse, and Mark Hitchcock is almost unrecognizable wearing a crisp buttoned-up shirt and with his hair and beard neatly combed.

Callum and Brayden, however, are both in costume. Brayden isn't wearing his wings, but he *is* in some of his Daxys armour, and Callum's wearing his House Osterion cloak and princely trousers and tunic.

Brayden slings an arm around Callum's shoulder and calls out, 'What do you think, guys? Do we win best dressed at the cosplay contest today?'

A series of whoops and whistles accompany the roar of laughter in the room, and he flashes a winning smile at everyone before the moderator gestures for quiet to start the panel.

If I didn't know better, I'd say Callum looked a bit nervous, raising a hand in greeting to the audience even as his eyes dart around the room and he fumbles to take his seat.

But obviously I do know better, and he'd just rather be anywhere but this 'crappy convention hall'. He probably thinks this is all totally beneath him.

The whole audience gets swept up in the panel, hanging off the actors' every word as they share the process of understanding their characters and taking them from book to screen, working alongside the authors and the writers' room. There are jokes about the anonymous authors behind the OWAR books, with some of the panel miming zipping their mouths closed and Mark Hitchcock shifting in his seat, which

I *know* is only going to feed the conspiracy theory that he's one of the authors.

After the moderator wraps up her half hour, she throws it over to the audience, and a few staff members walk around with microphones. There are questions about their favourite scenes to film, who they'd most like to see their character interact with next, thoughts on particular fan theories and cool props they've stolen from set.

Petra is the antithesis of her character – warm and charismatic, far from the cunning, ice-cold queen we see on screen. And Brayden is, as ever, a total hit with everybody, getting a lot of laughs from the crowd. Mark proves to be as grouchy and coarse as his character, but in that grumpy-old-man way that comes off as endearing.

And Callum is . . . an enigma.

Some of his answers feel clipped and short, but there's a hint of self-deprecating humour that reminds me of his Reddit AMA. At other times he gives thoughtful answers, almost making me believe he cares deeply about this show and, more importantly, its fandom.

Almost.

So when the moderator asks, 'Any other questions?' I suddenly find my hand shooting up, and she zones in on me with a smile. 'Great, at the back there!'

A microphone is shoved in my face, and the entire room turns towards me. There must be a hundred pairs of eyes on me, at least. *Including* Callum's, which seem to pierce right through everything else. A cold sweat trickles down my back, and my chest feels tight.

What am I doing?! I don't put myself in the spotlight. I don't put myself OUT THERE. Not like *this*!

But – I guess I'm not me, today. I'm Mida. A ruthless, self-assured sorceress who seizes her fate to forge her own path, after a life of being downtrodden by the crown.

'I just wondered . . .'

My voice comes out thin and raspy. I clear my throat, embarrassed.

The edge of Callum's mouth twitches up, like he's daring me to carry on.

'I just wondered,' I repeat, my voice stronger and clearer now, 'how it feels to have such a dedicated fanbase? Not just for OWAR as a series, but for *you* and your characters.'

'You kidding?' scoffs Mark Hitchcock, and grins. 'Bloody love it. Keeps me going when the going gets tough!'

Petra smiles magnanimously, sincerely. 'It's the greatest honour of my life.'

Brayden Brown nods, uncharacteristically serious for once. 'That it is. These fans – you guys – are my lifeblood. I could never have given all I have to this role without you. Knowing how many lives I've touched as Daxys . . . there's no better feeling. It's everything you dream of, as an actor.'

Everyone's attention turns to Callum.

I give him a smirk of my own. I picked up the gauntlet he threw down. Now it's his turn.

His mouth moves into that imitation of a polite smile he gave me and Cerys the first day we met him on set. The gleam in his eyes is more like something I'd imagine seeing from Kai on screen.

'It can be a lot of pressure, of course. And it can be really difficult at times, too. But you know what?' he drawls, leaning back in his seat, his fake smile widening. 'I'm just so *exceptionally grateful*.'

I look around, bouncing nervously on the balls of my feet. Come on, where *is* he? Jake should be easy to spot, he's tall enough, and with his giant wings! But he went to the toilet fifteen minutes ago, and the *Of Wrath and Rune*-inspired TTRPG one-shot is starting any minute now . . .

My phone buzzes, but it's not Jake – just Nikita in the group chat, asking what time Cerys and I will be back and if we want to hang out later. I grimace; Cerys has date-night plans with Max again, and I'm sure the *last* thing Nikita wants is to get stuck with me waxing lyrical about my nerdy day out. She'll probably make up an excuse to get out of it before I have to. I shove my phone back in my dress pocket without replying.

A body slips out of the crowd to stand directly beside me, leaning a purple-cloaked shoulder against the wall to face me.

'Nice costume, Fangirl. Who are you supposed to be, exactly?'

I scowl at Callum and debate simply ignoring him. Why does he keep seeking me out? He's only doing this to antagonize me.

Well, I won't give him the satisfaction.

But then he takes my character sheet out of my hand, and I'm too slow to snatch it back before he gets a glimpse.

Callum raises an eyebrow at me. 'Mida the sorceress. You play *Of Wrath and Roll*?'

I'm a little surprised he knows what the OWAR version of Dungeons and Dragons is called, but I just grumble, 'I'm a gamemaster, actually. If you *must* know.'

'And what, you came dressed as your character? That dress is . . .' He trails off, clearing his throat and averting his gaze sharply. 'It's, er, something alright.'

Rude! It's a *good* costume, is what it is. I don't normally wear red – purple's my favourite colour – but I can't deny that the deep scarlet suits me, and the cheap velvet fabric is made up for by all the alterations me and Nan (well, mostly Nan) made. Like the braided bronze belt, or the bits of embroidery to reflect Mida's spellwork, or the long, draped sleeves with chiffon inserts that cascade all the way down to my knees.

Instead of showing it off, though, I cross my arms over my chest defensively and give Callum's own costume a pointed look.

He rolls his eyes. 'It's really hard to talk Brayden out of an idea once he gets it into his head. A couple of the others who came along dressed up, too. We thought ... I dunno, thought it'd be fun.' He shrugs, trailing off, his voice sounding uncharacteristically small.

'I'm sure the costume department were thrilled.'

Callum meets my gaze now, with a hint of a smile. 'Yeah, we'll get an earful on Monday morning, but they can't stay mad at Brayden for long. He could get away with murder, I swear.'

'And you can't?'

'Apparently not. Nice line of questioning earlier, by the way.'

'Nice answer. Really ... evasive.'

He inclines his head in a noncommittal response I can't decipher, and I turn away with a huff. I wish he'd just *go away*. And where the hell is Jake?!

'Aren't you going in?' Callum asks. He gestures at the board nearby, signposting the one-shot campaign that's about to begin now in a minute.

'I'm waiting for someone.'

'Your friend from set?'

'No. Someone else. I have *multiple* friends, you know.' Except it sounds so childish when I say it out loud, he probably thinks it more likely they're imaginary friends. And then, and I don't know why, but I say, 'I'm waiting for A GUY, actually. His name's Jake.'

Callum lifts an eyebrow. 'Uh-huh.'

Is he laughing at me? Was that sceptical? Or just the tone of someone who deeply, sincerely, does not give a single shit who I'm waiting for?

Not sure what else to do but deflect, I snap, 'Are *you* going to play? There's already a Prince Kai character sheet ready-made in the handbook. I'm sure even you could pick up how to do it.'

He smiles again, but this one is wry and mirthless. Somehow, it's even colder and more closed-off than any of his Kai expressions. 'I'm sure I could. But nobody wants me there.'

I don't want him there, obviously, but . . .

'What do you mean?'

As if on cue, a man in his twenties walks past to make his way into the TTRPG session, and catches sight of us. He gives Callum a wide smile and a clap on the shoulder as he passes.

'Hey, mate, great costume. Prince Oscar, right? Nice!'

He's already gone before either of us can correct him, and I'm stunned he didn't recognize Callum – *in costume*, no less – but Callum just shrugs at me as if a point's been proven.

'Not everybody is as excited as you are about Kai.'

'But . . .'

But that's not the point, is it? Not for *this*, anyway. He wouldn't be swanning in to steal the show as some jumped-up actor (even if that's *exactly* what he is), he'd just be there to play, dressed up in character like the rest of us, immersed in a world we all love and collectively want to be part of for a little while.

We would all be someone else, someone . . . a little bit *more* than we are in real life. Does Callum ever feel like that when he's acting? Does he get that with Kai?

'Sounds like they're starting,' he remarks, nodding his head towards the room.

They are – but Jake isn't here yet, and . . . and I'm nervous to go in on my own. Despite my earlier excitement, now I'm worried that people won't like my character or my costume, that they won't like *me*. That I'll know too much about OWAR, or not enough. That I'll forget some obvious rule and make a silly mistake that annoys everyone. With ever-likable, charismatic Jake by my side, that all seemed a lot less intimidating.

And, for some reason, I hate the idea of Callum thinking I made up this guy I was waiting for. Even if it is only Jake. It feels like losing some kind of battle I regret fighting.

What, like a fake dating trope was going to help me . . . impress Callum? Make *me* feel better? As if.

Mida wouldn't care about any of this. Faced with disdain from Prince Kai Osterion, she'd give back as good as she got, and she wouldn't give a toss what he thought as long as she was sticking to her principles and her plan.

I clutch my character sheet tighter and square my shoulders before taking a step towards the room.

'Are you coming, *Your Highness*?'

I'm goading him, and the smirk Callum gives me as he pushes away from leaning against the wall tells me he knows it. The extra distance he puts between us makes me notice the sudden chill where his body heat was just moments ago. I search his face and find a glint in his eyes that seems almost cheeky, but when he speaks, there's an undercurrent to his voice that has me bristling.

'Enjoy playing pretend, sorceress Mida.'

'I plan to.'

I whirl on my heel and stride into the room, chin up and heart racing. I swear I hear Callum chuckle before he walks away – but I don't stop to dwell on it. I find a space at a table and sit down, relieved to find some familiar faces already there – Heather and Fern from the local South Wales OWAR Discord – trying their hand at some tabletop role play.

After a quick round of introductions to the group and our characters, our gamemaster for the next two hours sweeps us into an immersive fantasy adventure, and I lose myself in the game, exhilarated.

It doesn't matter if it's all pretend. The companionship and connection are all real, and I'm so glad I was brave enough to let myself be a part of it.

CHAPTER 17

Against all odds, Callum and I have clearly done too good a job at appearing at least halfway polite towards each other, because I get the absolute joy of being sent on even more errands involving him.

I can't really say *no*. With schedules still a mess and so many people away on summer holidays, everyone's being roped into tasks beyond their usual roles. Lisa has to lend the costume department a hand. Cerys gets purloined by make-up once they realize how talented she is with a paintbrush, especially when so many of the creature characters in the show aren't CGI.

Cerys loves it. She won't shut up about how enamoured she is with the whole thing, how exciting she finds it. The literal embodiment of the starry-eyed emoji.

'I could really see myself doing this,' she tells me in a breathy rush on the drive in. 'Like ... I'm *good* at this. You know? It's so much better than I could've imagined. My team are even helping me find courses to get qualifications for this sort of thing! Ugh, I'm just *so* glad we did this! Aren't you?'

'OH YEAH,' I say. 'TOTALLY.'

It's not that I *hate* it. If I did, I could just leave. I never came into this work experience with the same keen, career-minded focus Cerys did. If anything, her mention of qualifications makes my stomach tangle in knots. I've been avoiding thinking too much about the fact we'll have to start submitting our uni applications soon. I don't even *know* what I want to study, let alone figured out what I want to do for a job. Whenever Cerys tries to ask me about it and says I'm being awfully quiet or seem off, I just ask her more about her plans instead.

But I really *do* love being on set and being a real part of bringing my favourite series to life. There's magic in building the story with so many tiny details. Here, I don't have to pretend to be a little bit less than I am – I can let my inner nerd out unashamedly, and nobody ever looks at me sideways for it. Everyone here really is wonderful.

Well – most of them.

The Monday after the convention, I'm sent to deliver some new pages to Callum in his trailer. (I blame

Brayden Brown: apparently he's been telling people me and Callum 'hung out' at the con. Who knew *Daxys* would be such a gossip?)

Callum barely opens the door wide enough to peer out, and his hand slips through the crack to take the edited script off me before he slams the door in my face with a grunted 'thanks'. It's a far cry from the wide smiles and chatty small talk he exchanges with other crew members; I'm not even sure anymore if he's doing it purposely to wind me up, or just hates me that much.

Then I happen, by some cruel twist of fate, to be standing near him when filming pauses to move a couple of cameras to new marks. I'm fixing a sextant back into place on a table after one of the boom-mic operators accidentally knocked it over, and Callum says, 'I'd kill for a coffee right now.'

Charming! Sure, I've let some of the higher-up crew members boss me about on errands, but coming from *him*, it's something else entirely.

Especially when he didn't even look at me. Or say please. Or even *ask*, like a polite and normal person.

'Oh?' I bite out, smiling even as I glower at him. I swallow the urge to call him an entitled dickhead and tell him where to go. Callum deigns to meet my eye then. 'Your usual? Anyone else, while I'm there?'

Feeling *incredibly* petty, I go out of my way the next

afternoon to bring Callum a coffee. Iced Americano, with caramel syrup. I present it to him when he's loitering in the palace war room as everyone takes a break and the director talks to a couple of the lead actors.

Callum eyes the drink warily, like I've poisoned it.

I take a sip from the straw, then hand it back to him. 'Just caramel, don't worry.'

'I didn't think it was *poisoned*,' he scoffs, but takes the drink off me with a muttered *thanks*. He turns the cup in his fingers a couple of times, and I wait until he takes a drink.

It suddenly strikes me that his lips are on the straw, where my lips just were.

I'm not sure what to do with that thought, exactly, but I know it makes me feel some kind of way.

Probably just that I've overstepped, and that's a too-familiar and too-friendly thing to do, and *WE ARE NOT FRIENDS*.

So the morning after, when I'm helping finish up a new set – a council chamber in the Gilded Glade – it feels like retaliation when Callum strides baldly into the room and slams an iced Americano down on a cabinet next to me.

He smiles at me, all teeth. His eyes glint, but it's not mischief – it's more like triumph.

'Vanilla,' he informs me. 'Not poison. Thought you might be thirsty, Fangirl.'

I cross my arms, and he takes a sip to prove his point, not once breaking eye contact. Up close like this, I find myself lost in the depths of his brown eyes, the tiny flecks of hazel in them – but when I try to look away, my gaze snags on his mouth, lips pursed around the paper straw, and then the distinct bob of his throat and slight flex of his jaw as he swallows. It sends a weird shiver down to the base of my spine. When he holds the cup out to me, I'm aware of a few people looking over at us, so I force myself to smile back, and I take the cup and lift it to my mouth.

And I try really, *really* hard not to look again at *his* mouth, which was just wrapped around the same straw I'm now putting in *my* mouth. My stomach is in all kinds of weird knots. My face feels hot, too. My fingertips tingle.

The sweetness of vanilla hits my tongue, and I force down an appreciative noise.

Instead of *thanks*, I tell him, 'Don't put drinks down on my set. You'll leave condensation rings.'

He barks a laugh – which I take to be the equivalent of a sarcastic *'your* set?' – and doesn't say goodbye before he leaves.

*

We get stuck in this weird battle of back and forth, alternating between glaring like one of us has the high ground and going in for the kill with over-the-top kindness, as performative as it is.

He makes a point of calling out, 'Hello, Anissa, how's your day going?' when he sees me, like it's so bloody magnanimous of this sort-of famous actor to remember my name.

I nick a couple of highlighters and some sticky tabs out of a stationery stash and leave them on the top step of his trailer, along with a note that says: *For the next book you want to deface.*

I catch him bickering with the costume department at one point and overhear enough to understand they want to add some weapons to Kai's look, to emphasize how much more involved his character is getting in the show's plot.

Callum snorts derisively. 'The bow is a no-go, I've told you.'

'Nobody's asking you to use it! It'd be decorative . . .'

'There's no way Kai is carrying a bow around,' he snaps, and I'm startled. Normally he's so polite when talking to the crew.

I sidle over to say, 'But Callum, it's tradition for men of House Osterion to participate in all aspects of a tournament – the jousting, the melee *and* the archery.

In fact, all esteemed members of the royal court carry a bow and arrow, even if they never use it. It's a mark of their rank.'

The guy from the costume department shoots me a grateful look.

Callum stares me down for a moment before plastering on a bland smile. 'That's right, Anissa, thank you. But *actually*, you're wrong. Kai wouldn't have been trained the same way. His visions make him too much of a liability to shoot a bow – according to some people, anyway. That's why he's only ever seen in close combat. It's the only thing he's considered *able* to train for.'

'Well, now, that's –' the costuming guy starts, but Callum cuts him off.

'In fact, I'm *sure* there's a direct reference in one of Oscar's POV chapters in the eighth book about how it's easy to be the most proficient Osterion sibling at archery when only three of them learned. Which means Kai didn't. *Therefore*, nobody would bother giving him a weapon he can't actually use.'

I grit my teeth, irked at being out-nerded.

So much for *they're not his books*.

The costume department guy sighs. 'Right, then. Dagger it is.'

Callum gives me a toothy smile. 'But thanks, Anissa. That was a really *helpful* contribution.'

It takes all my willpower not to give him the middle finger and to storm off with a little dignity, silently counting down the days until I can put him far, FAR behind me.

Then Callum magnanimously volunteers to help me carry a bench when he sees me struggling to move it to its correct mark.

Actually, he doesn't so much help as jog over and say, 'Let me' and then proceeds to *pick the whole thing up*, and put it back down in the spot I point to.

His neck strains with exertion and his cheeks turn pink. His biceps flex under the long sleeves and layers of his costume, and I catch myself staring a bit too much. I get that tingly feeling in my fingertips again; this time, it spreads all the way to the pit of my stomach, right down to my toes. With the cloak and the sword belt and everything, it's giving high fantasy hero, Prince Charming vibes, my favourite kind of fictional love interest. But it's only the costume, the Kai of it all, *not* Callum.

And then he moves the bench again, and again, when I accidentally-on-purpose give him slightly wrong directions. He pretends like it's his fault and I'm not doing it to mess with him. I pretend like I'm so, so sorry about it.

'Might as well put all that hard work at the gym to good use,' I say dryly.

'I'm sure there's a bench press joke there somewhere.'

I scowl, lips pursed hard, but only because it *was* kind of funny, and I refuse to lose this ongoing battle by laughing.

When his cape snags on a decorative set of crossed swords we're intending to hang on a wall, I'm called over to assist. The swords themselves aren't sharp so there's no damage to his costume, but they *are* very delicately held together. It took one of my team a full forty minutes to get the balance of them right.

I bend down to untangle him and brace a hand against Callum's leg for balance as I lean around him, not realizing until he jolts that I've basically groped his lower thigh. I cringe, blurting an apology as I retract. I end up wobbling, perched precariously on the balls of my feet, and his fingers brush my shoulder.

Instead of shoving me away, though, he holds me up, helping me find my balance. His hand is gentle and firm, cool fingers pressing into the warm skin of my bare arm.

I look up at him and briefly consider that this is exactly the kind of compromising position that would lend itself to some raunchy scenes in a fanfic. Probably one packed with tension and thinly veiled lust.

But obviously, this is real life, and my face is on fire because I just touched this boy's leg, and my mouth is dry when I say, 'Er, thanks. Sorry again.'

'S'okay,' he says, and *his* voice sounds wrong, too. Rough. He clears his throat, and turns sharply away, staring blankly at the other side of the room – reminding me in no uncertain terms that I am nothing if not a total inconvenience to him.

I feel something snap in the air between us, air rushing back into my lungs and a cacophony of noise suddenly filling my ears. Was the room always this loud, this packed with other people?

'Don't move a muscle,' I bark at Callum, and shift onto my knees at his side so I don't topple over again.

'Should I be concerned you're thinking so much about my muscles?'

'Maybe if you didn't flex them at any given opportunity, you'd spare me the trouble.'

He snorts. 'So much for the moony-eyed fangirl who could barely string a sentence together.'

Oh, God, what was I even *thinking*, being so overwhelmed when I met him? Did I really think he'd have hidden depths like his character? Ugh.

It's actually just as well he blocked me on Instagram,

I don't have to see any of the too-polished crap he posts. I can't even properly enjoy going on Discord anymore, because my friends there talk so much about *Callum* rather than Kai – rumours and news about auditions he's got, new roles he's pinned for, the sudden surge of fanvids that have sprung up on TikTok after he got spotted buying a pile of books in Waterstones recently . . .

No wonder he's got this insufferable swagger about him and thinks so little of me. What does an obsessive fangirl mean to a rising Hollywood star? Although that would make a great fanfic . . .

I glance up at Callum, but the only heat I feel this time is blood-boiling aggravation. Why am *I* stuck with this insufferable boy slowly ruining my favourite character in my favourite fandom, instead of spending my summer falling head over heels in love like I would in a fanfic?

I can't stand to even *think* about him. My whole body feels like it's fizzing when I do. My heart rate gets fast and my skin feels hot and *I hate him*.

I finally get his cloak free; the delicate sword display is no worse for wear.

'Well,' I say, standing back up with a sickly-sweet smile. 'That was before I met you.'

GIRLIE POPS 2.0! ✨

Daphne from college
Girls I miss you all so much!!! Can't wait to reunite this weekend!

Boy update: Crap Daniel has been liking all my old insta posts and trying to slide into my DMs but I'm staying strong! Helps that you've all got me thinking of him as 'Crap Daniel' lol

And I think Raf is going to ask me on a proper date when I'm home! SCREAMING!

Evie Price from school and also now college
OMG THAT'S AMAZING NEWS

Cerys
Whooop! Rooting for Raphne!

Rafne?

Either way, I ship it!

Daphne from college
What's going on with everyone else? Fill me in!

Evie Price from school and also now college
I regret to say that dad's mistress/new wife is winning me around a bit . . . she's actually quite nice? Still not really getting on with my dad or anything but she's not so bad really

Kind of excited to meet my baby sister when she's born too

Chloe with the Twitch channel
Been so so so busy lately omg sorry I've been MIA but my channel's doing really well and I had a TikTok go viral last week and turns out I made a ton of merch sales off the back of it!

Nikita from college (Daphne's friend)
Yesssss take that, Chloe's parents! Who says this isn't a real job?! So proud of you!

Cerys
I'm sorry things are still rough with your dad Evie, but that's really nice you're getting on with your stepmum! And omg a baby sister will be SO cute?! Love!

No special updates from me tbh . . . things with Max are still going really well, OWAR work's AMAZING, I can't believe it's already almost over! But I'm excited for you all to be back home for a proper group hang soon!

@Anissa has gossip though

Me
Do I?

Nikita from college (Daphne's friend)
Does she?

Cerys
I mean, we can't ALL boast about our cute new actor bestie . . .

WHO BRINGS YOU COFFEE

Me
THAT WAS ONCE

HE IS NOT MY BESTIE

WE AREN'T

HE IS NOT

AGH

Chloe with the Twitch channel
Spill! The! TEAAAAA!

Nikita from college (Daphne's friend)
Yeah, spill the tea . . . just not his coffee. On him. Again.

Daphne from college
Omg have you kissed???? I'm having visions of you guys like, sneaking off to his trailer for a cheeky snog

(In a totally non-creepy way obvs lol)

Evie Price from school and also now college
Anissaaaaaaa omg you dark horse, obsessed with this for you

I've followed him on insta since Cerys said about your run-in with him lol, he is FIT to be fair

Chloe with the Twitch channel
Everyone shut up my favourite show is on

Team #Calissa

I can't believe you didn't tell us he's been flirting with you omg

Me
I promise, he is NOT.

And I'm not either!

We just like

You know

Work together?

Nikita from college (Daphne's friend)
V convincing

Tbf, cannot picture you flirting with him lol

OHMYGOD CHLOE STOP TEXTING ME

Fine

@Anissa I'm sorry if that was mean. I just meant, you never really talk about anyone you fancy

CERYS STOP TEXTING ME

THAT'S NOT MEAN IF IT'S A FACT

Me
Haha no you're right, I don't see me flirting with him either

Ever.

In any universe.

Cerys
If you say so . . .

OWAR Discord Kai-rry On My Wayward Son
General

> **@therunestar**
> Um ... did anyone else see Callum's Deadline interview?

> **@osterionprincess1**
> ????

> **@osterionprincess2**
> !!!!

> **@rubytherapscallion**
> YES OMG?!

> **@wrathfulqueen93**
> I ... did not like it.

> **@ladyanissadishipper**
> Why, what did he say??

> **@osterionprincess1**
> Hang on, I need to go find this

> **@rubytherapscallion**
> didn't realize this guy hated OWAR so much?

> **@osterionprincess2**
> can't believe he was so weird about the books. I mean, I know we all LOVE the show, but you can't be part of something this huge and essentially discount the entire original material?!

> **@wrathfulqueen93**
> He did NOT come off well ...

@rubytherapscallion
wonder if some of it got taken out of context? it was all around weird, bad vibes though

@ladyanissadishipper
Oh no! Yikes. I haven't seen it either, be right back...

EXCLUSIVE! Meet the young fantasy actor stepping out of the shadows and into the spotlight – an interview with *Of Wrath and Rune's* Callum Denver

Callum Denver's career has catapulted into the limelight recently, from his recent starring role alongside Dwayne Johnson to critically acclaimed series *Of Wrath and Rune* and a slew of unconfirmed rumours attaching his name to even more household actors, directors and franchises.

For instance, when asked if Denver *has* secured a leading role in the next Spiderman movie, he chuckled and said enigmatically that we would have to 'simply wait and see', but he hopes to be on more screens soon.

Of Wrath and Rune is a long-running, British-made fantasy series based on the books by the same name. Showrunners have OWAR's cult following and devoted worldwide audience to thank for it not getting cancelled; they are currently filming season six but it holds relatively low viewing numbers to date. Denver's role as Prince Kai Osterion is a new addition for the upcoming fifth season.

Ask anyone but the most dedicated fans to name his character, and they might struggle; Denver is the *fourth* actor to take on the role. Until now, Prince Kai has been deemed a minor character in the books, despite many chapters being from his perspective.

'There's been nothing to go off, really,' Denver says of the source material. 'Those are some dense, doorstopper novels; you'd have to be insanely dedicated to get through them all. But, you know, it's not as if *Of Wrath and Rune* doesn't have a lot of those kind of fans behind it.'

Indeed, *Of Wrath and Rune* boasts one of the biggest fan communities online. There are hundreds of forums dedicated to the series, and it is one of the most frequently updated fandoms on a popular fanfiction website, which Denver admits he finds 'unnervingly intense'.

When asked about the huge outpouring of support for the series, Denver said, 'It's a bit much, sometimes. I'm not sure any of that is really for me.'

That might change now he is securing new, more mainstream roles. To some degree, it already has: although he rarely engages online, Denver's social media accounts have exploded in recent months, and the majority of his audience are young women. One particular thirst trap of Denver went viral just last week.

'You could definitely call *that* flattering,' Denver comments with a laugh. 'Who wouldn't love the attention – it's what every young actor wants, isn't it?'

CHAPTER 18

I read the article a few times. Somewhere along the way, the burning feeling in my chest shifts from vindication to . . . something icky and uncomfortable.

I *should* be pleased that everyone else gets to see what a prat Callum is. Even to Cerys and Jake and Max, I've been loath to say too much. Although they're not as big Kai fans, I still don't want to taint their experience of OWAR like Callum has done for me. That doesn't feel fair.

The article quickly starts doing the rounds outside of Discord. Reddit finds it and it spreads like wildfire. People are calling Callum rude and dismissive, which feels like a win in our ongoing, unspoken battle. But they're also attacking him for daring to say anything less-than-positive about the books, and for dunking on the fandom in favour of celebrating his more 'conventional' success with other films or social media.

And worse, they're attacking *Kai*. Kai's nothing, and nobody, he's just *there*, and annoying, and nobody likes him or cares if he's in the show or not. His whole drama with his visions is insufferable anyway; they're bored of the same crap and why can't he get over it already?

Those comments bother me way more than they should, and I know I'm taking it way too personally. It's the same kind of stuff people have always thought about *me*. Why else did I get bullied at school so much, if not for being an annoying nobody who just couldn't fit in?

But Kai isn't real, and he's not the one who must be seeing this slew of horrible comments directed at him, ripping him to pieces, *bullying* him and turning on him, as if they ever knew him in the first place. No, that's all Callum.

I keep thinking about that book in his trailer. All the sticky tabs. The piles of notes.

If he hasn't poured over every inch of those books, how else does he manage to bring so much depth and personality to Kai? How else did he remember that one throwaway comment about archery?

It makes my chest feel tight.

I know how isolating it can be, when people treat you like this – like the laughter they'll gain from a hurtful comment is worth more than the pain it inflicts. For all Callum and I are at odds with each other, this time I'm on his side.

I might have messaged him to say as much, if he hadn't blocked me.

The costume department ask me to take a new dagger and thigh holster to Callum's trailer, since I have a spare minute.

'I thought he wasn't here,' I say. 'He's not filming today?'

'That's alright, just drop it inside for him. Thanks, Anissa!'

I'm almost done for the day anyway, so I finish up with some candles for a scene in the tavern, take the dagger and holster and grab my bag before leaving via the trailers. I'll meet Cerys at the car park after; she'll be done soon, too.

Outside by the trailers, I spot some of the cast and take a second to slow down and absorb it all. Ahead of me, the actors playing Téiglin, Lady Adanna and Roach are sat on the steps outside the Moonwalker's trailer, a game of UNO half-abandoned between them as they laugh about something. Brayden saunters out from the costume trailer then, slipping on the battered Seattle Seahawks cap I see all the time on his TikToks. It's still so surreal that they're all right there, not on the other side of a screen; that they're real, tangible, *human*.

Between the chaos of Cerys's harebrained scheme to get us here in the first place, and how full-on the work has been, sometimes I forget just how freaking *cool* this is. I'm here! On OWAR! I'm part of my favourite show, doing something *amazing*.

I turn away before I can get caught staring and am confronted by the piece of paper taped to a door that reads 'CALLUM DENVER | PRINCE KAI'. Okay, maybe he's *one* person I wouldn't have minded only knowing from the other side of a screen . . .

I knock, just in case. When there's no answer, I breathe a small sigh of relief and I let myself in. It's not even locked.

The trailer is cool, an air-conditioning unit whirring quietly. Once again, the coffee table is piled high with scripts – the papers marked with notes and highlighted lines – and two of the OWAR books. One is open, face down.

I scoot around the coffee table, setting the dagger and holster gently on top of the papers. I don't dare disturb anything; there's probably some kind of method to the mess, a system obvious to only Callum. I can relate to that.

Curiosity gets the better of me, though, and I take a peek at the script on top.

INT. NIGHT, THE PALACE. **OSCAR** STANDS IN A WINDOW OVERLOOKING THE COURTYARD/CITADEL. **KAI** LURKS IN THE SHADOWS.

PRINCE KAI
Another revolt on the outskirts of the city. The rebels are getting closer, just as –

PRINCE OSCAR
DON'T say 'I told you so'. Arrogance doesn't suit you, little brother.

PRINCE KAI
But I *did* tell you this would happen. Traitors inside the palace walls, rebels gaining ground *and* support. Even your plot to capture Lady Adanna failed, just as –

OSCAR *rounds on him, furious.*

PRINCE OSCAR
I'm warning you, Kai. Your so-called premonitions mean nothing but a wild goose chase, they always have. All you succeed in doing is making a mockery of this family. Your magick is more trouble than it's worth, to any of us.

PRINCE KAI
Your lack of faith in my cursed visions won't stop the smallfolk revolting, or noble houses turning their back on us. The rebels *have* to be dealt with. The Eldritch Crown –

PRINCE OSCAR
The Crown is well in hand, as you know. I hardly need lectures on such magick from *you*. And besides, one preacher tried and hanged is hardly a revolt.

PRINCE KAI
Hanged?

PRINCE OSCAR

Of course. He was no one. Hardly warranted a formal beheading. But we had to make an example of him all the same.

KAI flinches. We hear clashing weapons, see a flash of pitchforks raised against palace swords.

PRINCE KAI

No. You made a martyr of him.

A chill runs down my spine, the scene playing out in vivid detail in my imagination. Knowing the aesthetic of the show, I can just *see* the moonlight filtering in from a window, illuminating Prince Oscar while Kai is cast in shadow . . .

If I weren't so scared of upsetting Callum's organized chaos, I'd snatch the script up to read the next few pages. There are notes in round, cramped handwriting on the page, though, and I lean in to get a better look.

Downplay any arrogance/ be more vulnerable. Soft delivery. Used to being shot down and ignored. Frustrated the situation is growing more dire and nobody will listen even though he's consistently right. Debating how to manipulate his brother – Oscar has to think any plan/idea is his own and that he's railroading Kai as usual. Try to conceal the vision (getting harder to do as more frequent, and they're taking a physical toll). Refusal to be bullied into the background anymore.

There's a wild fluttering in my chest, and it takes all my willpower not to trace the words with my fingertip. Not because Callum wrote them, but because they feel so *accurate*. He's so in tune with Kai's entire character, and my heart swells to see the level of care and thought going into his performance. He gets it, gets Kai, and my whole body feels lighter knowing it's *not* just me and my sad silly fangirl brain running away with itself.

It's the way Kai has to mask it all. Downplay his whole self. Be so hyperaware of other people's responses to his words and actions that he's trained himself to walk constantly on eggshells just to make his visions and magick more manageable for *other* people's sake; to spare *them* some kind of hurt, even if it's at the cost of being honest, or himself.

It's exactly what I love about Kai. How I'd write his character in a fic.

It's so powerful, seeing it reflected here, that my breath shakes on an inhale. I have to sit down, perching on the edge of the sofa to steady myself. My gaze settles then on the open OWAR book, turned down, spine cracked. The cover is worn and fraying at the corners. Sticky tabs protrude from some of the pages.

The rest of the collection is stacked haphazardly on the floor nearby, just within reach.

I don't hesitate this time: I grab the open book, poring over the cramped handwritten notes spilling down margins. Certain words are circled, whole sentences devoted to unpacking one single action and all the implications behind it. I hold my thumb in place so I don't lose Callum's page and flip through the book. There are different-coloured pens and different thicknesses of ink, like the notes have been added to over time. Some sections are so heavily annotated that there are Post-it notes stacked one on top of the other on the page. It's not even just the sections mentioning Kai or the Osterions – it's the entire book.

And it's the same handwriting as on the scripts. *Callum's* handwriting.

Why did he tell me this book wasn't his, when I asked? Why did he make it sound like he'd never deigned to look twice at the source material in that recent interview?

He must've read the series dozens of times over. His copy of the seventh book (arguably the one with the most Kai content) is practically falling apart.

I don't understand. Why did he lie? He can't be *ashamed* of it. He works on the show, for crying out loud.

It doesn't make sense.

I only look up when the trailer door swings open. Callum is silhouetted in the doorway against the afternoon sun, his dyed hair highlighted in a vibrant halo of red, his expression indecipherable as he takes in the incriminating scene.

'Anissa,' he says in a low voice. It doesn't sound like him. It's quiet and mild and with an undercurrent that sends a shiver down my spine. It's *Kai's* voice: a specific cadence and delivery I just read notes on and have heard hundreds of times over in the season five trailer.

My heart thunders, and my palms start to sweat.

'I suggest you get the hell out of here before I call security.'

CHAPTER 19

Actually, *all* of me starts to sweat.

'This isn't funny,' Callum goes on, his voice as rigid as his posture. 'I mean it. Get out.'

'I – I wasn't – I haven't –'

He storms over, the door swinging closed behind him, and when I stand up to meet him, he snatches the book right out of my hands. When he puts it on the table, face down again, it's surprisingly gentle. His face is pale and a muscle feathers along his jaw.

I'm frozen to the spot; Callum's furious, but he's also cold. Removed somehow, like he's performing as Kai rather than being himself, and all I can do is stammer some more. I mean, obviously I *was* sort of snooping. He caught me red-handed. I could get fired. Oh, God, I could get *Cerys* fired, or at least tarnished by association, and this means so much to her . . . And my parents are going to be *so* disappointed in me . . .

But on the other hand, it was *literally* just some annotations in a copy of OWAR, it's not like I was stealing his socks or something.

'You can't just barge in here and go through my things!' Callum exclaims, each word bitten off, sharp. 'It's – you're . . . You know, I almost *believed* you, when you said it wasn't you who went to the press about my AS levels. So what are you doing? Looking for *more* things to sell to them? Stuff you can leak to your sad little obsessive fandom friends so *more* people can take the piss out of me online and rip me to pieces?'

It's the fandom comment that gets me. I flinch, blood finally returning to my body after forming ice in my veins. I snatch the book back up off the table before I retort.

Callum's eyes widen a fraction in alarm, and even though it only lasts a split second, I *know* that look: the possessiveness, the fear, like he thinks I'm going to tear this precious, ordinary thing of his into pieces with my bare hands. Like it holds a piece of his soul.

I shove the book back into his chest. Hard. He fumbles for it, taking half a step back. I file the thought of how firm and muscular his chest feels far, *far* away into the depths of my brain where it can get lost in the archives so I never have to think about it again.

I snap, 'And *I* almost believed *you* when you said

these books weren't yours. So much for "dense, doorstopper novels". If you ask me, the only sad little obsessive fanboy here is *you*. How "insanely dedicated" do you have to be to have read these books so many times they're practically falling apart?'

Callum pales, and for a moment I think he might genuinely be sick. I almost feel bad for throwing quotes from that horrible interview back in his face. Almost.

'FOR YOUR INFORMATION,' I barrel on, breathless, 'I *wasn't* in here to go through your things. Costume asked me to drop your new dagger off. They said you weren't going to be here.'

'But you thought you'd take a look around anyway.'

I bite the inside of my cheek, embarrassed.

Callum's eyes dart to the holster on the table. He frowns, like he's not sure whether to believe me or not.

I fumble in the pocket of my dungarees for my phone, unlocking it and opening the photos app to shove at him. 'There. See for yourself.'

He gives me a hard look, as if trying to figure out what kind of angle I'm playing – but eventually he must realize there isn't one, because he sets his book down (safely far out of my reach, I notice) and hesitantly takes my phone. He holds it like it's going to explode, and scrolls delicately with the point of his index finger, boomer-style.

There's a bitter tang of panic suddenly on my tongue, realizing I have no idea what's in my recent camera roll.

Callum helpfully informs me: 'You screenshot a lot of memes.'

'Oh. Yeah, I guess.'

'A lot of OWAR memes.'

I shrug. I like to save my favourite ones.

And then, in spite of himself, the scowl disappears for a moment and the corners of his mouth tug up. It totally transforms him, like he's shaken off the mask of Kai, and is back to himself.

'Is this your dog?'

'Oh! Um, yeah. That's Harley. She's a regular little chaos demon.'

'She doesn't *look* very little.' He taps the screen, and a video plays. Harley's wild, enthusiastic barking suddenly fills the trailer, along with the sound of me and Mum screaming with laughter and a lot of splashing. I know exactly which video it is, and I grin when a second later, Dad's voice in the video shouts, '*HARLEQUIN MATHILDA O'SHEA, YOU GET BACK HERE RIGHT – NO NO NO HARLEY, WAIT – AAAAH!*'

A laugh bursts out of Callum as he watches Harley chase something along the bank of the boating lake and take a running leap at Dad – bowling him over and sending him flat on his bum in the shallow water. I giggle, remembering it, so glad I caught it on camera.

'*Mathilda?*' Callum questions, handing my phone back, still chuckling.

'It's my nan's name. Apparently she was a bit miffed when I was born and her name wasn't passed on to me, so my parents promised they'd use it for their second child. Which turned out to be the dog.'

Callum makes a small, thoughtful noise in the back of his throat. 'They seem nice.'

'Oh. Uh, yeah, they are. I mean, I like them. I think they're fun to be around. I don't know if that's a bit weird, actually? But I didn't exactly have a lot of friends growing up. Or still. I mean, you know, until quite recently, but you didn't ask about that. Haha. Um. But yes, they're . . . they're nice.'

I snap my mouth shut. As if Callum needed to think less of me. Now I'm the snooping, starry-eyed blabbermouth fangirl who *also* has no friends. Wonderful.

Why, WHY, can I never seem to control what I say around him? I've literally never had this problem before.

This is probably the point in the conversation where I should ask about his family – and I suddenly realize that I don't know *anything* about them.

I have no idea if we're still fighting but it feels like that dam might have broken, so I say, 'Do you, um . . . Are your . . . ?'

Callum's expression darkens, his guard coming back up. He half-turns away from me, picking up the holster for his dagger and turning it agitatedly in his hands.

'Thanks for dropping this off.'

'Callum –'

His phone starts ringing, and he flinches. I hesitate.

'I said *thanks*, Anissa. I have to take this.'

This time, I leave. Outside the trailer, I close the door and pause on the steps long enough to hear his phone ring out. It starts up again immediately.

'Screw you, Richie,' Callum spits out. Then he answers the phone and says more politely, 'Richie, hi . . .'

The rest of the conversation is too muffled to hear. I remember he was on the phone to this Richie guy before – his agent or manager or something. Callum's tone sounds irritable, though. Kind of exhausted.

Maybe his other auditions and fancy new roles are suffering from the backlash he's been getting from that *Deadline* interview? *Maybe* he shouldn't have been so mean about the series, when he's so obviously massively invested in it.

Or maybe ... Callum is full of hidden depths just like Kai, after all.

I'm starting to think I'd like to find out.

CHAPTER 20

The end of summer crashes in all at once. Jake seems to suddenly remember how many vague plans the four of us had started to make back in July and insists on squeezing them all in – a barbecue on the beach, a cinema trip, even sacrificing our TTRPG session in favour of a sweaty hike up Pen y Fan. The girls from college all come home and I find myself roped into a brunch at Daphne's house that turns into an entire day of swapping stories about their summers.

I didn't think I had much to contribute – since I doubt they'll want to hear about things like the drama my team had over soy vs wax candles, even if *I* found it really interesting – but they keep trying to grill me on Callum, with pointed looks that make me squirm.

There's nothing to tell though.

He's – insufferable! Everything I *don't* want in a romance. I want swoon-worthy chivalry and epic gestures and dedication, *devotion*. The kind of stuff I read about. Not constant one-upmanship and snide, sidelong smirks, and never knowing where we stand with each other.

And I definitely *don't* fancy him.

I deflect by saying, 'As if. ANYWAY, I bet he's the kind of guy who uses monkey-face emojis unironically.' And that gets them talking about Crap Daniel and Daphne's flirtationship with Raf (with an actual proper date still pending).

Between Cerys and Max being totally loved up, Daphne talking herself in circles about her crushes, and Jake firmly in the talking stage with Teddy, I feel . . . *lost*. It's not like when I was a loner at school, stuck on the outside but preferring it that way because it meant I didn't get bullied as much. It makes me want to beat my fists on the invisible wall keeping me from experiencing this and scream *let me in!*

I never used to feel like this. If I saw couples at school, I didn't feel jealous. Boys sending 'u up?' Snaps hardly compares to the sweeping, gut-wrenching romance of a 'who hurt you?' trope.

It's never really been on my radar in such a real, raw way until now, I guess. It always felt like some vague future thing that *would* happen – eventually.

Chloe says she has no time for crushes and

relationships between her showjumping classes and Twitch channel, and Evie's still sore from being cheated on in Year 11. Nikita's constantly talking about 'fit boys', but she's also always so self-assured and unbothered, she's done with them at the first hint of a red flag.

It's on the tip of my tongue to say some of this stuff out loud to the girls. That I'm pining for *something* – if not with anyone in particular – but I have no idea what to do about it, how to even start . . .

It's my last day on set before college starts back up next week. Cerys and I both got cards signed by our teams and even Brayden, too, with good luck wishes and heartfelt goodbyes, and official OWAR T-shirts to mark our brief time here.

As of this evening, I will no longer be involved in the behind-the-scenes making of *Of Wrath and Rune* season six.

And I will never – *ever* – have to see Callum Denver again.

It's bittersweet, leaving, but that last thought is the one that keeps me grounded.

My main tasks are all done by mid-afternoon, so I'm sent on a couple of errands for the costume department and then asked to run call sheets out to the trailers. It's still exciting to see the actors up close and my legs feel like jelly when I speak to the Moonwalker or Téiglin or Lady Adanna, even if it's just to say, 'Here you go!' But I can't hold on to the feeling, because nagging at the back of my mind is Callum.

I save his call sheet for last. Mostly because I want to avoid him. Definitely not because this will be the last time I see him. Anyway, maybe he isn't even here – I haven't seen him at all since our run-in last week.

But when I trudge up to his trailer and knock, he shouts, 'Come in,' and I grumble a little under my breath before opening the door.

Callum's trailer is such a mess that for a second I think it's been ransacked. But then I see the tripod and ring light set up with a microphone attached and a sheet hung up to act as a plain backdrop, and I realize he's just shoved his usual pile of books and scripts, along with some of the furniture, to one end of the small space. He's filming an audition tape.

The fangirl in me is dying to know what for. But I've learned better than to ask.

I poke my head round the door, dropping the papers just inside. 'It's only me. Call sheet.' Then, biting my lip, I decide to add, 'You won't have to worry about me darkening your doorway again, by the way. Today's my last day before I go back to college. I'd say it was nice getting to know you, but ... well. Goodbye, *Your Highness*.'

Great job, me. EGOT-worthy, actually. Just sassy enough to feel like I'm not leaving in defeat. And let that be the last I ever say to him!

'W-wait, Anissa.'

And I do, if only for how unusually nervous he sounds. Callum stands up from the chair in front of the camera and drags a hand through his hair, teeth worrying at his lower lip. The pale blue of his T-shirt makes the red in his auburn hair look that much richer, his brown eyes that much darker ... his arms that much *more* ...

Okay, nope, definitely NOT following that train of thought.

I tear my gaze back to meet his, but luckily, Callum's too busy looking wretched and torn up about something to have noticed my ogling. I move inside the trailer and pull the door shut quietly behind me.

Does he want to say a proper goodbye? Tell me it's just as well I'm leaving because now he won't have to get some kind of restraining order against me? *Apologize?*

But when he doesn't say anything at all, I ask, 'Are you alright?'

'Y-yeah, I'm . . .'

'You don't *look* alright. You don't sound it, either.'

A dry chuckle rips out of his throat, and Callum's shoulders sag before he finally looks at me. 'I'm embarrassed, okay? I don't . . . *ugh*. Fine. Okay. I need . . . *I need your help, please.*'

He grinds the words out so stiffly, it takes me a moment to register them. I cross my arms, suspicious. 'With what?'

'I have to send in an audition tape,' he huffs. He reaches for a script, which he hands over to me. 'For this movie. It's an adaptation of this YA book . . .'

'Ooh, which one?' I flick through a couple of pages but don't recognize the characters' names. A glance tells me it's not dystopian or fantasy, though. It reads more like a romance.

Int. Treehouse – **Abi** *sits looking out at the lighthouse, contemplating. She's still in her ruined homecoming dress.*

Cole climbs in to join her.

COLE

I thought I'd find you here

ABIGAIL

[smiling] You always find me. How did you know?

COLE

This is where you come to think.

'I just need someone to read lines with me,' Callum says, and the look of shock on my face must be priceless. He's *got* to be joking.

'You're surrounded by actors! Couldn't you ask one of them? What about, um, Sienna? Lady Adanna?' I'm still never sure whether to call people by their actual name, or their character's name. I guess it won't matter after today anyway.

He grimaces. 'She'll only give me tips and direction, and I don't even *want* ... Look, it doesn't matter, alright? All you have to do is read Abigail's lines. You don't have to perform them or anything; you won't be on camera.'

'Wait. *You're* playing the love interest?'

I clamp my mouth shut. I didn't mean for it to come out like that. It's a *huge* deal. A leading role like this would solidify him as a heartthrob – it's what his fans have been crying out for.

He rolls his eyes. 'Can you just read with me? Please?'

I chew on my tongue for a moment, but give him a curt nod of agreement. Callum returns to his seat in front of the camera. I perch on the edge of the pushed-aside coffee table, so we're roughly level with each other.

He starts recording, and stares somewhere between me and the camera. 'I thought I'd find you here.'

'YOU ALWAYS FIND ME.' My voice is stiff, and I'm projecting way too loudly for the tiny trailer; I'm immediately taken back to being Narrator #6 in the school nativity. 'How did you know?'

'This is where you come to think.' He sighs heavily. 'Abi, I'm so sorry about what happened earlier, at the homecoming game. You didn't deserve any of that. I know I should've warned you, but I didn't realize how far they were going to go – and you were so excited when Preston asked you out . . .'

He sounds fed up, and I frown, not sure that seems right for this type of scene. Cerys has made me watch enough romcoms to understand the pattern they tend to follow, and skimming ahead a little my suspicions are confirmed: this is the big heart-to-heart moment right before the *will-they-won't-they* vibe culminates in a kiss.

Crap, Callum can't be expecting me to snog him on camera for his audition, can he? Or is that why he asked *me* instead of someone else?

Do I . . . want that to be the reason?

No, that can't be it. Obviously. I'm spiralling – again – and catch myself just before the pause becomes too noticeable. 'You're my best friend, Cole. I thought I meant something to you.'

'Don't you see?' Callum leans forward in his seat, voice more urgent, lower, an edge to it. 'That's exactly the problem. I've always just been your best friend, Abi, and you . . . you don't just mean something to me. You mean everything to me. Don't you know how much it hurt when you said yes to Preston? When you –'

'Whoa, sorry, hang on. Can you . . .? Er, cut?' I say awkwardly, making a gesture with my arms like the clapperboard they use on set. Callum blinks at me a few times before a disbelieving snort slips out.

'You did *not* just tell me to cut my own audition tape.'

'Only for a second! It's just . . . I mean, you're playing the love interest, right? Based on this scene, it's obviously a friends-to-lovers storyline, probably with a bit of a love triangle and some unrequited love . . . But you're playing it as if she's wronged you!'

'She has! She's gone to homecoming with some other guy –'

'No! I mean . . .' I stand up, suddenly too energized to sit still. 'Where's the *yearning?* The passion! She isn't your enemy, she's the great love of your life, or whatever, and even if you're upset, isn't that coming from a place of longing?'

Callum scoffs, leaning back in his seat. 'If I wanted feedback on my acting, I would've asked someone else. Just read the scene, Anissa, please –'

'You're a good actor, Callum! You're a really *great* actor, actually.' His eyebrows lift – it might be the first actual compliment I've ever paid him, but I'm too het up about him butchering this sweet romance scene to dwell on it. 'But you're performing like you've never even heard the word "ROMANCE" before.'

'And you're the expert? With that guy from the convention the other week, right? *Jake?*'

Crap, I forgot I even made that comment about waiting for Jake when Callum found me, as if he was my boyfriend or something. I'm surprised he even remembers. It makes me bristle, though, the way he insinuates I don't know anything about romance. It stings.

Because he's right: I don't.

'I bet your idea of being in love comes from OWAR fanfics,' he adds smugly, and I *hate* that he's right again. I glower, my jaw clenched, hands balled into fists at my side, and when I stand up to toss the script aside,

Callum rises to meet me with a smirk on his face, and I collide with him.

I'm also, again, not thinking about the firm wall of muscle where my hand plants against his chest, or how soft his T-shirt is. Or how his mouth looks, curved up on one side while his brown eyes dance with amusement.

Or that he's so close I can smell his deodorant. Fresh, like eucalyptus.

'Meanwhile,' I bite out, 'YOUR idea of romance is probably posting a manufactured thirst trap to see if any fit girls comment on it. How is *that* any more real than reading about love?'

Callum's jaw works furiously, and the look in his eyes shifts to something heated. I think it's a challenge. I stick my chin out and push closer to him, to prove some kind of point.

Finally, he says in a low voice, 'Isn't that exactly the kind of girl you were, though? Commenting on my posts, waiting to be noticed?'

'That was *one* time. As if I'd *ever* want you to notice me now I actually know you.' My heart is hammering and my fingers feel tingly again, I'm so wound up. 'I hope you don't get the role, you know. I'd feel sorry for whatever poor girl has to kiss you with that horrible ego in the way.'

Callum scoffs, raising a hand to rake through his hair; the movement makes his chest bump against mine. Not counting a cwtch with Jake, who's always openly affectionate and loves a good hug, this is the closest I've ever been to a boy.

But neither of us step back. It'd be admitting defeat somehow.

Callum's breathing is heavy, his pupils dilated, a faint flush painting his cheeks. His heart races wildly; I can feel it against the heel of my hand pressed against his chest. My heartbeat matches his pace, and my skin is tingling all over now, noticing where his clothes touch mine and the brush of his breath on my cheek.

The only coherent thought I have is: *This sounds like a kiss scene in a fanfic.*

'I bet you'd be lining up for the chance to kiss me,' Callum says, and there's a bite to his words. 'I bet you've thought about it. Probably written fanfics all about it. You can't even get through reading a few lines with me without getting all tangled up.'

'Believe me, you're the *last* person I'd want to kiss.'

Callum smirks. That glint is back in his eyes, like a challenge.

'Sure. You keep telling yourself that, Fangirl.'

I'd like to say it all happens like an out-of-body experience, or that I don't know what possesses me, but

I'm all too conscious of my every movement and the definitive choice that I want to accept his challenge – and prove him *wrong*.

So I grab his T-shirt near the collar to close the last tiny sliver of distance between us, and press my closed lips against his.

One of us takes a sharp intake of breath. I have no idea who.

His mouth is softer than I was expecting it to be. Warmer. His hair tickles my forehead.

He lingers, and I feel his hand ghost against my hair like he's about to rest it on the back of my head, sink his fingers into my hair, but I'm already shoving us apart. My lips are tingling, matching the sensation in my fingertips, the small of my back, my toes. I feel like I just got electrocuted, heat radiating from the pit of my abdomen.

There's a split second where he looks a bit dazed too, a bit softer, like he might draw me back into him. But I blink and his hand has fallen away. He's as closed-off as ever, shrugging his shoulders back and looking at me as if to say, *And?*

I bite the inside of my cheek, then snap, 'See? *Nothing*. Good luck with your audition.'

I march out, letting the door swing open and then shut noisily behind me, and I don't stop until I'm far out of sight of the trailers and can lean against Cerys's car to wait for her.

Shit. I can't believe I just robbed myself of my own first kiss – by kissing *Callum Denver*.

I touch a trembling finger to my lips.

They taste like caramel.

CHAPTER 21

The first morning back to college is ... weird. On a LOT of levels.

First and foremost, I have *people* now; friends to sit with, have *lunch* with, to hang out with during study breaks in the common room or library or on the field. I will have people to *talk to during the day*. (Downside: when am I going to work through my TBR pile and all the fanfics I've downloaded to read? This friendship lark is very distracting and time-consuming.)

I spent the last couple of months of college before summer hanging out a bit with Daphne and co, but the fresh start September feeling is really making that sink in. The newness of it is terrifying. Intoxicating.

The Girlie Pops 2.0 chat is a flurry of activity in the morning and I watch the messages flood in while I shovel down breakfast.

What would they say if I told them about the kiss with Callum?

I'm bursting with the need to tell someone, but I know it'll become a whole thing because he's a sort-of famous actor . . .

And it was *so* stupid. Heat of the moment, totally ridiculous. I can GUARANTEE it didn't mean anything to him. He'll probably laugh about it – at *me*, if he even thinks about it at all.

It was barely a kiss, anyway. Just a peck, really. Harley shows me more affection when she boops her wet nose into my face. So it's not like there's anything to tell, is there? *Definitely* no mortifying 'I threw myself at a boy who thinks I'm a pathetic weirdo' tale to recount . . .

Oh, God. I can't *believe* I was so reckless and stupid. It's a good job work experience is over and I'll never have to see him IRL again.

Nan strides into the kitchen and looks almost surprised to see me there. 'Come on, you, get a move on! Your friend's waiting outside!'

'What?'

'The girl with the red car. Isn't she here to pick you up?'

Speak of the devil – my phone lights up: Nikita from college (Daphne's friend), informing me she's outside.

What? Why is she here? We're not even friends, more like ... mutuals. But I text her back to say I'll be right there and abandon the rest of my breakfast to finish getting ready, dashing back and forth between rooms with my toothbrush hanging out of my mouth, feeling like I've forgotten how to be a functional human.

Nan stops me before I can rush out the door. She's got my parents on a FaceTime call to wish me luck for my first day back. They're at the airport on their way to India, to visit some of Mum's cousins in Jaipur who she hasn't seen since my grandparents took her when she was little.

After gushing about how it's my last year of school already and how grown up I am and how time flies, etc., etc., Mum says, 'We'll be back soon, I promise!'

'Not if Auntie Neha's cooking is as good as she claims it is on her Insta. You'll never want to leave,' I joke.

'No amount of Rabdi could keep us from coming home to our baby,' Mum croons, only half-teasing.

Dad snorts. 'Speak for yourself!'

They say a quick goodbye to run to their boarding gate, and Nan strokes my hair (more dry shampoo than anything else – I stayed in bed too long this morning doomscrolling) and offers, 'Shall I do you a tarot reading later? Or some oracle cards maybe? See how your last year of college is going to go?'

The question that flashes in my mind is more along the lines of 'WHAT ABOUT CALLUM AND THAT KISS?!?' but I just nod and say, 'Sounds fun. Thanks, Nan!'

Then I finally launch myself into Nikita's passenger seat with a breathless, 'Hi, thanks for the lift.'

She says, 'Hi. You've got toothpaste all round your mouth, you know.'

I pull down the sun visor to check in the little mirror, and scrub my mouth furiously with the back of my hand. Nikita starts driving, and the music is turned up a little too loud for conversation, but I can hardly sit in silence the entire drive.

'Did Cerys put you up to this? You never gave me a lift to college last year.' Cerys is usually the first to call Nikita out if she's being a bit blunt or standoffish with me, although it's been nice to see the others have started to follow suit lately, too.

Nikita snorts, which doesn't exactly sound like a denial and isn't exactly encouraging. 'Actually, Daphne and Evie told me to pick you up. You're on my way. It makes sense.'

Has our friendship reached that point now? Begrudging and somewhat petty small acts of kindness towards each other?

Why do I seem to keep accumulating people where

that is the entire basis of our relationship? First Callum, now Nikita?

I must have a problem. I must *be* the problem.

This cannot be normal.

I can't offer her a lift in return since I don't get to borrow my dad's car that often, but I can at least say, 'I like your shirt. It's really cute.' It is – the bright red and soft linen fabric really suits her, especially with her curly hair pulled back in a tousled bun. It makes her blue eyes pop.

I don't know how much of that is a bit full on to say, though, so leave the compliment at 'cute'.

'Thanks.' She glances my way briefly. 'You wear a lot of purple.'

'Oh! Yeah, I guess. It's my favourite colour.'

She snorts softly. 'Never could've guessed.'

Then Nikita bumps the music up a little louder. I spend the rest of the drive scrolling Discord and checking to see if any of the in-progress fics I'm reading have updated.

We're almost to college when my ears perk up, my head bobbing in time to a song I recognize – it's one of my favourites, by a band Jake introduced me to called Argonauta. They're three women from Leeds, and all their songs are inspired by Greek myths. The way they use violins really scratches an itch in my brain.

Their folksy, indie-rock sound is a stark contrast to the new Sabrina Carpenter song that was just playing, and Nikita seems to notice I've clocked the song change, jabbing a button on the console to skip to the next.

'*You* listen to Argonauta?' I blurt, and it comes out more judgemental than I intended. I'm just surprised. I'd say they don't seem like Nikita's style, but I guess I don't know all that much about her beyond our surface-level interactions.

'They kept coming up on my TikTok. They're kinda cool.'

They're *very* cool, if you ask me. But that's usually a marker of a thing being actively uncool.

I venture, 'Me and Jake saw them last year, when they played at Cardiff's student union.'

'I know.' After a beat, she adds, 'He posted a photo of you guys there. We were all stalking his socials at the time because Cerys had such a big crush on him, and we were massively invested, obvs.'

After a moment, she skips back to the Argonauta song. Nikita nudges the volume up again, but throws me a smile and says, 'I bet they were really awesome to see live.'

'They really were.'

'Maybe – maybe if they're in town again, I can tag along with you and Jake?'

'Totally! Yes!' Nikita's hardly my favourite person, but my enthusiasm for the band eclipses that. It's so *exciting* to have someone to share this stuff with! Even if that someone *is* Nikita.

I guess she feels the same way, because she tries and fails to fight back a smile.

Instead of the last couple of minutes of the drive being spent in not-quite-companionable silence, we both belt out the lyrics at the top of our lungs, screaming them with everything we've got.

The girls seem to have hit a reset button and decided to go all in rather than just have me as some kind of part-time, fringe acquaintance. Daphne came to get me when she spotted me in the canteen, so I could join them for lunch. Nikita *voluntarily* sat next to me in French; she even smiled at me.

It felt like a prank. Like any second they'd all burst out laughing, mocking me for ever thinking they wanted me around.

Which didn't happen, obviously, but it didn't stop me from overthinking every word I said.

It's different with Jake. We can talk for hours and hours and still have so much left to say. We can repeat stories we've already told each other a bunch of times and it's still funny. Cerys is easy to be around and I feel like she *gets* me; and at least with Chloe, we have some common ground in nerdiness – even if I don't know that much about Pokémon and she's not much of an OWAR fan.

I'm constantly on guard though. Monitoring myself. Fighting to keep all the noise in my brain in check. Even if the girls have been nice to me so far, it's hard to shake off the shame I've carried around so long from being bullied at my old school. Back then, nobody cared what I had to say. Sometimes I'm scared they still won't.

On top of all *that*, my brain is fried from the jarring return to a timetable of classes and having to sit in one place for hours at a time, forcing myself to focus on something I'm told to care about. It makes me miss the wonderful chaos of being on set – always having something to do, some fun project to get stuck into, a million things being talked about at once . . .

I must jinx it, because I'm just starting to feel sorry that I won't go back when Cerys comes hurtling down the hallway to accost me as I leave the classroom with Nikita.

'I have the BEST news,' she shouts, breathless, her eyes bright and cheeks flushed. 'Lisa just phoned, and she said they've agreed to extend our contracts! They're so desperate for the extra help on set that they want us to stay on, even if it's only a few hours after college or on weekend shoots! Isn't that *amazing*?'

She's bouncing on her toes she's so excited, and all I can do is gawp at her as the blood drains from my face.

'Babe, that's incredible! Love this for you!' Nikita gushes, giving Cerys a hug, and shooting me a sidelong glance that says, *WTF is wrong with you???*

Right. Yes. I'm supposed to be excited too. This is great news. *Whoopee.*

'WOW THIS IS GREAT NEWS,' I yell, like volume will compensate for a stunning lack of emotion – because, actually, it's taking everything in me not to scream or throw up or both.

How am I supposed to go back after I kissed Callum? After that whole . . . *scene*, in his trailer? But how am I supposed to explain to anyone why I *can't* go back? That's not an option either.

So I just give Cerys and Nikita a rigid, toothy smile, and die inside.

When I finally get home from college, I'm a husk. I feel like I've been running at a hundred and thirty-two per cent capacity all day long, my brain switched on constantly in a way that I haven't had to do all summer.

The very inconsequential not-even-a-proper kiss with Callum is still buzzing at the back of my mind, intermingling with the back-to-college stress. I can barely think about the fact that I'll have to go back to work experience soon and potentially face him. I don't even have the energy to dissect my day with Nan when I get in, or watch all the videos of food Mum's sent me from Auntie Neha's kitchen; instead, I escape to my bedroom, hunker down, and opt for the white noise of my favourite fandom to soothe my tired brain.

OWAR Discord Kai-rry On My Wayward Son
General

@rubytherapscallion
yoooo @ladyanissadishipper how'd the first day of college go? Happy Last Year of School!!!! are they harping on about your uni applications yet lol?

@osterionprincess1
Ugh I legit do not miss that at all haha, still scarred from all the intense UCAS assemblies my school did and it's been two years

@osterionprincess2
I'M still scarred from having to attend your UCAS assemblies tbh

@ladyanissadishipper
It was good thanks! Turned out to be a really nice first day for once? Who knew that having friends to sit with in class would be such a gamechanger lol

@ladyanissadishipper
And how did you know?! Literally first thing they said in assembly this morning was 'THIS IS THE MOST IMPORTANT TIME OF YOUR YOUNG LIVES, EVERYTHING HINGES ON YOUR FINAL YEAR OF SCHOOL' etc etc

@wrathfulqueen93
lmao no it doesn't

@wrathfulqueen93
take it from a former gifted child and burnt out zillennial, it absolutely tf does not

@wrathfulqueen93 ...
but maybe like, don't try to coast. It is still kind of important ☺

@osterionprincess2
yay for a good first day back! we had an extra teacher training day so I don't start til tomorrow, DREADING IT

@osterionprincess1
You'll be fine, 2. Year ten's a walk in the park! Just don't mess it up, yeah? Auntie will kill me if she thinks I encouraged you to take it easy lol

@therunestar
Also @ladyanissadishipper did I see you literally just uploaded a new Kai one-shot?!??? Fab work. Honestly, reads like poetry!!! And so many hits on it already! LOVED that bit about him not learning archery too? So genius. Just wish a certain someone (cough Callum Denver cough) understood the character half so well . . .

I Can't Help But Wonder by **ladydishipper**

Prince Kai Osterion, One-Shot, drabble, Canon, fated magick, Kai Osterion visions, mentions of Prince Oscar Osterion

Kai can't help but wonder what life might have looked like if he wasn't – well, him.

Words: 438 Chapters: 1/1 Hits: 637

Sometimes, Kai wondered what might have been.

What life might have looked like for him, in another world. Another place, another time, another *him*. If his magick hadn't been warped and corrupted before he could even learn what magick was. If he hadn't been born with magick at all. If his brother Oscar, the pride and joy and glory of House Osterion, had been the one cursed with these visions and this power instead.

It wasn't power, not really. It rendered him power*less* too often for that. Magick might have been a force to be reckoned with for anybody else – for the Moonwalker, for scum like that Rascal, Roach, or her ladyship Adanna di Silver. But not for Kai.

Not when it marked him out as different – as unpredictable and abnormal and some quandary those around him couldn't quite understand. He was troublesome, burdensome. He was a challenge; a complication; a calamity.

No. He wouldn't wish his corrupted magick on Oscar, no matter how complicated his relationship with his eldest brother could be – but what *if*? Would they have treated their precious Oscar like a pariah for being different? Would they have taken the time and care with him that nobody ever seemed to have for Kai?

Would he have been a different person, in that universe? He couldn't help but wonder: would he have fought and played and trained more diligently? Would he have used a bow and arrow, rather than being told it was too risky due to the unpredictable nature of his visions? Would he have been highly regarded by the court and council for his ideas and insights? Could he have earned their respect instead of eliciting their fear?

Would he have had friends, comrades? People close to him, dear to him?

Would he have been dear to other people?

If he could have controlled the visions, quieted his mind, not lost huge swaths of time in the blink of an eye or been judged as scatterbrained and haphazard when he was simply trying to maintain a sense of order amongst the disorder, he might have simply ... fit in. Or what if there was a world where he was even seen as *normal*, the visions something ordinary and acceptable and simply part of who he was, if people didn't vilify him for it?

In another life, would he have been ... happy?

It was all so unfathomable, and no matter how often he might turn over such questions in his mind, none of it ever served to make Kai feel any better.

But still.

He couldn't help but wonder.

CHAPTER 22

I'm greeted by the most terrifying words anyone can hear in real life: 'So I read your fanfic.'

I startle so badly that I throw my entire cup of iced coffee. Most of it ends up all over my feet, the cup landing with a hollow plastic rattle, but not before I manage to accidentally launch some of it at Callum Denver.

And to think, I'd done such a *good* job of avoiding him like the plague over the past week ... and now we're right back where we started. Ugh.

He doesn't seem surprised to see me. Did he already know I was back? Was *he* avoiding *me* until now, thinking I'd weaselled my way on to set again just to be near him after our kiss? Or, God, even worse, did he think I was so affected by our not-*really*-a-proper kiss that I HAVE to avoid him, lest I throw myself at his feet and proclaim my undying love for him?

Callum is too busy to notice me cringing hard enough to spontaneously combust, though. He wipes his sleeve over his wet face, licking his lips. *I've kissed those lips. I felt them against mine. He leaned in like he wanted to keep kissing me back.* Has he thought about it since?

Not that *I've* been thinking about it, obviously ...

He breaks me out of my reverie by saying, 'Caramel? Oh, Anissa, don't tell me that coffee was for *me*.'

'They were out of vanilla syrup,' I grumble.

Cerys and I both have Thursday afternoons completely free on our new college timetables, so we bunked off at lunch to come to the studio for a few hours – something she volunteered us for before I could stop her. Right now I'm on hand to help reset some of the set dressing in between takes of a rowdy tavern scene.

Noticing someone already kindly making their way over with a roll of blue paper towels to clean up my spilled coffee, I grab Callum by the elbow and drag him out of the way. I've already drawn some attention by dropping my coffee. I do *not* need anybody hearing the rest of this conversation.

'What do you *mean*,' I hiss, my face a bit too close to his, 'you *read my fanfic*?'

Callum grins in a way that can only be described

as 'shit-eating'. He looks downright *gleeful*, the smug arsehole, like this is all one great big joke. One that I'm obviously the butt of.

The pit of my stomach falls away. I can *feel* the blood draining from my face – my whole body.

Oh, God. I didn't think anybody would ever find them. Not anyone who knew me in REAL LIFE, anyway. Has he sent my fanfics to other people? To other cast members? Do people *know*? Have they all read it, are they snickering at me behind my back? Do they all think I'm the obsessive, pathetic fangirl Callum obviously does? Is this vengeance for the kiss, for coming back to set?

And they're about Kai. All twenty-eight of my published fics. They're ALL. ABOUT. *HIM*.

I want the ground to swallow me up and spit out my bones, and then swallow my bones and grind them to dust.

I simply cannot.

'You have a lot of Kai fanfics,' he says, not very quietly.

All the blood comes surging back to my face, and my skin feels like it's on fire. I scowl and tug Callum even further away from everyone else. To my surprise, he doesn't resist.

'You did say you really liked the character – I

guess I shouldn't have underestimated you. I read the comments on your latest one, too. People *really* liked your insight about how he didn't learn archery, huh?'

I pinch my lips together, hard. Callum grins even wider.

'Glad to see I've had such an impact.'

I manage to unclench my jaw enough to bite out, 'Maybe if you weren't so secretive about what a dork you are for this series, *you* could take the credit for the archery thing.'

A muscle ticks near his eye. 'That's okay. Just surprised to see you *do* value my opinion. Your other fanfics were interesting, too.'

'Interesting,' I echo.

'Kind of . . . an insight into your brain. It was funny, reading them and knowing *you* were behind them.'

Did he read all of them? The modern AU I abandoned after five chapters where Kai was a transfer student at a new school, Oscar the golden child jock and him the lonely outcast nerd? Or the short, eleven-chapter canon-divergent fic where Kai takes the Eldritch Crown for himself? What about the one-shot from a few weeks ago where he's lurking at the ball in season three, watching everyone else enjoy the party?

Did he read the one-shot I wrote as a spin-off of

someone else's fic where Lady Adanna is sent to the palace as a suitor for Oscar and they fall in love (it was a classic enemies-to-lovers, arranged-marriage AU, I was begrudgingly obsessed with it), and Kai watches them fall in love feeling jealous and confused and like that's something he'll never have or understand?

It's one thing to post them sort of anonymously online, when total strangers read it, and even with my Discord friends, who are still sort-of strangers but also *get it* and won't judge me.

But Callum?

CALLUM DENVER? Absolutely not. I regret everything.

I feel hideously, horribly exposed.

This is a thousand times worse than kissing him.

'How did you even find –?'

'Your screenname's really similar to the one in some of the Discord servers.'

'Wait – hang on – *Discord*? Are you – do you –?'

Holy shit. Callum Denver's a lurker! He has a secret sock puppet account to lurk anonymously in the *Of Wrath and Rune* fan forums!

He carries on quickly, 'I mean, "Lady Anissa di Shipper" wasn't exactly *hiding* your identity. And there aren't a lot of people consistently posting Kai-centric stuff. I'd seen some stuff on Reddit about the archery theory. It wasn't exactly much of a rabbit hole to go down to find you.'

'Why?' I whisper desperately. 'Are you going to – I don't know, *blackmail* me with it?'

'What? No!' He blinks a few times, and his grin falls away. 'I just . . . I thought they were interesting, that's all.'

'Yeah. You said.'

We hit a stalemate, and I don't know how to move past it. Callum seems unusually sincere, which is not entirely reassuring, if I'm honest. I don't *think* he's going to share it with everyone else here . . . But why read them? Why mention it?

Is it anything to do with the kiss?

My questions must be written all over my face because he mumbles at last, 'It just . . . seemed like a good way to get inside your head.'

'Do you *need* to get inside my head?'

Callum gives me a long, indiscernible look that's so intense it sends a shiver down my spine. His pupils are dark, and his breathing seems a little more shallow than usual. When did it become so hard to look away from him?

If I read that line in a fanfic, it'd be followed by something like *'Yes – because I can't get you out of mine,' he said in a gruff voice, and grabbed her and kissed her, deeply*, etc., etc., which obviously, absolutely, isn't what's happening here.

We've ended up standing a bit too close to each other. Again. I move back half a step.

Callum clears his throat, looking away.

Somewhere across the room, the director yells, 'Cut!' and fresh air seems to flood the room. I take a deep lungful, and for some reason, now can't look at Callum as I do.

'I'm away next week,' he says after a moment.

'Where are you going?'

'LA.' He grimaces, though, like he can't imagine anything worse.

'Auditions? Is this for that YA movie?' I ask, and he nods. I'm almost surprised he admitted it; that he isn't going to accuse me of leaking news about him again. 'Richie's earning his pay cheque, huh?'

Something flickers in Callum's eyes at the mention of his agent, manager, whatever Richie is. But even though I clearly only know Richie's name from eavesdropping, it's not the wary, accusatory look I'm used to getting from him – in fact, this one's not aimed at me at all. It's more exasperated. *Tired*.

'Well,' I say, 'good luck.'

'Thanks,' he replies, a bit miserably.

I have a thousand and one questions I want to ask

him, but before I can ask any of them, he adds, 'Just thought I'd let you know. In case you're thinking of snooping around my trailer again.' His voice is deadpan but I think I see a wry flicker in his eyes. 'Try not to miss me too much.'

I snort a laugh. 'Me? I would never.'

'Oooh,' Nan says, turning over a thick, worn tarot card. 'The Knight of Cups! Now that's one for the romantics. A noble, handsome man comes charging in on a white horse. An emotionally mature man at that, if you're lucky.'

She laughs, the sound cracking as she coughs. She *claims* she stopped smoking twenty years ago, but I'm sure I've seen her bury a lighter in her cardigan pocket when she comes in from 'watering the garden'. Luckily for me, she's too busy hacking up a lung to notice the way I turn bright pink. I rush off to the kitchen to get her a drink of water, buying myself time to look normal again. I'm glad my parents aren't here; I can never keep secrets from them. At least while they're far away, I've got a bit of space to process things before they see it written all over my face.

When I was little, and even at my last school, there were rumours that I was a witch, because people knew how superstitious Nan is. She's given me evil-eye bracelets over the years since they're meant to be good luck charms. If they break, it's a sign they've done their job and warded off some bad luck. Kids at my old school thought they were an actual evil spell. Someone thought I'd *cursed* a boy who picked on me in PE class after he broke his nose that same day due to a particularly aggressively thrown rugby ball I genuinely had nothing to do with. And there I was, thinking the bracelet was just a sweet gift from my nan that matched my style.

Nan's always said she has a sixth sense for the 'spooktacular', but right now, faced with the Knight of Cups, I'm tempted to tell her she's a total charlatan and taking the mickey out of me.

'Except there isn't a boy,' I tell her firmly, looking at the tarot card face up on the coffee table, taunting me. 'Much less a noble, emotionally mature one.'

He *is* handsome, though. Just a bit. I can't argue with that.

Nan shrugs, dismissive. 'To be honest, it usually means being in tune with your own feelings and being creatively inspired, but most people aren't interested in hearing that. Can be a sign that you're making decisions with your heart instead of your head.'

'Wow. Super convincing. You're really good at this, you know.'

She flicks my ear in reproach. 'Helps when the subject is invested in the answers they're seeking. What answers *are* you seeking, Anissa?'

She shuffles the tarot deck again, waiting, but my mouth dries up and I don't have a response. I don't know what I'm asking.

Or maybe I do, but I'm very sure that I don't *want* to ask it.

CHAPTER 23

The first week and a half of college is over in a blur, and I want to sleep the whole weekend away. But duty calls, and so on Sunday morning I take a seat at our usual spot in the cafe, and unpack all of my notes for the next part of our adventure.

In all honesty, the last thing I want to do is immerse myself in *any* kind of fantasy involving Prince Kai Osterion, but I've missed playing this game with the others recently, and I can't let a few silly interactions (or one *extremely* misguided kiss) with Callum take that away from me.

Besides, today should be fun – there's quite a lot of stuff in the official *Of Wrath and Roll* handbook about the palace dungeons, so I've got all kinds of booby traps and puzzles ready for our party . . .

*

'Go ahead,' drawls Prince Kai. 'I assure you the path is clear of flaming arrows. If you don't believe me, why don't you have your sorceress here cast a truth-telling spell on me?'

'As if I'd waste my precious spells on *you*,' I snap.

'Make him go first,' Cailean suggests. Some of his hair is singed after a flaming arrow shot out of a wall down the last corridor, but his pride is wounded more than anything else. The Moonwalker was sliced so badly by a swinging axe that our cleric, Wreevo, had to use a major healing spell on him, and I'm limping after getting nicked by the same swinging axe.

'But we might need him to break into the vaults and get the crown,' says Wreevo.

Begrudgingly, the Moonwalker agrees. 'I don't trust him either. Wait a moment.'

Max rolls a D20 to investigate, and it's a nat twenty, the best he could roll. He punches the air.

I breathe out a sigh of relief. 'Thank God for that!' I laugh. 'I was starting to worry for the fate of *all* our characters . . .'

The Moonwalker rises from his low crouch on the floor. 'Some of the tiles are raised. We'll have to avoid them if we don't want to trigger a booby trap.'

Wreevo snorts. 'He said *booby*.'

'Follow me.'

The Moonwalker goes first, moving deftly from one flagstone to the next. The balls of light I cast offer a pale-blue glow in the otherwise dark corridor, bobbing gently before us. Lord Syxos goes next, managing to make it across with reasonable ease due to his long legs and wide strides. Wreevo follows, lumbering a little, and puts a foot wrong about halfway along.

The row of flagstones drops away as he hops along to the next safe spot, leaving a gaping black hole in the floor. Several seconds pass before we hear the stones hit the ground. It'll be a long, awful drop to almost certain doom if we fall.

'I thought you said there were no traps!' Wreevo shouts back to the prince.

He smiles thinly. 'I said there were no flaming arrows.'

Cailean goes next, but he's encumbered by some very heavy (stolen, too-large) armour and several (also stolen) weapons, and he stumbles several times. More sections of the floor drop away, leaving a patchwork path behind.

'You're next,' I snap at Prince Kai. His hands are tied in front of him now, and I've put a binding spell on his magick. It won't last forever, but it'll help us get most of the way through the dungeons without him causing too much trouble. '*Your Highness.*'

'My lady is too gracious,' he quips, but goes ahead. He's barely worse for wear after our previous battle – unless you count the bruise my dagger hilt left on his temple – and quite athletic thanks to all his courtly combat training, so he manages to get across without issue.

Prince Kai shouts back to me, 'Your turn, my lady.'

I roll my D20 and wince. It's not great.

'You have disadvantage, remember? On athletics checks, because of your injured leg,' Max points out, ever a stickler for the rules. But he's right, so I roll again, knowing I'll have to take the lower of the two rolls . . .

And this one's even worse.

'Shit,' says Jake, staring at the die.

'*Shit*,' Cerys echoes, looking at me with wide, horrified eyes.

I barely manage the first half of the path – or what's left of it, anyway. Huge black chasms yawn all around me, threatening to swallow me whole at the slightest wrong move.

I gather myself, brace against the pain in my injured

leg, and take a leap at the final gap to get to the other side with the rest of my party.

My foot catches the edge of the stones, my leg buckles and I fall backwards into open air.

'Mida!' the Moonwalker cries in alarm.

'Who's closest?' Jake asks frantically, snatching at dice and character sheets.

'Kai was last over!' Cerys makes a grab for Max, as if pleading with him for mercy.

'No!' I cry. 'I'm not having *him* save me.'

Jake hoots with laughter. 'I *love* the beef between Mida and Kai. It gets me every time.'

'I'm surprised you're not nicer to him,' Cerys says, eyes narrowing slightly. 'I thought you'd want us to see why you like Kai so much, instead of keeping him a villain.'

'That wouldn't be very in character for Mida,' I point out, which is mostly true. It's also weirdly cathartic for venting some of my endless frustration at Callum, but she doesn't need to know that.

The longer I don't tell her about everything that's gone on between me and Callum – specifically the kiss – the more monumental it all seems. If I explain now, it'll be like one huge secret I've been keeping and less like a series of micro-events to gloss over.

The truth bubbles up inside me, threatening to come spilling out, but I squash it back down and wave for Max to carry on. He gives me a nervous, grave look, his mouth pinched, and rolls a D20 to seal Mida's fate.

Prince Kai's hands grasp the front of my dress and haul me up over the edge of the sheer drop. We go sprawling on to the floor together. Wreevo and Cailean cheer, relieved I'm safe. I barely have time to register my near-death experience; I'm too busy scrambling off the wretched prince.

'You ought to be thanking me,' he says. 'Even if I only saved you because this blasted binding spell of yours will become permanent if you die.' It won't, but I told that particular lie so convincingly that he believed it, and he isn't familiar enough with how magick *normally* works to know any better.

'Well, thank you for your selfishness, *Your Highness*.'

'I'm sure you're more than used to it from your time as a palace servant, sorceress.'

He's infuriating, and I hate to be belittled.

So I deliver a swift kick to his shin, which he barely notices, but leaves my foot (on my remaining good leg) bruised, with a sorely stubbed toe.

*

After we pack up, Cerys and Max make excuses to leave so they can spend the afternoon *as a couple*, politely yet pointedly disinviting us so they can snog each other's faces off in peace.

Jake has other plans, however, and coaxes me to come shopping in town with him.

'Special occasion?' I ask while we wait for the bus, and he grabs my arms with a huge grin plastered on his face.

'Nis, I've got huge news! The biggest! Max and Cerys already know – I told them on the drive over. I meant to tell you earlier but then we got straight into the game . . . Anyway! You know how Ginny's going back to uni this weekend, for her second year? Well her friend's having a house party, and *we're* all invited! It's going to be really low-key, I promise, but some first-years are going . . .'

'Let me guess.' I'm already grinning back. 'Teddy's going to be there?'

'Yes! Gin said you and Cerys can stay in her room, she'll bunk with a mate, and me and Max can kip on the sofas. Max said he'll drive us, too. Please say you'll come? You have to! It's our first PROPER party!'

'You've been to loads of house parties!' He's been to at least *five* since I've been friends with him, which is loads in my book. 'I don't know, Jake, that's . . . I mean, this is different. This is with *uni* students . . .'

'Which is exactly what we'll be, this time next year! Well, as long as I pass that maths resit . . .' He trails off absently, and doesn't notice my uncertain grimace. I've been browsing courses and prospectuses but still haven't decided if I even want to go to uni yet. 'Plus, Ginny's going to show us around campus, so it's *basically* like an open day – not like our parents can object, is it?'

I snort. As if my parents would *ever* object. They'd be bundling me out of the door and wishing me a good time, thrilled to know I had plans with friends. Jake misreads my reaction as scepticism though, and his face falls.

'Please, Nis? I really don't want to go without you.'

There's a pang somewhere in my chest, but it's more heartwarming than anything else. This feeling of being *wanted*. Relied on, needed, by a best friend.

So I nod, and Jake pulls me into a quick cwtch just as the bus arrives. We disentangle from each other's arms to climb onboard the bus and soon enough find ourselves mooching around the shops. Jake fills his arms with piles of clothes to try on, determined to find *the* perfect party outfit. I've never seen him like this, but it's endearing.

I sit on one of the little chairs by the dressing room to offer second opinions on his looks, and feel like I'm in a montage scene in one of Cerys's beloved romcoms. Finally, Jake emerges in a coral T-shirt that complements his fair complexion and makes his blue eyes pop. It makes him look taller, too, and emphasizes his lean build.

I tell him all this, and Jake beams. 'You think? It's nice, right? Plus, feel it! It's *so* soft.'

He comes over so I can rub my fingers against the fabric. It's smooth, pleasant, and I hum in appreciation. Comfortable fabrics and insufferably itchy clothes are something Jake and I have bonded over plenty. He'll often end up changing several times before leaving the house just to find something that feels right, whereas I'll just buy multiples of something I know I like so I don't have to worry about that so much.

Daphne once told me that she envied how I'd 'perfected the capsule wardrobe'. I haven't had the heart to explain that's not exactly it.

'Think Teddy will like it too?' I tease Jake.

He grins, looking unusually shy before the moment passes. 'How about you? Do we need to find you something to dazzle and beguile a cute older boy? Or girl. Or person.' He holds up his hands like he's apologizing for assuming.

'Yeah, right! Don't worry, I don't think anybody's in danger of *me* flirting up a storm any time soon . . .'

CHAPTER 24

My usual escape into fanfic and fandom has been snatched out from under me, now I know Callum might see them. College work makes me think – and stress – too much about uni. I can't talk to my friends because it would mean having to talk about the kiss. So I'm left with just one option: Red Wings Studios.

It's late on Wednesday night, and hardly anyone else is here. Nan thinks I'm here to prep for a night shoot, so I was allowed to borrow the car for once.

The reality is, I'm hiding.

Everything is just . . . a lot, right now.

I'm currently waiting for call sheets to print so I can highlight them for different departments or actors, which is pleasantly mind-numbing. I have a Dungeons and Dragons podcast playing on my headphones, and the steady *whirrrr-kachunk!* of papers printing in the background and the *schhhick* of my highlighter rhythmically dragging across the page are soothing.

No college coursework to worry about, no new friends I have to stay on my best behaviour for, no uni applications looming over me . . . and *definitely* no attractive but impossible boy to deal with.

I breathe easier. My mind feels nice and blank, like a computer that's just booted up and has no programmes open and running yet.

Eventually the sheets are ready to go, but just as I round the corner to start dropping them off, someone runs smack into me so hard my headphones bounce off. I barely catch them as I stumble back, and a hand reaches out to steady my elbow.

It's Callum.

'Are you too famous now to watch where you're going?' I blurt, then – 'Wait, aren't you supposed to be in –?'

'Callum!' calls a jovial voice from the other end of the corridor.

And then I'm yanked sideways.

Everything is pitch black and my back's against a door while Callum whispers, 'Don't say a word. Please, Anissa. Just – *please*?'

I'm too stunned to speak anyway. My newly quiet

brain is struggling to process this abrupt change in circumstance.

My eyes adjust to the darkness and I make out a few shapes – a ladder, a mop. I take a small step and something plastic clatters to the floor, which I immediately trip over and Callum has to catch me again.

'Oh my God, please. I'm literally begging you, just – *don't*,' he hisses, sounding less like he's actually pleading with me this time and more like he's going to spontaneously combust if I blink too noisily.

I pull a face at him, even if he can't see it.

Outside, the voice gets closer. 'Come on, Callum! This isn't funny.' He sounds familiar, but it's only when he calls out, a little more tersely, 'Ghosting Favreau is one thing, kid, but you're not going to shake me that easy. Let's just talk about this, huh?'

It's Richie. The agent-slash-manager-slash-whatever.

I look at Callum, aware my mouth is hanging open.

I feel him cringe more than I see it. The hand holding me upright clenches, and I shift so I can grab his sleeve. Maybe for balance. Maybe to convey a question, like, *Why on earth did you drag me into this cleaning cupboard you lunatic?* But maybe also to let him know that I realize he must have a good reason for not being in LA like he's supposed to be, and I won't rat him out.

Callum's whole body tenses as Richie's footsteps pass right outside our hiding spot.

My thumb strokes a reassuring arc along his arm. His bicep, specifically. Because that's apparently where my hand ended up and where my thumb is now moving back and forth along a defined curve of muscle. Along *warm, bare skin*, because Callum's only wearing a T-shirt.

Add that to the growing list of things about him I'd be better off ignoring . . .

He's stood so close that I feel his chest brush against mine as his breath hitches, the warmth radiating off his body. The slight tremble that's rippling through him.

If this was a coffee shop AU, this would be the part where we'd kiss.

Richie's wheedling voice grows quiet again, doors opening as he checks rooms nearby. Callum relaxes, sinking against me for a moment.

I don't think he means to. I think, mentally, he's out there in the corridor with Richie, not in here with me. I don't think he even notices the way his chest presses into mine or the handful of call sheets I brace against his torso when the weight of his body pushes me gently back into the door again.

His T-shirt is soft. I can feel the cool texture of a printed logo against the backs of my fingers.

A sigh rushes out of him – the classic loosing of a breath he didn't know he was holding – and for a small moment, he leans his head forward and presses his forehead to mine.

It's intimate but innocent; my brain is scrambling to process this new type of closeness.

There's a funny swooping feeling in my stomach and my toes clench.

His breath tastes like caramel.

'Callum,' I say softly, his name half a question on my lips.

He moves away abruptly like he's just been electrocuted.

'Sorry,' he blurts, voice barely above a whisper. It's a tiny space in here, but he's far enough away now that I suddenly feel cold and have to wrap my arms around myself. My heart is racing – although I suppose that's a common side effect of being bundled into a cleaning cupboard by a sort-of famous actor who plays the comfort character in your favourite TV show.

'Sorry,' he repeats. 'I panicked.'

'I gathered.' I have to fight to keep my voice sounding normal. I have no idea what any of that just was, but I do know it was definitely NOT the kind of 'classic romcom Moment, *capital-M*' that Cerys always likes to talk about. *Definitely* not.

'Aren't you meant to be in LA?'

'Yeah.' Callum coughs. 'Meant to be.'

'Did you cancel it?'

'I . . . decided it wasn't in my best interests.'

'But the auditions –'

'Don't,' he says sharply, but there's no anger in it. 'You sound like Richie.'

'What happened? I mean, isn't that kind of . . .' *Career suicide* sounds a bit overdramatic, but Callum seems to get what I'm saying well enough.

'It wasn't in *my* best interests. I don't know how many times I have to tell him; I don't *want* –'

But he cuts himself off with a sigh. His shadowy outline reaches up to tear at his hair, and he starts pacing in a tight circle in the limited floor space available. I watch him for a few moments, unsure what to ask first. Why doesn't he want the auditions? Why is he avoiding Richie rather than just talking to him – doesn't Richie work *for* Callum, not the other way around? Does this have anything to do with his secretive dedication to OWAR? If he doesn't want the auditions, why is he taking them at all?

'Please,' he says at last, 'you can't tell anyone about this.'

I scoff. 'Oh my *God*. I'm not –'

'No, I don't – I don't mean "don't blab to the press

or Reddit". I mean, don't tell *anyone*. Even your friend who works here, or your boss, or Brayden, or anyone. Especially Brayden, actually ... Please. I just ... I need ... some time.'

'For what?'

He doesn't answer, though.

'How come you're here, anyway? Even if you're not in LA, you're not filming this week.' I should know – I just printed the schedules.

Callum hesitates, then mutters, 'If you must know, I was hiding.'

'Hiding?'

'Yes, alright? Hiding! I – I thought if I hunkered down in my trailer for a bit, I'd fly under the radar. But Richie apparently knows me too well – he knew exactly where to find me.'

I laugh, I can't help it. It's just so ridiculous – especially because I'm here doing the exact same thing. Callum grumbles something I don't catch because I'm too busy giggling, and when I calm down I get the sense he's scowling at me. His arms are folded across his chest.

'Are you finished?'

'Mm-hmm,' I say through pursed lips, another laugh slipping out.

'Look, please, just keep this between us? I'll – I'll owe you one.'

He sounds so desperate, it sobers me up. 'You don't have to owe me anything. I won't tell.'

'Yeah, but –'

'Just because you don't like me doesn't mean this has to be – I don't know, *transactional*.'

'I don't like you?'

'Yeah, alright, you don't have to rub it in.'

'No,' he says. 'No, that's not . . . What makes you think *I* don't like *you*?'

'Do you?' I challenge, and the beat of silence that follows says plenty. 'Exactly.'

'Maybe if you weren't so up yourself –' he starts, annoyingly straightforward, like that's a perfectly reasonable thing to tell someone.

'Maybe if *you* weren't so abrasive!'

'Or if you weren't so out of touch . . .'

'*Out of touch?* That's rich, coming from you, Mr Hollywood!'

'Says the girl so consumed with fandom that she can't separate what she sees on TV from reality –'

'Well you don't have to worry about me separating *you* from anything, since you blocked me on Instagram. It's alright for *you* to be able to stalk *me*, though. Tracking down my usernames. Reading my *private* things –'

'It's not private if you post it publicly.'

'Anonymously! And, what, you think you *know me* from a few fanfics I wrote? That's totally different.'

'No, it's not. You think I put my whole life online?'

Honestly, it hadn't occurred to me until now that might be the case. That the glossy, superficial posts are only a small piece of the picture. But I barrel on, 'For the record, you *don't*. Know me, I mean. Whatever "insight" you think you got by reading my fics, forget it. You don't know the first thing about me.'

'I know you're in your own head too much,' he says evenly, taking a step towards me. 'Chronic overthinker. Less of an introvert, more like ... self-imposed isolation.' Another step.

My breath snags in my throat, a flood of outrage coursing through me. Who does he think he is? What right does he have to psychoanalyse me like this?

And be *right* about it?

'I know you've never had a proper boyfriend, or even kissed anyone before, and romance feels like something only other people get to have. You wouldn't be able to write it half so brilliantly if you didn't *mean* it.'

Rude. I mean, he's absolutely correct, but still.

Callum doesn't step closer again, but I push away from the door so I don't feel so emotionally cornered – only to find myself face to face and toe to toe with him. I grip the call sheets furiously. Even in the dark, I'm near enough to make out Callum's self-righteous smirk.

'I know you're lonely, and you hate it.'

My face burns. I'm *not* lonely. I have *loads* of friends. I'm part of two different group chats! Plus I have the Kai-rry On My Wayward Son Discord and the local OWAR one Cerys first introduced me to. I have – I have . . .

An all-consuming fear that it'll be snatched away from me at any moment. A total and complete inability to let myself believe these friendships are solid and real and genuine, sometimes. A lifetime of being alone that's shaped me and made me smaller and is so, so hard to shake off.

'And,' he says, 'I know you'd rather escape into a fantasy world than ever have to face reality.'

I jab a knuckle into Callum's chest. The call sheets in my hand rustle against his T-shirt.

'Maybe. But you wouldn't be hiding in the cleaning cupboard if you weren't doing the *exact same thing*.'

CHAPTER 25

I'm still seething from my latest spat with Callum when I storm back to my car later that evening, after finally being told to pack up and go home by one of the production assistants.

Where does he get off, picking apart my personality traits, when *he's* a mess of contradictions himself? A dedicated actor one minute and shallow arsehole the next, then also a secret nerd sabotaging his own career . . . And he can't act like he *hates* me, then try to kiss me back, then say things like *that*!

He doesn't know me. Not one bit.

Not . . . in the way I'd want someone to know me, anyway.

He doesn't even know *himself*.

'Psst . . .'

I wish I'd never let Cerys drag me into this whole work experience thing. Sure, I would've missed the chance to help build something amazing and be behind the scenes of my favourite show, but at least I'd have kept my love of Kai untainted.

'PSST . . .'

I wish Callum Denver would just bloody go to LA and never come back, I –

'Anissa!'

A hand catches my shoulder, and I shriek and whirl around.

My elbow hits a moustachioed stranger right in the sternum and he stumbles back with a startled groan. He's wearing a boiler suit and cap, and I think: *I'm going to end up on a true crime podcast. Cause of death: fangirled too close to the sun. Also: murdered in a car park.*

Coughing, he says, 'Bloody hell, Anissa!' and it's not a stranger – it's *Callum*.

My hands fly to cover my mouth. 'Ohmigod I'm so sorry! Wait – no I'm not. That's totally your own fault for sneaking up on me. What are you *doing*?'

'I was *trying* to get your attention,' he says, rubbing the middle section of his ribs. 'But you were miles away.'

I scoff. Like I need ANOTHER round of him telling me that I'm in my own head too much.

'I wish I was. Miles away. From *you*.'

'Hilarious. I need a favour.'

'Unbelievable!' I exclaim. 'You really are something else. Dragging me into cupboards, belittling me, and now you have the *gall* to ask me for a favour. Try someone else. Maybe a fangirl who *is* actually so besotted with you she doesn't mind putting up with all your crap.'

He grimaces, and for once, doesn't argue back. '*Please*. I just need you to drop me off somewhere.'

'Absolutely not!' I cry, and Callum shushes me frantically. The car park is lit by floodlights that cast sharp, stark shadows across his face, and where the light does hit him, he looks pale and drawn. There are deep circles beneath his eyes that haven't been painted on by the make-up department this time.

I get a better look at his outfit now: a grey jumpsuit I think is a woman's, a Seattle Seahawks cap that's too big for him, slipping down his forehead, and –

'Are you wearing a *fake* moustache?'

I mean, I know he is; I can see it right there on his face. It's a thick reddish one that's giving Magnum P.I., Nan's favourite cop show. The fake moustache sits wonkily above Callum's upper lip. It's too big for his face; I'm pretty sure it's one that his in-show father wears.

Callum smooths his fingertips over the moustache self-consciously, only succeeding in making it wonkier than it already was. 'I raided one of the costume trailers. I needed a disguise.'

'A *disguise?* What next, you need a getaway car?'

He doesn't deny it.

A laugh bursts out of me. 'No WAY! I'm not . . . Do you even hear yourself right now? As if I'd do *you* any favours, after *everything*.'

'Please? Please. I'll really owe you one.'

'I don't *want* you to owe me one, Callum. There are plenty of drivers around, ask one of them –'

'They'll tell Richie, if he asks.'

'Then call an Uber!'

He shakes his head. 'I'd have to wait out front by the reception. Someone will see me. Please, Anissa. Just, I don't know, drop me off somewhere on your way home. I'll get an Uber then.'

I hesitate. It's *weird* that in spite of how little he thinks of me, he's acting as if I'm some kind of lifeline.

Also weird: that I'm tempted to help him out.

But in the dodgy car park lighting and in his stolen, haphazard disguise, Callum doesn't look like the up-and-coming Hollywood heartthrob who winds me up relentlessly. He looks like a tired, scared teenager, and . . .

And *damn him*, he looks like Kai. All beleaguered and run-down and like he just needs a quiet five minutes somewhere with a cup of tea and someone to pat him on the shoulder and tell him that he's a cinnamon roll of a human who must be protected at all costs.

'Oh, bloody hell, alright,' I huff, and gesture for him to follow me.

Callum sighs, says quickly, 'Thank you!' and hurries along at my heels. He scrambles into the passenger seat of my car, where he hunkers down so low he's practically sitting in the footwell, hardly able to see over the dashboard.

'Really helping me feel better about the whole "smuggle you past your agent and the security guards" thing here,' I mutter, getting into the driver's seat like a normal human being.

I smirk as I switch on the ignition. Oh, how the turns have tabled! How nice to feel like *I* am the normal one, and *he* is the weirdo with serious issues. I'm sure I'll relish this later when it's over.

Despite Callum's extensive attempt at subterfuge, it turns out to be completely unnecessary. The few other people who are heading to their cars don't even notice us, the security guards barely spare us a glance on the way out and, even though Callum is tense and glancing frantically around, Richie doesn't come charging out shouting his name and chasing after us like a bad cartoon villain.

As getaways go, it's very unremarkable.

After a few minutes, Callum relaxes and shuffles up in his seat.

'Thanks,' he says, a bit shakily. 'I –'

'If you say you owe me one –'

'I owe you an apology,' he interrupts.

'Bit late for that. I've already helped you escape.'

'Still.' He clears his throat. 'I'm sorry.'

'For?'

'Huh?'

'If you're apologizing, it's *for* something. What are you sorry *for*?' I'm not trying to be nasty – I'm genuinely curious. 'Is this a general "sorry about my bad attitude" apology, or specifically about our argument earlier?'

'Can't I just *be* sorry?' He huffs, exasperated.

I shrug. 'I suppose. It's not much of an apology, though.'

'I'm *sorry* you're always so bloody prickly,' he mutters, not entirely under his breath. I glower in his direction, and Callum squirms before saying, 'Alright. I'm sorry for all the stuff I said about you being lonely and too caught up in the fandom. It . . . wasn't nice.'

He doesn't pretend he didn't mean it, or doesn't think it's true. But I think I appreciate the apology more genuinely for it. At least he's not lying.

'And I'm sorry for putting you out, making you drive me off set. And dragging you into the Richie drama. It's . . .' He trails off, apprehension rolling off him in waves. I almost feel a rush of sympathy for him – *almost*, because then he mumbles, 'Never mind, you wouldn't get it.'

'Oh, yes, I'm sure it's the sort of important, impressive thing a lowly fangirl like me could never understand.'

'That's not –' Callum scrubs his hands back and forth over his face. The fake moustache falls onto his lap. 'Do you think that just *once* we could have a genuine conversation without going for the jugular?'

'I don't know. Are you capable of it?'

'I'm not the one who starts it!'

'Mm-hmm.'

'I'm not!'

'Whatever you say . . .'

Callum makes a few unintelligible, grouchy sounds that make me giggle in spite of myself.

I go on, 'Maybe we could have a genuine conversation if you didn't look down on me so much all the time.'

'I don't look down on you.'

I cut him a look. 'Please. You completely wrote me off the first time we met.'

'You did sort of yell in my face.'

'And you made it *perfectly* clear earlier just how much you think of me.'

'I . . .'

It's way too satisfying to leave him floundering for words like this, when I feel like I'm too often scrambling to maintain some sense of 'I swear I'm a functional human being'.

'Well,' he says defensively, 'you've made it plenty clear you don't think too much of me, either. Especially after . . .' He cringes, averting his gaze, and I flush. *The kiss. He's talking about the kiss.* I can hear my heartbeat suddenly roar in my ears. 'Anyway, you're always quick enough to try and take me down a peg or two, or find new ways to annoy me.'

I toss him a sickly-sweet smile, even though my heart is still pounding. 'I do my best.'

He might not *always* start these back-and-forths between us, but I almost always finish them.

I drop Callum back at the apartment that the OWAR production team have put him up in. It's more like a self-catered hotel, he tells me, with tight security, a doorman and a concierge; most of the cast and higher-ranking crew are staying there.

It looks modern and sleek, with huge windows everywhere. Callum mentions something about the heated swimming pool and rooftop tennis court. Apparently Brayden Brown has a sign-up sheet for rotating matches, which I bet must be brilliant fun. It sounds too surreal to be true. Magical, almost.

'Do your parents not mind moving around with you?' I ask, the thought only just occurring to me. If I had to move around for shoots like Callum, drag my parents away from work along with me, make Harley live in a hotel or something . . . I can't even imagine.

'It's just me. Mum lives in London and Dad's . . . in Leicester? I think?'

'You don't *know* where your dad lives?'

Callum shrugs. 'He moves around a lot. Consultant.'

'Oh, well, that explains it.' (And by 'it', I mean *nothing*.)

I find a spot to pull into opposite Callum's building.

'That must be really weird,' I muse out loud. 'Is it scary?'

'What, Brayden's tennis tournaments?'

I roll my eyes. 'Living on your own at seventeen.'

A harsh bark of laughter rips out of his throat. 'You know, I think you're the first person who didn't assume it must be really *cool* to live on my own. No adult supervision, no one nagging me to do my homework or not leave my socks on the floor . . .'

No Dad to make me a cup of tea while I tell him

about everything I learned in class that day. No Mum experimenting with some fairly straightforward recipe and ultimately butchering it. No episodes of *Married at First Sight Australia* that Mum and I will watch avidly and Dad will inevitably get sucked into, no matter how much he claims to 'not be watching'. No Nan to chat about art-and-craft projects with, or send YouTube videos to about niche dramas in the online tarot-reading community.

It sounds awful, to be honest. I don't say that, because it's a deeply uncool take, but the quiet that settles between us feels softer, more understanding. I wonder if he thinks it's pretty awful, too.

'Anyway. Thanks for the lift,' he says quietly, one hand on the door handle. 'I'll, uh, see you around.'

'Yeah. See you around.'

I drive home in a daze, trying to wrap my head around the whirlwind of this evening. Jake will *never* believe any of this.

If not for the auburn moustache abandoned in the passenger footwell, I wouldn't believe it either.

OWAR Discord Kai-rry On My Wayward Son
General

@osterionprincess1
no jokes, I am lowkey devastated

@rubytherapscallion
??? what's up?

@osterionprincess2
OMG HAVE YOU NOT SEEN OMG I'LL FIND THE LINK NOW

@wrathfulqueen93
Hot off the press (and by press I mean the whiteboard conspiracy girlies on TikTok) . . .

@therunestar
Wait. CALLUM DENVER HAS A GIRLFRIEND?!?!!?

Video transcript from @boarderlinebabe – posted 12 September

IS CALLUM DENVER DATING SOMEONE?! Lock in and buckle up, because today on the whiteboard we've got a brand-new celebrity dating conspiracy theory for you, all about the up-and-coming fittie from the fantasy show *Of Wrath and Rune*, and his top-secret girlfriend...

The theory: Callum Denver is dating someone.

The evidence: FIRST! The secretiveness on social media. He used to post regularly! Which begs the question, why *isn't* he posting much these days? What – or who! – could he be hiding? And more importantly, where is our soft launch, Callum Denver?!

A couple of blind items released about gossip on the set of OWAR – where there is always fun drama to report on, because this fandom is SO invested! – suggest that Callum's been getting particularly friendly with a certain girl on set. She must be a crew or cast member if she's around often enough to spend time with him, since OWAR's employees are so stringently vetted... anyway! They have coffee dates, or so the rumour goes.

We also have THIS recent photo from an anonymous source... You can see a girl (the same girl?!) really blurry in the background as Callum is just exiting his trailer looking VERY, er... well. Let's just say, someone had their hands in his hair. Cheeky! Sneaking off for a kiss between takes, perhaps?

Finally there's THIS photo from a fan staking out the cast's accommodation just the other night, showing Callum leaving a car. You can't really make out the driver since it's too dark and far away, but it's *definitely* a girl! The same girl? I'd be willing to bet yes! She must have been driving him back from a date night...

Now, if my theory's correct, this relationship started back in August, when filming moved to a new production studio...

nerds unite 🗡

Max
idk how weird ha-ha or weird gross this is, but I just found this TikTok doing the rounds on an OWAR Reddit thread and I think it's about you Anissa?

It's about that guy Callum who plays Prince Kai

Cerys said he brings you coffee all the time

Jake
I'm sorry wHAT

Cerys
Oh my God. ANISSA. EXPLAIN YOURSELF?! How long have you been Callum Denver's secret girlfriend?! Hahaha

Me
Omg this is too funny

> Believe me, if me and Callum Denver were secretly dating, you guys would absolutely be the first to know

> I promise you, NOTHING is going on

> NOTHING.

GIRLIE POPS 2.0! ✨

Chloe with the Twitch channel
Okay super random but a video just popped up on my fyp about that guy you like from OWAR and his secret girlfriend and I SWEAR TO GOD @Anissa that's your dad's car in one of the pics??? It's got the same RSPB parking sticker in the window?

ARE YOU SECRETLY DATING THE HOT ACTOR?!

Evie Price from school and also now college
Shut. Up.

Cerys
This is so funny, Max literally just sent the video in our group chat! Plot twist they ARE talking about Anissa lol (Callum brings her coffee, I think it's a running joke between them after she spilt his on our first day?)

But good point about the car Chlo, what is UP with that @Anissa????? Did you drive him home?!?

Me
I'm sure loads of people like to support the birds

You guys know what these internet conspiracy things are like, it could be anyone

Daphne from college
Okay but WAS it anyone!?

Me
I was literally just giving him a ride home

The drivers were all busy or whatever

IT'S NOT THAT DEEP I SWEAR

We were definitely NOT coming back from a date

Nikita from college (Daphne's friend)
~~There's no way it WAS a date like pls, have we all met Anissa~~ *Nikita from college (Daphne's friend) deleted this message*

~~Shit wrong chat~~ *Nikita from college (Daphne's friend) deleted this message*

CHAPTER 26

'Something on your mind, love?' Nan asks, appearing in my bedroom doorway on Saturday afternoon and making me jump out of my skin. I automatically minimize the window with my Word doc and ongoing fic out of habit.

Cons of your family supporting your nerdy interests: they would *absolutely* want to read my fanfics to 'encourage me' or whatever, and I would simply rather DIE.

'Did your crystal ball tell you that?' I joke.

Nan clicks her tongue. 'Don't be silly. No, that video you were listening to finished ages ago and you've been sitting up here in silence. That's not like you. You love a bit of background noise.'

'Huh.' That's true; I do work better with background noise. But I got too sucked into my current project: a story about Kai forming an unexpected friendship with Roach, and the pair bonding over their messy and unpredictable magick. It was only meant to be a quick break, but somehow it's been hours already.

'Nothing's on my mind,' I lie. 'I'm just, you know. Homework. Locked in.' I gesture, hands either side of my head, and Nan nods, understanding. She does this, too – loses entire days to a single knitting project, or reads an entire book in one go. Sometimes I even forget to stop for lunch.

Nan puts a cup of tea and a plate of custard creams down on my desk, nudging them into the tiny bit of space among all my stuff and then takes a seat on my bed.

'You can always talk to me, love, you know that. And if you don't, I'll just ask the crystal ball to tell me,' she adds with a cheeky look.

I laugh, but a curl of discomfort licks up my spine. Not because I think she can see all my secrets – but because I kind of *do* want to talk about something that's been bugging me for the last couple of days.

I suck in a breath. 'I have this ... friend. Sort of. We don't *exactly* get on. But I, um, think I'm a bit ... worried about him?'

'About *him*,' Nan echoes, in a tone that makes me regret opening my mouth at all. I narrow my eyes at her and Nan's eyes sparkle mischievously back, but she manages to say in a sensible enough tone, 'Is he in trouble?'

'No! Nothing like that. It's more ... I think ...' I grimace, an uncomfortable feeling in the pit of my stomach, weighing me down any time I think about my last interaction with Callum. 'I think he's ... lonely? He doesn't exactly have much family around, and ...'

The glint in Nan's eyes is snuffed out, and her face falls. 'Oh, poor lamb! Well, why don't you invite him round? I'm doing a roast tomorrow. I've got more than enough potatoes ...'

I burst out laughing. 'That is *not* happening.' I don't know how to explain that I can hardly invite an honest-to-God TV actor for Sunday lunch at my house (especially since the only way I *could* contact him is on Instagram, where he's blocked me) so I just settle for saying, 'We aren't *that* close, Nan. He's just ... I don't know, different.'

'Well.' She sets her hands on her knees, her gaze thoughtful. 'Maybe you ought to try reaching out a little bit more. You of all people know how difficult it can be to find your way in and make friends when you feel different.'

Her comment hits me like a punch in the gut. Nan gives me a soft smile and pats my shoulder as she leaves me to my laptop – though all my earlier intense focus has suddenly vanished.

When I stare back at the pages I've just written, I realize that it's not me I find reflected back in Kai this time. It's the sad, scared boy in a fake moustache in the car park.

'Here,' says Callum, finding me while I'm stapling some fresh, fake bloody upholstery on to a chair. 'A peace offering.'

He's handing me an iced Americano. I already know it'll have vanilla syrup.

I put down the stapler and stand up to take it. This is the first time I've seen him in over a week: he's only just returned to set after his abandoned trip to LA. It's difficult to look at him properly. The harsh words he said in the cleaning cupboard are still rattling around in my brain, but so is the quiet, aching feeling that he carried the whole drive back to his place.

Callum draws a sharp breath, but I get there first – 'You found a better hiding place, then? You didn't come back to set.'

'Why, did you miss me?' His tone is sceptical rather than scathing, and I snort.

But I also crouch back down to finish sorting out the chair, because I don't trust my face to make the right expression.

'Brayden let me crash on his sofa for a couple of nights – I told him my schedule got rearranged and they were doing some maintenance in my room. Then

Sienna – you know, Lady Adanna – was away for a premiere in New York, and I said I'd look after her cat, so I hid out there for a bit, too.'

'You didn't tell them what happened?' Not that I know the details of why he's avoiding Richie so much, but . . . I get that heavy sensation again. Sympathy for how lonely that must be.

He shrugs. 'Didn't feel like getting into it.' And clearly he still doesn't, because he doesn't offer any further explanation. 'I, um – I wanted to talk to you actually. It's kind of important. If you have a minute?'

'Sounds serious.' My mouth turns dry, but I don't stop working or look up. I put a staple in the wrong place and mutter a swear.

'There's a video. Going around. About me. About . . . *us*.'

'Oh, THAT!' The laugh that cuts out of me is unexpectedly dry – but I suppose I should've seen this coming.

Objectively, it's hilarious. A series of micro-interactions, taken out of context and shuffled together to tell one particular story. And I know if it were about anyone else, I'd eat it up too. But knowing it's about *me and Callum* – it's laughable. Eye-rollingly absurd.

'People think we're, you know.' He squirms, like the idea is so unfathomable. '*Hooking up*. They even got that photo of you leaving my trailer after we ... after we kissed.'

Oh, God, *now* he wants to talk about that? *Here?*

I stand up so quickly I knock the chair over. I know it draws people's gazes, but I'm too busy glowering at Callum and hissing, 'Shh! Do you *want* everyone to know? What is this? Are you asking me if *I* leaked that photo? I know you think I'm out of touch, but I promise you Callum, I'm not *that* delusional.'

He scowls, a muscle feathering along his clenched jaw. 'That's not what I'm trying to say.'

'And for the record, that was barely even a *kiss*, alright? It was – it was nothing.'

It was *not* the proper first kiss I still haven't had – the first kiss I've been waiting for; the swoon-worthy moment I'll hold dear for the rest of my life.

'Understood,' he says through his teeth. 'But actually, I just wanted to check if *you* were alright. I know it's weird to see yourself plastered all over the internet, so I wanted to make sure you were okay. But clearly, you're just your usual bubbly self, so I'm wasting my time here.'

'Wait, Callum –'

I reach for him. I *reach for him*, like an idiot, like *that's* not the sort of photo taken secretly on set that paints some pretty little lie about our 'romance'. My fingers barely graze his sleeve, but a voice calls out and I'm not sure whether he stops for them, or for me.

'THERE you are! Oh my goodness! *Anissa!*'

Cerys comes running over, freckled cheeks flushed and blonde ponytail swinging wildly behind her. She skids into me and seems only then to notice I'm not alone.

'Oh, Callum! Hello! Sorry, am I interrupting?'

'No, we were just –'

'Anissa was just filling me in on her latest TTRPG adventures.' Callum gives Cerys a polite smile, his posture suddenly relaxed, and I bristle at the lie. The fact he even knows to mention it . . . It makes us sound like better friends than we are.

Even if Cerys agrees how silly our 'secret romance' sounds, I don't like the idea of her believing we're actually friends. I don't like lying to her.

But I can't call Callum out without getting into *everything* with Cerys right now, so I just force out a smile and say, 'Like I said, you're welcome to join us any time you want. You could use all your in-depth research to really bring Prince Kai to life.'

Cerys gasps. 'Are you going to play with us? We haven't been able to make time for it lately, but . . . Oh shoot, we're not playing this weekend either, are we? We've got that party.'

Callum tilts his head, politely inquisitive. 'Oh?'

'Our friend Jake's sister invited us. It's at her uni . . .'

'Jake?' Callum echoes, pinning me with a look, and *shit*, why does he remember about Jake? 'Right. I remember. He's your . . .'

'He's our other best friend.' Cerys beams. 'But obviously Anissa's already told you about him! Hey . . . do you want to come? It's just a house party, but –'

'Oh, Callum can't –'

But he suddenly perks up, looking genuinely surprised. 'Really?' And damn that soft, vulnerable look on his face. Damn *me* for letting it get to me. I blame that conversation with Nan. 'D'you mean that?'

Cerys nods, grinning. 'Of course! It's nothing fancy like you're probably used to, and I don't think anyone there is a particularly big OWAR fan . . . Well, except Jake and my boyfriend Max. They're huge fans, but they won't be weird, I promise.'

'No,' Callum drawls, and smirks in my direction. 'Throwing coffees on me and screaming in my face is Anissa's thing, isn't it?'

Cerys giggles like it's a huge joke we're all in on together, a silly fond memory to share. She winds an affectionate arm around my shoulders. 'Tell him, Nis! He's welcome to tag along, isn't he?'

The whole interaction feels like an out-of-body

experience I'm watching from afar. Somewhere, another version of me is frantically rolling a twenty-sided die and hoping for the best on a persuasion check when I'm already at some kind of disadvantage.

'Well, yeah, sure, but . . . don't pressure him, Cer. I'm sure Callum's got *way* better things to do this weekend than tag along with us . . .' I look him in the eye to inform him, 'Jake's sister is giving us a tour of the uni, too. Bath. Basically like an extended open day; you'll probably find that really boring, won't you?'

The grin that splits Callum's face cheek to cheek is toothy and crinkles his brown eyes at the corners. There's a mischievous glint in them that feels like a challenge . . .

My stomach sinks the second before he tells Cerys, 'Sounds brilliant. I'll be there.'

I hear the imaginary D20 landing on a mocking *one*. Critical fail. I have to smile at Callum when he says he'll message me for the details, and I fake thank him for the coffee I now want to throw in the bin out of sheer spite. He leaves and I try to focus as Cerys gushes about Lisa agreeing to be a reference for her uni applications and how exciting this all is.

It is exciting, and I'm over the moon for her.

But I'm also furious, because now Callum's stolen my time with my friends – one of the last little bits of sanctuary from him that I had left.

CHAPTER 27

Callum graciously unblocks me on Instagram to get details about the party. I'd tell him to go kick rocks, but being *that* level of petty feels like losing our never-ending battle, so I just let him know that Max is happy to pick him up on our way down to Bath, and that yes, the others agree to his polite request (*cough* DEMAND *cough*) to pretend he's simply a friend from college.

I wonder if he's going to bring another ridiculous disguise in fear of more run-ins with screaming fangirls.

The boys promise they'll keep their cool after Cerys practically threatens them, but they're both vibrating with excitement over spending a weekend with an actual member of the OWAR cast.

I'm dreading it. I'm dreading spending so much time with Callum and having to save face for the others' sake, and I'm dreading *them* finding out what an arsehole he can be and him ruining their love for the series, too.

Callum comes sauntering out of his building, a weekend bag slung over his shoulder, calling a cheerful goodbye to the doorman, and I'm forced to budge up into the middle seat – right between him and Jake.

Cerys introduces the boys, and while Max says a rather shy hello, Jake leans over me to exclaim, 'Dude, hi, this is going to be *the* best weekend *ever.*'

Callum laughs. 'Good to meet you, Jake. Anissa's told me *loads* about you.'

'She has?' Jake grabs me in as much of an embrace as he can when we're all buckled in, and smacks a noisy, playful kiss on the side of my head. 'Glad to see the bright lights of Hollywood haven't made you forget about your bestie, Nis!'

'Well. The bright lights of *Cardiff*,' Max jokes, making the boys laugh. Callum looks between me and Jake, more observant than calculating. My skin itches. I never expected to get caught out in something that was barely even a white lie. I never *said* Jake was my boyfriend . . .

But Callum and I both know I implied it, and that's more than enough.

The journey feels endless. The boys have a million and one questions for Callum about what life on set is like. How does he fit in college, or exams? Does he go to loads of cool parties? Is it true that the actors playing Lady Adanna and her faithful guard Devon are *actually* dating?

Cerys cringes and tries to apologize on their behalf – she has an even weirder aura than *me* on this road trip, for some reason – but Callum only laughs and says he doesn't mind, and he really, genuinely, doesn't seem to. He answers all their questions (except the one about Lady Adanna and Devon, claiming even *he* isn't sure), and asks some of his own: what they're studying, their plans for uni, how they got into OWAR and even asking for stories about our TTRPG adventures, which everyone's happy to regale him with.

He especially enjoys hearing all about the way I wove Prince Kai into our campaign, and the beef my character Mida has with him.

Laughing, Jake recounts Prince Kai saving Mida from falling to certain doom and how Mida kicked him in the shin afterwards, bruising her own foot. 'It's even funnier because obviously you've met Anissa! She was always dead quiet in school, you barely even knew she was there. And even now she's not exactly . . . well, you know.'

He gives me an affectionate nudge, even if he trails off a bit awkwardly.

Callum, though, just looks at me with a wry smile. 'Sure. I couldn't imagine Anissa *ever* being a bit argumentative. She's a real . . . *wallflower.*'

The word is one thousand per cent a pointed reference to my Kai fanfic with the same title, and I cringe and sink lower into my seat.

This weekend cannot end soon enough, and it hasn't even started yet.

Ginny's waiting for us on the doorstep, waving us over with a big smile and wrapping us all in big hugs. The resemblance between her and Jake is so striking: their long noses, blue eyes and sandy hair; even their similar thin-framed glasses and lean, narrow builds.

She whisks us inside, and a stale smell like damp and fajitas and WKDs hits me all at once. The house is a three-storey terrace. She points out the kitchen on our right, the downstairs bathroom and the living room with saggy, brownish-grey sofas where the boys will be sleeping, then takes me and Cerys up to her room so we can drop off our things.

'You didn't mention the other guy was so cute!' she says as soon as we're out of earshot. Ginny's never gotten into OWAR the way Jake has, so all she knows is that Callum's another fandom friend we've brought along. 'He seemed to have a bit of an eye for you, Anissa!'

I scoff. 'I probably just had something in my teeth.'

Ginny and Cerys share a look. I recognize it as the kind she shares with Daphne or Evie when they're gossiping about boys, and it turns my palms clammy.

On our way back downstairs, I corner Cerys. 'Is everything okay? You seemed kind of off on the drive here.'

The smile she gives me is blank, and her eyes are distant. 'Yep! Totally fine! Come on, we can't keep the others waiting.'

At the front door, Ginny plants her hands on her hips as she faces us all. 'All ready to go? We've got ages before we have to get ready for the party, and I'd be a terrible big sister and host if I didn't do the mandatory "show you around campus" so everyone can pretend this is an *educational* trip . . .'

Ginny takes us to see some empty lecture halls, the student union, a campus pub and the library. I look around with mild interest. Like this, uni doesn't seem as intimidating and scary as I've been building it up to be in my head. Actually, it's unnervingly easy to picture myself tucked into a booth in the library surrounded by books, my laptop and a podcast playing quietly through my headphones while I study . . .

Callum walks around like he's in a daze, with greedy eyes that drink in every last tiny detail. He asks Ginny endless questions on everything from how the dining plans work to what tutorial groups are like, making her laugh.

'Someone's keen to move out! Bloody hell. I thought you'd all be more excited about pub crawls and the Dungeons and Dragons society than how the online coursework portal works!'

Callum flushes, an uncharacteristic display of vulnerability that the others laugh off, and I can't stop thinking about even hours later. He *did* seem to care a lot about his exam marks, but I never really thought about whether he'd go to uni. When the others asked him about it on the way here, he never gave a straight answer . . .

Is he here just to spoil my weekend with my friends? Or is there something else that pushed him to accept Cerys's invitation; something that has nothing at all to do with me? Something even bigger than maybe just being a bit lonely?

And WHY do I want to know so desperately?

I'm still thinking about it when Cerys, Ginny and I get ready afterwards, clambering past each other to reach for make-up brushes and curling irons. Ginny pours us each a glass of cheap rosé wine that stings my nose but tastes like fruit cordial, and I let their gossip about the night ahead wash over me. We follow Ginny's lead of a cute-but-casual striped jumpsuit: Cerys wears jeans with a cropped sheer blouse that she's borrowed from Daphne, and I opt for a lilac corduroy minidress, layered over my Argonauta band tee I got from their concert last year.

'Love you in purple,' Ginny tells me. 'It's so your colour.'

'I should hope so. I wear enough of it.'

She squints at me from where she's crouched on the floor, doing her make-up in a full-length mirror propped up against the side of a wardrobe. 'Have you thought about dying your hair? You'd look so badass with purple hair.'

I grimace. 'I tried last year actually. It went *so* wrong. I tried to bleach it first and totally fried my hair. Ended up with a really dodgy haircut for a while.'

Cerys blushes, and I throw her a reassuring smile. I remember overhearing her and the girls from college talking about how terrible my hair was, and laughing with each other about it. I kind of don't blame them. It *did* look atrocious.

'Maybe I'll try again some time,' I muse, catching sight of my reflection as I put my jewellery on. I wear my favourite ear cuff shaped like a snake, a mismatched dangly pair of moon and star earrings, and a couple of rings on my fingers.

It was easier at school, when conformity was the norm. We all had the same uniforms, I would pull my hair back in a ponytail and nobody took too much notice of my jewellery if I didn't wear much of it. It was one more way to fly under the radar and not get picked on.

But going to college where there's no uniform has been freeing. I've felt so much more like *myself*. It's been fun to experiment with ways to express myself after keeping so much of me under wraps for so long.

It feels a little bit like revenge, too. A middle finger to the people who *would* bully me for being different. Like I get to own it now, and not let them take it away from me.

'I could help you, if you wanted?' Cerys offers. 'I've never dyed hair before, but Daphne and the girls would help, too! Nikita's always helping her mum dye her hair at home; she'll know exactly what to do.'

I beam at her. Maybe it's a little liquid courage from the wine, or maybe I'm finally letting myself feel like part of the group, but when I say, 'I'd love that', I mean it.

CHAPTER 28

The tight hallway and small rooms at Ginny's friend's house are quickly filled to bursting. Music pours out from two different speakers, the conflicting beats and lyrics making it too distracting to focus on any one conversation for a while. Callum flies totally under the radar in our group. Nobody would expect to see him here, and out of costume, with his hair more red than brown, he's practically unrecognizable.

Cerys is brought easily into the fold with Ginny's friends, asking them all about the uni experience and giggling over their stories, and it's only then that I realize what's been up with her all day – she's avoiding Max.

Did they have a fight? What's going on? They didn't hold hands *once* during Ginny's campus tour, which is so unlike them.

Max and I cling to the wall near the kitchen for a

while, tucked out of the way. Jake is being his usual excitable, extroverted self and darting from one conversation to the next with a surprisingly keen and relaxed Callum in tow – although Jake always stays in sight of the front door.

Max gestures at him with his Diet Coke. 'Place your bets now: will he calm down once Teddy *does* finally arrive, or be even more like an overexcited puppy?'

'Definitely the latter.'

Max chuckles, and clinks his drink against mine in agreement. 'How about you – or have you only got eyes for your secret boyfriend Callum Denver?'

I know I'm supposed to laugh and crack a joke, but what comes out is – 'Never mind me. Has something happened between you and Cerys?'

Max grimaces. 'I'm not sure I should be talking about it . . .'

'I'm *your* friend, too,' I point out, which seems to catch him off guard. Max and I formed a friendship over Discord around the same time as Cerys and I got close, though we don't ever really hang out just the two of us. He's usually busy being Cerys's boyfriend or Jake's best mate, or it's all four of us hanging out together.

I hate the idea of something being off between them; I want to help.

Eventually, Max sighs. 'We had a fight this morning. About Callum.'

I swear my heart stops cold, and I glare across the room at Callum. I *knew* he'd ruin everything. I wish I'd never met him.

'Well,' Max goes on, 'not *exactly* about Callum. Just . . . Cerys was really pushing me not to geek out too much, like I was going to embarrass her. And I get that she was worried it might affect her work experience on set *now*, but at the time it just felt like she was ashamed of me being, you know, a nerd.'

I wince. I can see why that's a sore spot – Cerys was kind of judgy about fandoms until pretty recently, and Max can get really defensive sometimes.

'But you'll make up, right? You can't stay mad at each other forever.' I grab his arm, feeling suddenly frantic. I know it's silly, but I think if *Cerys and Max* can't make things work, how could I ever hope to? 'You two are PERFECT together. You're like, the EPITOME of epic romance. My IRL OTP. You're not going to break up over this, right?'

Max's mouth curves upwards, but it's tinged with . . . sadness? Pity? I'm not sure. 'No relationship's perfect, Nis. It's not all like it is in the stories.'

Embarrassment squirms through me, but Max glances off towards the kitchen, where Cerys is giggling, and this time his smile is softer, more sincere. 'I'm sure we'll figure it out. It's not like it's the first time we've argued.'

It's not? That's news to me.

But maybe I've pried enough for one evening – and if Max has faith in their relationship, I should, too.

Does it make it better, knowing they can fight and still come through the other side? Does it make their love stronger? More – real? I guess I never thought of it that way before now ...

Quiet settles back between us, and it's nice. Low pressure. I think this is how it would feel to have siblings – shared personality traits and no need to chat to understand each other. Max's arm leans lightly against my shoulder, and for several minutes we just sip our drinks and people watch.

He and Jake are similar in a lot of ways, but they're definitely a bit of a black cat/golden retriever set when it comes to social interactions. I'm grateful for it now, though, so I have someone to loiter with on the periphery.

It's only when Teddy walks in with two other brand new first-years that we both shift, laser-focused on watching Jake have a nervous breakdown in the space of 0.3 seconds. Teddy is every bit as cute as the photos on his socials, with a dimpled smile and brown eyes that immediately search the crowded hallway. He brightens when he sees Jake and raises a hand quickly in greeting, then seems to lower it awkwardly as if trying not to look too overenthusiastic.

He's wearing a short-sleeve shirt and chinos, looking more like he's going out for a posh dinner with his parents than to a house party, and I smile into my wine glass. He's made the effort for Jake; it's so sweet to see.

Callum turns away from the chat he's having with a small group of people to give Jake a nudge, saying something nobody else can catch. Jake tosses him a smile before lunging forward so abruptly that he trips over his own feet and spills someone's drink as he stumbles to a stop right in front of Teddy. They're close enough that I hear him breathe, 'Hi.'

'Hi,' Teddy says shyly. He's blushing.

Jake nods. He smiles. He gulps. He smiles again.

Callum is watching from afar, and his eyes meet mine. I'm surprised when he grins, like he's as excited for Jake in this moment as we are. I'm smiling back before I can think about it.

Max whispers to me, 'I don't think I've ever seen Jake lost for words. That boy never shuts up.'

I grab Max's arm and drag him over. I hardly ever put myself out there like this – my skin is crawling and my stomach roils, but I push it aside. I'm doing this for Jake; it's what Mida would do if a member of her adventuring party was in trouble.

'Hi! We're Jake's friends. I'm Anissa. This is Max.' When I glance over, I find Callum with his back turned to us – to *me* – already talking to some other people.

Teddy says, 'Yes! Of course! And these are my flatmates, Dave and Keon. Jake's told me loads about you guys. Your friend Cerys is here too, right?'

'I think she's been adopted by Ginny,' Jake laughs, and it's the dam breaking before he falls into his usual pattern of easy, enthusiastic chatter. He and Dave bond over the struggles of further maths at A level, and when Teddy mentions I've got work experience on a TV set, Keon – a drama student – moves closer so he can ask all about it.

Then Dave excuses himself to go chat to some people he knows and I notice Max, on the fringe of both conversations now, slink quietly away to find Cerys. Keon's so interested in hearing about my work experience that I don't have much choice *but* to keep chatting to him.

I keep glancing over at Jake and Teddy. Jake's laughter sounds easy and relaxed, and Teddy keeps fidgeting with his Afro or smoothing down non-existent creases in his shirt. Keon follows my gaze at one point and smiles at me. 'Were you brought in to wingman too?'

'Is it that obvious?'

'This is all he's been talking about, you know.'

'Jake, too.' I cringe. 'Don't tell Teddy I told you that, though.'

Keon mimes zipping his lips, laughing. He has a nice laugh: warm and sweet, like honey in hot tea. He's tall, his jawline smooth, with dark hair that's shorter on the sides than on top, and his teeth are the kind of perfect only achieved with braces that make me self-conscious of the gap between my two front teeth.

Keon puts a hand on the top of my arm. 'Should we leave them to it for a bit, and grab some drinks?'

I don't want to drift too far, in case Jake needs backup – though, as I watch, Teddy reaches up to touch Jake's arm casually, his hand lingering there a bit, and the points of Jake's cheekbones turn bright pink. They're doing just fine on their own.

I look down at Keon's hand, still on *my* arm.

He's the kind of obviously and objectively cute guy that girls would automatically fancy, and it's quite nice, I suppose. Flattering. But it doesn't *feel* much different to if it was Jake or Daphne touching me.

I lift my gaze, wondering if I should say something to Jake before disappearing, but somehow my eyes find

Callum instead, further down the hall. He's looking at me.

Looking at Keon's hand on my arm.

'Sure,' I say, once again channelling the kind of Mida confidence I usually only bring to our TTRPG. 'Let's go.'

See? No sad, pathetic, lonely fangirl here. Take THAT, Callum.

I find Ginny's bottle of rosé in the fridge and top up my glass halfway. There's a buzzing sensation in my head, but it's probably only because of the two different playlists blasting. It gets a bit quieter when I take a sip of the cheap alcohol.

Keon cracks open a beer and lifts his drink to me. 'To the wingmen – and women – of the night.'

'To us.' I clink my glass against the neck of the bottle, and Keon asks more about my work experience at the studio. He's chatty and funny, and even if he really couldn't care less about me or OWAR, he listens actively and asks questions. I try to remember not to get too swept up talking and ask him questions, too.

I have no idea where Cerys and Max have ended up or if they made up after their fight this morning, and whenever I notice Jake he's so busy chatting to Teddy that I know it's best to leave them be.

I keep catching glimpses of Callum, too. He always

seems to be talking to someone different whenever I spot him, and he looks like he's having fun – maybe even a little tipsy? He's a *lot* smiley.

It's ... hurtful. Knowing he's capable of that. Of *this*. That he can be nice and friendly, and I rarely get to see that side of him.

I guess I never show him that side of *me*, either, but still.

Callum catches my eye at one point while I'm leaning against a wall out of everyone's way. Keon's telling me a hilarious story about a nosebleed he got during a school play, but the way Callum's dark eyes bore directly into mine makes my spine straighten. There's a tingling in my fingers, but that's probably just the wine.

His head tilts slightly, questioningly, but I don't know what he's asking me.

A shiver rolls down my spine, but I say to Keon, 'Shall we go outside?'

The tiny patio is blocked in by rickety fences, and there's one lone, rusty deck chair neither of us suggest sitting in. Instead, Keon perches on the step outside the back door, and pats the space next to him for me to join. It's only when I sit down that I realize how small the space is, and I end up flush against his side.

Our ankles touch. Our knees, our thighs, our hips,

our arms. I can feel the fabric of his jeans rough against my bare shin, smell the woodsy scent of his cologne mingling with the malty smell of beer on his breath.

Distantly, I register that this is the stuff of giddy daydreams and fanfics: being at a party, sitting alone with a cute boy, the touch barrier broken and some kind of romantic tension building to the inevitable kiss scene. *This* is what my teenage years should be. *This* is how the main character gets to fall in love.

I stare at Keon, wondering if I want to kiss him.

His mouth looks nice. Soft, smiley.

He tucks a piece of hair behind my ear, and his fingertip brushes against the snake cuff. 'This is cute.'

'Oh, thanks. It was a birthday present.'

Is he making a move?

Do I *want* him to be making a move?

Keon leans in, closing his eyes, and I have a split second to realize – *it's happening*. I'm finally getting my *proper* first kiss. This is it, my Moment; I'll finally get to be just like everybody else and it'll be brilliant and wonderful and – *crap, I hope I'm not a bad kisser*.

I remember to close my eyes, too, and let his lips land softly on mine. There's a small *clink* as Keon puts his beer bottle down to settle his hand on my leg – very respectfully near my knee. I follow his lead and put my free hand on his shoulder, using it to lean a bit further into the kiss. The taste of beer on his breath isn't great, but I don't think the cheap wine on mine is much better.

Every romantic scene in every fanfic I've ever read starts running through my mind: noses slotting side by side, teeth grazing lower lips, tongues fighting for dominance and firework sensations . . .

He pulls away slightly to catch his breath and moves in to kiss me again. I part my lips this time, and he takes the invitation to drag his tongue lightly against my lower lip. I open my mouth wider and tilt my head so he can deepen the kiss.

It is, I consider, a perfectly decent kiss. There's no weird washing-machine swirling of his tongue and no gross noises or anything. It's certainly *more* of a kiss than I shared with Callum in his trailer.

But it feels a bit like it's happening to someone else.

All I can think is – *is that it?* Is this what I've been building up in my head all this time, wistful for? It doesn't make me feel *anything*. It's about as exciting as a trip to the dentist, and I feel like a complete idiot.

The kiss finishes and Keon smiles at me sweetly. We go back inside to rejoin the party.

CHAPTER 29

I stand in front of the fridge, not seeing any of its contents, and touch my fingers to my lips.

I always thought I'd feel . . . *changed*, somehow, by my first kiss.

I thought it would be exciting. I thought *I* could be exciting. Like Cerys or Daphne. That I could be the kind of girl who'd go to a party and meet a cute boy, be flattered by his attention and kiss him and fall madly in love in a whirlwind romance.

But I just feel sort of . . . frustrated. Not because of Keon, but because I'm annoyed at how much I'd built this up in my head, and how silly I feel for believing that real life could ever live up to all the sweeping romance fanfics I've read.

Callum was right: I'm a delusional fool who lives more in her own head than facing reality. To paraphrase only *slightly*.

I slam the fridge door shut, making the cans and bottles inside it rattle. I feel so *stupid* to think I could be like everybody else. Things were a lot easier when I was just the weird loner kid stuck on the outside. At least then I didn't get everything so wrong. My life was small, but it wasn't messy like it is now.

I don't even want to *be* here. I only came for my friends, but they're nowhere to be seen now. And I don't think I can stay, knowing I'll have to avoid Keon for the rest of the night.

The party is raging all around me. The crowd seems to have doubled, tripled in size, and music is blaring so violently I can feel the pulse of it inside my chest, down to my bones. I squeeze my way out of the kitchen, into the hallway and manage to make it to the front door. It's already open; the cacophony of the party pours out into the street.

The fresh air hits me – refreshing, sobering. My breath is shallow, and I don't know if it's the bass that's pounding so hard in my ears or my own pulse.

The further down the street I get, and the further away from the party, the better I feel. I make it to the end of the road before the tension in my body unspools all at once, and I have to sink on to a low brick wall at the front of somebody's garden. Leaning over my knees with my arms tucked over my head, I wait for the world to go back to normal.

Footsteps stop nearby.

'Are you alright?'

I groan, not even bothering to look up. 'Go *away*, Callum.'

He doesn't, but since when has Callum Denver ever listened to anything I have to say? He comes to sit on the wall next to me – not quite touching me – and I feel his hesitation before he asks, 'Did something happen?'

'No. Yes. I don't know.'

How do I admit that *reality* happened? That he's right: I've sunk myself so deep into my identity as an OWAR fangirl that I forgot I'm *not* strong and bold like Mida. That girls like me don't get to have sweeping, epic romances; that the fun nights out at house parties kissing boys don't belong to us, and I fooled myself into thinking I could have those things.

That reality is not what I imagined, and I've got only myself to blame.

I suck in a breath and push myself to my feet. In his jeans and plain white T-shirt, his auburn hair a bit dishevelled and a sheen of sweat at his temples, the faint smell of cider mixing with his deodorant, Callum could be any seventeen-year-old who tagged along to a house party. He looks like exactly the kind of person I *don't* feel like; I can't bear it.

'I'm fine. I'm just tired. Overwhelmed. That's all. I'm going back to Ginny's – you should go back to the party. Enjoy the rest of the night.'

'But . . .'

I start walking, certain Callum won't follow me. Why would he? He never has before. These conversations – *confrontations* – always end with us storming in opposite directions.

'Let me walk you back, at least.'

I stop, shocked, and pull a face. *'Why?'*

Callum lets out a noise that's somewhere between a grunt of frustration and a laugh. His tone is surprisingly gentle when he responds, and it ignites something warm in my chest.

'Probably for the same reason you smuggled me off set the other week. Because it feels like the right thing to do.' He holds my gaze, arms hanging at his sides, looking both awkward and dead set on coming with me. I sigh and this time carry on walking with Callum at my side.

Hating the silence, and worried that if I'm too quiet he'll ask why I left the party, I decide to go on the offensive and ask: 'Did you have a good time?'

'Yeah, actually – I did. I liked feeling normal for a change. And I like your friends. They're really cool.'

In spite of myself, I smile. I'm both glad he thinks so and a little amused; I'm not sure Max – an introverted nerd with long hair who loves cosplay – is the typical definition of 'cool'.

Then Callum says, 'Why did you tell me Jake was your boyfriend?'

'Actually, I only ever said he was my friend. Who is a boy.'

'You let me think it, though.'

I can't deny that. I bite the inside of my cheek.

'What happened with that guy tonight? The one you went out to the garden with.'

My heart rate picks up a bit and I avert my gaze to study my feet, watching my trusty lilac Converse moving one step at a time along the pavement. 'We kissed. It was fine. And then I left.'

Callum snorts, and I round on him with a glower.

'Yeah, I know, alright? *Hilarious*. Someone like *me* kissing a cute guy at a party is a real joke, I get it –'

'What? No! I was just . . .' He shakes his head softly, then chuckles and scuffs the toe of his shoe against the ground. 'I was wondering if you ran away from every guy you kiss. I thought maybe I was special.'

'I didn't – I don't . . .'

Shit, I kind of did though, didn't I?

'What's the joke, though?' Callum asks. When I look at him oddly he clarifies, 'You said the idea of someone like you kissing a guy at a party is a joke.'

The smile I give him is thin, brittle, and the backs of my eyes sting.

'I know you think you've got me all figured out from reading a few of my fanfics, but you don't. I've told you, Callum, you don't know anything about me. This just proves it.'

I stalk ahead down the street, but not before I swear I hear him say, 'I'd like to, though.'

CHAPTER 30

It's eerily quiet back at Ginny's house with all her housemates at the party, too. Callum and I stand in the narrow galley kitchen with a glass of water each, leaning against opposite countertops.

After walking the rest of the way in total silence, we both cave and start talking at the same time.

'Why did you bail on going to LA –?'

'You were trying to use Jake to make me jealous, weren't you?'

We both blink, taking a second to process what the other just said. My face burns, while Callum looks away with a scowl – although I don't think he's upset with me, exactly. His shoulders roll back, squaring, and it's body language I recognize from when Prince Kai is faced with a difficult decision.

I decide to throw him a bone for once, and answer first: 'I think I just wanted to prove to you that I wasn't a total outcast who doesn't have any friends. And pointing out that I was waiting for a guy . . . I guess it made me feel . . .' I squirm, trying to figure it out to explain. 'Normal. Wanted. Part of something that wasn't just the OWAR fandom. Something *real*.'

Saying it out loud, I realize that's exactly why I went outside with Keon tonight, too. Why I kissed him. Why I even agreed to get a drink with him in the first place, when Callum had been staring at us in the hallway. It makes me feel even more humiliated about the kiss than I already did.

But Callum nods, a thoughtful look on his face even as his eyes burn into mine. There's an intensity to his gaze that makes me feel like he's looking for all the parts of me I keep squirrelled away, to study them one by one like jigsaw pieces.

He tells me hesitantly, 'I bailed on my audition because I want to be a writer, like you –'

'Like *me*?'

He rolls his eyes, irked at the interruption, but it feels unusually good natured. 'Oh come off it, Anissa. You're a natural storyteller. I've read your fanfictions and your prose is fantastic; you clearly know how to use a strong character arc to influence the plot, and your understanding of world building is really impressive . . . Your TTRPG campaign sounds exactly the same, the way your friends rave about it.'

I can't help but pull a face. Even if it's nice to have a compliment on my writing from someone who isn't Cerys or a stranger online, it's also weird to have any kind of compliment from *Callum*.

'I wouldn't exactly call myself *a writer*.'

'I would.'

He sounds so sincere, but it feels like too big a statement for me to know what to do with right now.

'I want to be a writer,' he carries on, his voice more solid now, more sure. 'I give a lot of feedback on the scripts when I get them. I know it's not my place, but it's mainly to point out when they've got a character really wrong, or if they've done something for a cool visual effect that conflicts with OWAR lore.' His hands curl tighter around his glass, and he leans forward. 'Like, this isn't some low-key fandom. If they get that stuff wrong just to pull off some a big dramatic moment, there'll be *huge* backlash about it.

'Richie hates when I do it though. He keeps saying, "Stay in your lane, unless you want to get written out." And I guess he's got a point. Nobody really wants some jumped-up, bit-part actor interfering.'

'You're not a bit-part actor –'

Callum gives a thin smile. 'Maybe not anymore. I'm only getting more screen time these days because Richie's doing his job and making me a star.' This time, there's no denying the resentment in his voice.

'Can't you just tell him that's not what you want?'

'It's complicated. He's been with me since the start of my career. He's family. And I *did* love it back then. And I *love* being Kai and being part of this show; the role was a *dream*. I've grown up hooked on these books. The cast feel like family to me. I don't want to give that up. Richie's got ... other ideas, I know. He only ever saw OWAR as a stepping stone to bigger and better things for me. But I don't want to take on any more new roles.'

'What about that movie you did? And you're in that new Netflix one, the thriller ...'

He grimaces. 'I hated it. I mean, they were cool jobs, the people were great and all, but my heart wasn't in it. I didn't want to be there. And I spent the whole time feeling like a piece of shit for taking that away from someone who did.'

I guess imposter syndrome gets to us all. *Celebrities: they're just like us.*

'I want *this*.' Callum gives an all-encompassing gesture at the kitchen. 'I want to go to uni and house parties and make friends my own age and get in trouble for not finishing my coursework on time or staying out too late. I want to be *normal*. Feel part of something real, like you said. And I get it, Richie's just doing his job.' Callum sighs, resigned. 'And he needs *me* to do *my job*. But I've tried telling him I don't want to carry on outside of OWAR. He just doesn't get it. He thinks this is what everyone wants.'

'Isn't it?'

I thought that's what everybody dreamed about: being recognized and loved and seen and admired by countless people, being welcomed and *wanted* everywhere you go. Having the world at your feet.

Being the girl flattered by the attention of a cute boy at a party, and kissing him on the patio steps.

I stare at Callum, taking in the bags under his eyes and his messy hair. For all the gym muscles he's built for the show and his artificially white teeth, he looks . . . fragile.

Maybe Kai isn't the cosplay.

Maybe Callum Denver is.

He pushes away from the countertop, moving to stand beside me. I can feel the warmth of his body on my skin even though we're not touching; it makes the hairs on my arms stand up and sparks a sensation in the pit of my stomach that makes me feel dizzy. I take a drink of my water, draining the glass and discarding it on the side.

'Why Kai?' he asks me. 'Of all the characters, all the fandoms . . . Why him?'

Oh, the verbal essays I could give.

A little voice in the back of my head reminds me of the bitter animosity between us and how this will probably only give him more fodder against me . . . but in Ginny's empty, shabby student kitchen in the dead of night, I think I *want* to tell him – open up to him, the way he has to me. There's a lump in my throat that I swallow, and my voice comes out soft and quiet when I finally answer.

'Because he makes sense to me. Sometimes there's just *so much* going on inside my head – like when Kai gets his visions – and I don't know how to make it stop. And I feel like there's all these social cues and expectations that everyone else got the memo about except me. Don't be too loud or too quiet; don't like *that* thing, like this one instead; don't be yourself, but if you are, don't be surprised when people make fun of you for it. Me and Kai . . . we're both stuck on the outside for things we have no control over. So he makes sense to me. He makes me feel less alone.'

I risk glancing up, and find the corner of Callum's mouth has quirked up. I'm possessed by the sudden urge to trace that curve with my fingertip. I clamp my fingers around the edge of the counter instead.

Then he sighs, setting his glass of water down to brace against the kitchen counter like I am, his pinkie finger barely a hair's breadth away from mine.

'What I said, about you not separating OWAR from reality ...' He hesitates. 'A lot of people feel like they know me just because of some parasocial relationship they've formed over social media, and it makes it hard to know when people are being genuine. It's part of why I don't want to keep acting, and why I haven't been posting much lately. I hate it. The attention. The fakeness. That stuff I said to you was ... I guess I was trying to push you away a bit.'

Can't relate, obviously. I'd never do anything like that.

I would never, for instance, flake on group plans at the last minute because of a crushing sense of imposter syndrome, or run away from a cute boy so that he can't reject *me* first.

Never. Literally, could not be me.

'Sometimes, I think ...' He sucks in a deep breath, and looks me in the eye so intensely I couldn't turn away even if I wanted to. 'Sometimes I wish I could be more like you.'

'*Me?*'

'Well, yeah. Whenever I see you, you're always so unafraid to be yourself. Unapologetic about who you are.'

I'm too stunned to reply. I'm *constantly* afraid of being myself, but hearing it from Callum, someone who only ever sees the worst of me and sees it as a *good* thing . . . I'm speechless. I'm *touched*.

He carries on, 'When I accused you of being lonely, before . . . I was just projecting. You're not lonely, Anissa. You might feel that way, but I've seen the pictures you post when you're hanging out with friends. The way you talk about your family. And you have the TTRPG. People love you on set, too. Everyone knows you; they rely on you. They *like* you. You're one of the most passionate people I know.'

'Even when I'm winding you up?'

Callum smiles. 'Especially then, I think.'

I find myself smiling back and suddenly the endless confrontations, the one-upping each other, the petty rivalry, all feels like some silly joke the two of us are in on together. He hooks his little finger around mine, the faint tan on his hand against my brown skin, and for several moments, neither of us speaks. We just stand there, side by side, holding on to this unspoken pinkie promise.

It feels like a tide shifting; like something settling in the aftermath of a long storm.

It makes my heart beat faster, and something flutters deep inside my chest.

This is how it should have been. This is the moment I wanted – no, the *Moment,* capital 'M'. The heart-to-heart, the vulnerability of bringing down our walls and letting each other in; the feeling of being the only two people in the entire world and this instant in time belonging so entirely, completely to us.

The way his lips part with a soft exhale and his eyes devour mine, and the electric feeling racing across my skin like goosebumps, making me lean in closer . . .

Is *this* how it happens? There is warmth spreading from my chest, my stomach, and the hitch of breath in my throat is so loud in the silent kitchen that it makes his pupils flare larger, darker, and I wonder how I look to him in this moment. I wonder if he feels untethered the way I do, snared in the tension between us that's so different to every other heated moment we've shared so far.

It feels strange and wonderful all at once, and Callum's chest just barely grazes against mine as he turns more fully into me. His free hand comes up to brush against my bare arm, and I let my eyes flutter shut.

The front door bursts open. Voices shout and laugh and overlap; feet pound as they run inside. There's the faint noise of a siren.

Callum and I spring apart just as Ginny's glazed eyes light on us and she cries out in relief. 'THERE you are! OMG! Total anarchy! The neighbours called the *police* on us!' She comes running up and throws her arms around me. 'I was worried I'd have to tell your parents I accidentally got you arrested or something, ha! What are you guys doing back here? Anissa! I thought you were totally hitting it off with Teddy's friend!'

'I, um –'

'I wasn't feeling too well,' Callum interjects smoothly. 'Anissa volunteered to come back with me.'

'Aw! She's such a sweetheart, isn't she?'

Callum's smile looks awkward, and he won't quite meet my eye, but there's a faint blush staining his cheeks that makes me sure it wasn't all in my head – that *something* just happened between us.

He mumbles some excuse about finding his phone charger and goes off towards the living room. Ginny's brought some friends back with her from the party and now they pour into the kitchen, all chattering loudly about their daring escape from the police.

And it's only then, watching him leave, that I realize –

Shit.

I've got a crush on Callum Denver.

CHAPTER 31

It's the end of the night, and Cerys is a giggly, giddy drunk. She hugs everyone goodbye and makes loud promises to see some of Ginny's friends again soon, then Max and I help her stumble upstairs where she flops on to the middle of the bed, laughing over something about shoelaces.

Max just shakes his head, sighs, and drops a kiss on the corner of her mouth. They've apparently made up; I'm relieved for it. 'Tell us about it in the morning, yeah? Night, Cer.'

'Nos da,' she croons, and I close the door behind Max. Cerys blinks a few times, then gets up on wobbly legs to change into her pyjamas. 'Where's Jake? Why didn't he want to say goodnight?'

'He's still downstairs talking to Teddy. They've been inseparable all night.' It's so sweet. They even shared a few tender kisses, which I'm sure we'll get a full debrief about tomorrow on the way home.

Cerys sighs happily. 'Teddy's so lush. I hope it works out. You and his friend looked pretty cosy, too, though. Hanging out together *aaaaaall niiiiight*.' She pulls a face, her eyes huge and lips pouted, swaying back and forth before she starts giggling again.

'I kissed him.'

Cerys shrieks, then clamps a hand over her mouth and shushes herself. Her eyes are glazed, but they focus squarely on me. 'Shut up! What! When? How was it?'

I shrug. 'In the garden. Before I left. It was . . . fine, I guess.'

Cerys's smile falls dramatically. 'Was he not a very good kisser?'

'No! Not like that. The kiss was great, you know, objectively speaking.'

'Do you not like him?'

'He was nice.'

'Then what's the problem?' Her tone isn't accusatory, I only wish I knew how to explain it to her.

I wish I knew how to explain it to *myself*.

We finish getting changed for bed, passing a bottle of Cerys's micellar water back and forth while we take our make-up off, and then we crawl under the covers side by side. I've had a few sleepovers with Cerys; our late-night chats are always fun and *always* take some deep, existential turn.

So I know she won't mind me asking, 'How did you know? With Max?'

'How did I know what?'

'That you ... liked him. Fancied him. Wanted to kiss him.'

Cerys thinks about it for a few long seconds and I look over, half worried she's fallen asleep. But she's just staring up at the ceiling, mouth twisted to one side as she mulls it over.

'I don't think I did, for ages. I had such a big crush on Jake, I don't think I even realized I had feelings for Max. Obviously it turned out that I'd been messaging Max the whole time I thought I was messaging Jake, and by that point, my feelings were more attached to the person I'd been talking to than, you know, *Jake* . . .'

'But you kissed Max at that party last year, on Bonfire Night. Before you knew it was him you were talking to on Discord.'

'Yeah . . . I mean, he *was* really fit. And I was trying *not* to notice,' she adds with a laugh. 'Which was so silly, looking back. I could've saved loads of time by just accepting that I did fancy him. He's got this way of looking at me that just gives me butterflies. And when he holds my hand, I just *know*, you know? Like, he *gets* me. Like he's my person.'

I think about all the couples I've seen at school or college. Every time I've seen Cerys and Max be romantic with each other. Jake and Teddy, blushing and awkward and giddy with anticipation. All the fanfics I've written, trying to make sense of this feeling that feels so alien when it's such a universal experience.

I kept thinking I was too much of an outsider to understand, or that because I'd always been the weird kid at school I just hadn't got round to it yet. But kissing Keon tonight, that wasn't groundbreaking or earth-shattering or anything else.

It felt like I was missing something.

It felt like . . .

Like the kind of thing I found with Callum in the kitchen.

Which is so silly, because we didn't even kiss. We barely even *held hands*, and it wasn't even romantic like that. But it felt . . . monumental, somehow. Like I could finally make sense of things. Seeing him, and knowing he saw me, too.

What would it be like, if I kissed him instead? Properly, this time – not some petty, heat-of-the-moment, fleeting thing? If, instead of Keon's hand on my leg, it had been Callum's, the sweetness of his caramel breath on my tongue?

'But how did you *know*?' I ask Cerys. 'How could you be *sure*? How did you even know he liked you back, when you kissed him? When you told him all about how you felt?'

'I don't think it was so much about knowing,' she says softly. 'I just knew the "what if?" was going to eat me alive if I didn't do something. Imagine being stuck forever with the regret of *not* taking that risk and it working out. I can't imagine anything worse.'

I can: the regret of taking the risk and it *not* working out.

The shame would eat me alive.

But I only say, 'Yeah, I guess so.'

Within a few minutes, Cerys's breathing evens out and she's fast asleep. I stare at the ceiling for a long while, thinking I might be perfectly happy to lose any shot of something more with Callum if it means keeping my dignity and sanity intact. After tonight, we seem to have broached a genuine friendship at long last. That could be enough. That *can be* enough.

I've made my life smaller plenty of times before,

squashed down a lot of thoughts and feelings to make sure I don't stand out or do something wrong.

This doesn't have to be any different.

Still, I think sleepily, my eyes finally starting to grow heavy: it might be nice to wonder *what if*, just for a little bit.

What If It's You? by **ladydishipper**

Lady Adanna di Silver/Sir Grayson 'The Moonwalker', Lady Adanna di Silver, Sir Grayson 'The Moonwalker', Devon Smith, Moonsilver, one shot, drabble, s3 ballroom scene, Lady di Silver can unalive a man in the blink of an eye but kiss one and she turns into a wreck

After one fateful meeting, as their paths cross during a ball, Lady di Silver starts to wonder if this is the adventure she's been searching for all along. (AN: not my usual Prince Kai-centric stuff, but more of that soon, I promise! And sorry to all the Silversmith shippers. I promise I'm not bashing Lady Adanna/Devon as a pairing; it's nothing personal!)

Words: 522   Chapters: 1/1   Hits: 602

How long had it been, since she felt this way?

Had she *ever* felt this way?

Devon was her closest companion, her dearest friend, and there had been many occasions over the years and on her journey when Adanna had considered that perhaps things might one day shift between them, as things so often did. A path already written, well-trodden by many before them, of two people's lives so intertwined that something *more* was, ultimately, inevitable.

Until the end, they always said, and there were times that felt so true it made her heart ache.

She had thought, occasionally, about kissing him, to see what it might be like. If her heart would thunder the way she'd heard it did for young women in love.

Once or twice, she even wondered if she *was* in love with Devon. He was devoted to her – had even left his position in her father's guard to accompany her on her quest to find the Eldritch King! – just as she was devoted to him. If she lost him, it would level her. If he was hurt, she would feel the blow like it was she who had been harmed. If his mood was dark, she wanted to soothe it.

Was that love? She was sure it was. But – was it the same as being *in* love?

Now, she was convinced: she was not in love with Devon, and she could never be with him in that way.

Because now, she was being spun around the dance floor at the Osterions' extravagant masked ball, and the room was still spinning even after she had stopped. She was encased in a pair of strong arms, leaning against a body honed into a lethal, graceful weapon. His breath tickled along the back of her neck, sending a shiver down her spine.

This time, when she wondered what it would be like to kiss him, it did not seem so abstract or ordinary.

To kiss the Moonwalker would be... *incandescent*.

Even the mere idea of it was dizzying.

She wanted to hate him, on principle if nothing else. He was her rival in a thousand and one ways. This jaded, ruthless assassin with his own magick had been the cause of endless strife. While Adanna had wanted to mend the realm through diplomacy, *he* would rather raze it brick by brick. He was stronger; she was smarter. He was quicker; she was better. He was more powerful; she was more skilful. He was the night; she was the dawn.

But he had looked into her eyes tonight and seen every terrible, lesser part of her, all the things she tried to hide or improve. And she had seen those same things in him.

Yet here they still stood, with his lips at her ear whispering some fresh taunt, and a smirk on her lips as she debated her retort, already anticipating the fire it might spark in his dark eyes.

The Moonwalker was the bane of her life, a near-constant thorn in her side.

And she realized she would not have it any other way.

Your Direct Messages

Callum Denver *@callumdenver_owar*
Saw your latest fanfic

Anissa O'Shea *@thatfangirloverthere*
Stalker

I only posted it two hours ago

Callum Denver *@callumdenver_owar*
What can I say? I'm a big fan

If you're not careful, I might spill coffee all over you and scream in your face

Anissa O'Shea *@thatfangirloverthere*
HILARIOUS. (Will I ever live this down???)

Callum Denver *@callumdenver_owar*
I thought so (and no, you won't)

I was just wondering though

It's not what you usually write

Anissa O'Shea *@thatfangirloverthere*
Not about Kai, you mean?

Callum Denver *@callumdenver_owar*
Romance

Anissa O'Shea *@thatfangirloverthere*
I guess so

Callum Denver *@callumdenver_owar*
I liked it. For the record

Anissa O'Shea *@thatfangirloverthere*
You did?

Callum Denver *@callumdenver_owar*
Was it about someone?

Anissa O'Shea *@thatfangirloverthere*
My OTP, Moonsilver. Lady Adanna di Silver and the Moonwalker are meant to be together and I will die on this hill

Callum Denver *@callumdenver_owar*
You know what I mean

@thatfangirloverthere is typing...

@thatfangirloverthere is typing...

Callum Denver *@callumdenver_owar*
Sorry, I guess that was overstepping

Anyway, thanks again for letting me tag along this weekend, I had fun. I really needed it. Was great to meet Jake and Max too

PS. Glad to see you got home in time to take your dog for a walk, I liked your story of her chasing the ducks

@thatfangirloverthere is typing...

@thatfangirloverthere is typing...

Anissa O'Shea *@thatfangirloverthere*
We're going for another dog walk after college tomorrow

Maybe you could tag along?

I could tell you then? x

Callum Denver *@callumdenver_owar*
☺ it's a date x

CHAPTER 32

Alright, pros of telling Callum I have developed a crush on him:

1) It is always flattering to know someone fancies you (I think??? In my limited experience)
2) THIS IS HOW ROMANCE WORKS, ALL THE BOOKS HAVE TOLD ME SO
3) There is a chance he will say, 'Yes, Anissa, I have a crush on you also, you're right, we definitely had A Moment in the kitchen after you snogged another boy'
4) I will not have to suffer this absolutely diabolical feeling of *what if* that Cerys put in my head (I see why they call it a crush, I am squashed under the weight of this, I hate it)

5) At least if he says, 'No Anissa, I don't like you that way' I can move on and get rid of this horrible feeling

Cons of telling Callum I have a crush on him . . .

1) HE MIGHT NOT FEEL THE SAME. IN FACT HE QUITE DEFINITELY DOES NOT.
2) VERY EMBARRASSING
3) WILL HAVE TO CHANGE MY NAME LOSE ALL MY FRIENDS AND THE TTRPG GROUP AND START OVER SOMEWHERE REMOTE LIKE POINT NEMO
4) Will get very nervous and sweaty trying to tell him and that will give him the ick and be the sort of thing he will tell everyone else about and I will never live down and (see point 3)
5) He'll think I'm even more of a deranged fangirl than he already does and (see point 3)

Somehow, it doesn't feel like a very balanced list.

I'm dying to run it all past Cerys and Jake and even the girls, beg them for help and try to figure out how much of all this is in my head. So what if we sort of kissed that one time and sort of held hands in the kitchen and he said 'it's a date' with a kiss at the end?

That doesn't mean anything, does it? It's. He's just. I'm not. There isn't –

UGH.

Harley looks up at me, tongue lolling out of her mouth, head cocked to the side as if to ask why I'm scowling. I'm feeling judged even by the dog, wonderful. I heave myself off the bench to pace around a bit.

I'll just walk off some of my nervous energy. It's fine. It's no big deal. I'm not even nervous.

As soon as I'm on my feet, Harley starts bouncing around and barking, eager to get moving. She practically tugs my whole arm out of the socket, so I walk briskly to keep pace with her.

'Callum,' I mumble to myself, to practise. It's always been helpful to process my tangled thoughts by saying them out loud. 'I think you're really interesting, and I've obviously noticed you're quite attractive. Even though we don't always get on, I think I like you. So. There's that.'

No, that's crap.

I could go more the fanfic route? The hopeless, die-hard romantic?

'Callum, I've never met anybody who sees me the way you do. Sometimes I think you bring out the worst in me, but that's not true – you just let me be all of me, even the messy parts I'd normally hide, and I think I do the same thing for you. You're always on my mind and in my head, and I believe we could have something truly special. So if there's even a chance you might feel the same way, it's worth taking this risk and putting it all on the line to say . . . I like you.'

Ugh, I can FEEL the nausea rise in the back of my throat. There's no way I could say that to his face! People don't talk like that in real life, do they? He'd just laugh at me, or worse, think *I* was laughing at *him*.

Harley sniffs at some flowers near the pond for a good spot to wee, so I come to a stop to wait for her. I exhale loudly, shake out my arms and straighten my spine.

'Okay, you can do this . . . *Callum*, part of me feels like I've always known you because I'm so attached to your character, to Kai. And getting to know the real you has been . . . an experience. Not always a very good one. You can be sort of snobby but I think also that might be an act to hide what a nerd you are. If anyone can recognize a bad defence mechanism, after all, it's me.

'Anyway, sorry, I'm not actually here to talk about me. I just wanted to tell you that having gotten to know *you* better recently, I've come to the conclusion that I've unfortunately developed a bit of a crush on you. If you'd rather I didn't fancy you, that's alright; it's not very pleasant for me, either. And I know you said this was a *date* but there's a good chance you meant it in a casual, friendly way? So, if that is the case, I think we should just keep a bit of distance between us. You can block me on social media again and I won't hold it against you, or against Kai in any fanfics I write going forward.'

I mean, I can't say *that* either, bloody hell. A rambling, oddly formal monologue? Calling out his crap behaviour at the same time as saying I fancy him? I'd die.

'Well,' says a voice behind me, 'that was quite the speech.'

Oh my God, I *have* died.

I am dying.

I am going to jump into that pond and never resurface. Forget the Arthurian legend of the Lady of the Lake, I shall become the Lady of the Pond, distributing branches to stray dogs. It'll be a better fate.

I freeze, not turning around even when Harley bounds past me to greet him, yanking hard on the lead. I can't turn around. My heart is stuck in my throat; I think I've forgotten how to breathe. In fact, as long as I *don't* turn around, he isn't there, and he didn't hear any of that, and it's some random stranger who just thinks I'm an oddball and will carry on their merry way.

I'm so very aware of Callum, out of sight behind me, bending down so he can fuss over Harley. His voice floats up towards me, his tone so serious it borders on sardonic. 'That *is* all deeply unfortunate, Anissa. I am so dreadfully sorry to have caused you this inconvenience.'

'Go away.'

'But –'

'*Please.*' I cringe. I have a newfound respect for Cerys, spilling her guts to Jake (actually Max) about how she'd fallen in love with him. 'Leave me alone.'

'I thought we were making sweeping declarations about fancying people, though. I didn't even get a turn.'

'*Hilarious.*' My feet are still rooted to the spot, but I screw my eyes shut now, too. I don't want to see him even in my periphery. 'You weren't meant to hear any of that! Obviously. So you should just go, and you can mock me from a safe distance where I don't have to hear it.'

'And you won't hold it against me, *or* Kai in your future fanfics?'

I'm *definitely* going to steal the Moonwalker's sword and hack Prince Kai's head off in our next TTRPG session. Then maybe have Mida plunge to her death down that pit, for good measure.

Callum steps somewhere, but I'm distracted by Harley careening off in the other direction, pulling me sideways. My eyes fly open as I stagger to try and stay upright – only to discover she's done a full loop back in front of me, wrapping my legs up completely in the lead.

I topple over.

Right into Callum.

In the proper romantic version of this story, this is where I told him I fancied him and swooned right into his open, waiting arms, ready for a kiss.

But this is not a fantasy, this is reality.

So I pitch sideways so violently that when Callum catches me, he stumbles back. Harley thinks it's all a brilliant game and jumps at him too, her weight sending us all crashing to the ground in a tangle of limbs and a wagging tail. My hands get squashed between mine and Callum's stomachs, I accidentally headbutt him in the chin, and one of Harley's paws lands right between my shoulder blades and knocks the breath out of me in a gasp.

It takes a few minutes to disentangle ourselves, during which Harley somehow manages to unclip herself from her lead, and bounds happily off into the pond with a huge splash.

I sigh, sitting up and collapsing over my knees, pressing my hands to my face. The wet dog covered in pond scum and algae is a problem for later me. Current me just . . . needs a minute.

There are gentle hands at my legs, and I look up to find Callum unravelling the lead from around my shins.

'Thanks,' I mumble, taking it back off him once he's done.

He takes a seat in the grass next to me. Close, but keeping a little space between us.

'You know, I'm not sure anybody's ever admitted they liked someone by saying how unpleasant and unfortunate it is.'

I grimace again, but say, 'May I refer you to Mr Darcy's first proposal to Elizabeth Bennet?' Callum tilts his head, conceding the point.

'Am I that bad?'

'You're –' I huff, leaning back over my knees again. '*No*. That's why it's *annoying*.'

'Right, well, that absolutely clears everything up.'

'I wanted to like you when you were just this ... *concept* of a person playing my favourite character. And then I met you and we didn't get on and that was fine, because I knew where I stood. And then I got to know you better and it started to all make sense, *you* started to make sense, and it's like I *stopped* making sense, and ...'

I feel so, so stupid. I wish I'd had crushes before so I knew how to deal with this one. I wish I'd never snooped in Callum's trailer and realized he was a genuine OWAR fan and never stayed in the kitchen with him after the party.

I wish I'd never met him in the first place.

I could've gone my whole life *not* suffering this feeling, and it'd be fine. Totally fine.

The silence between us is broken only by Harley splashing about in the pond and a couple of ducks quacking irritably at her.

'Listen, I *did* write you off at first,' he says, 'but I'm sorry for that. You thought I was belittling you, but the truth is – I was worried you'd do that to *me*. Reduce me to –'

'The bits and pieces you posted online?'

'Exactly! But you were always so belligerent and nothing like I expected, and you made me question things about myself. I didn't ... really *like* who I'd started to turn into. I didn't used to be this guarded and cynical. That's – sort of a recent development, since I started getting a bit famous. It's been hard admitting to myself that acting's not all I want to do – that *that's* not who I want to be. That I'm not wrong for, you know, being a nerd, or wanting to write instead of perform. Having you call me out on it ... It's been nice feeling like someone gets me.'

I mock-salute him. 'Fangirl, at your service.'

'And I see *you*, standing up for yourself, not taking crap from people –'

I cut him a sardonic look, and Callum inclines his head with a chuckle.

'Alright, from *me* ... And throwing yourself into doing things you're really passionate about, getting so lost in it...' He trails off and when I glance over, unable to help myself, Callum's blushing. He catches my gaze and rolls his eyes. 'Look, I'm going to be cringey but it's *enchanting*. You have this way of totally lighting up; it's beautiful. But then sometimes you catch yourself like you realize you're being yourself too much, and you fold it all back away into a box.'

I shrug, not really sure how to respond to that; part of my brain is still caught on the fact he finds me *enchanting*.

'I wish you wouldn't,' Callum says softly, and he reaches up to tuck a piece of hair behind my ear, looking at me like he *is* enchanted. It makes me *feel* beautiful. It makes me shiver, blush, melt into a puddle; it's a good job I'm already sitting down. 'I wish you'd let everyone else see you the way I do. I wish *you'd* see it. It's one thing if I'm pretending, that's my job, but it's sad to think you feel you have to.'

A small laugh slips out of me. 'Right back atcha.'

'What if we made a deal? No more pretending.' Callum sits up straighter, facing me fully, and sticks his hand out to shake. The seriousness of his tone is at total odds with how innocent and childlike the suggestion is, but I reach out and take his hand.

'Okay, deal.'

We don't shake hands. His fingers just wrap around mine, warm and solid, and they stay between us, a lifeline.

'In the interest of not pretending,' he adds slowly, 'I should probably let you know it turns out I actually really like you, too. And I was hoping this might have been more of a date in the traditional sense. Not the casual friend type.'

Oh.

Oh.

'You probably didn't factor in what a menace Harley is.'

Callum cracks a grin. 'I don't know. I did hope you might be swooning into my arms at some point.'

The laugh that bursts out of me is sudden and bright, and it makes Callum laugh, too. He lets go of my hand, but only to scoot himself closer, his arm half around me and his hand braced against the grass near my hip. By the time we've stopped laughing, I realize we're leaning against each other, and I turn my face towards him to say something.

I don't have the words, in the end, but that's okay. Callum smiles at me, his eyes searching my face, and it's not the through-gritted-teeth smile we normally give each other on set. It's soft, vulnerable and hesitant, and I answer it with the only thing that feels right in that moment: I lean the rest of the way forward, and I press my lips to his.

My hands slip around his broad shoulders to anchor myself before I float away, and one of his hands cards through my hair with such tenderness, such reverence, as he holds me closer, that it makes my breath hitch in my throat. The kiss is slow, months in the making, and I'm lost among the riot of sensations of his mouth, his tongue, his hands, his heartbeat fluttering wildly like mine.

This time, it's everything it's supposed to be. And it is *incandescent*.

OWAR Discord Kai-rry On My Wayward Son
General

@rubytherapscallion
um... guys?

@rubytherapscallion
@ladyanissadishipper are you there????

@wrathfulqueen93
Oh my God I just saw.

@therunestar
The comments on the fic are brutal.
@ladyanissadishipper don't bother looking and turn off your email notifications, I'm on it. We've got your back.

@osterionprincess2
OMFG I JUST SAW THE LATEST UPDATE FROM THE WHITEBOARD CONSPIRACY GIRL ON TIKTOK AND RAN HERE

@osterionprincess2
IS IT TRUE???

@osterionprincess2
CAN'T BELIEVE YOU WOULDN'T TELL US ANISSA OMG WHAT

@rubytherapscallion
look @ladyanissadishipper you don't owe anyone an explanation but obviously we're here for you if you need anything/want to talk about it

@wrathfulqueen93
I've just started a new thread to mass-report some of these comments/the video. Am doing the same in some other forums too. Like @therunestar said Anissa, we're on it x

@osterionprincess1
I'm still catching up but I'm sorry, is Anissa DATING CALLUM DENVER?????????? There's pictures of you snogging him in a park, this is wild! Get ur man girl lol what is HAPPENING

@osterionprincess1
Wait I just saw 2's texts

@osterionprincess1
Oh, shit . . .

What If It's You? by ladydishipper

After one fateful meeting as their paths cross during a ball, Lady di Silver starts to wonder if this is the adventure she's been searching for all along. (AN: not my usual Prince Kai-centric stuff, but more of that soon, I promise! And sorry to all the Silversmith shippers I promise I'm not bashing Lady Adanna/Devon as a pairing; it's nothing personal!)

Words: 522   Chapters: 1/1   Hits: 18,928

COMMENTS

@fictionfaun
Sorry is this supposed to be a self insert??? I don't get it. Weirdo.

> ### @therunestar
> It's literally just a Moonsilver fic? Chill

@runewarrior012
Oh look, another delulu fangirl living out her fantasies via fictional characters because she's so desperate to get the man irl. Pathetic.

> ### @wrathfulqueen93
> Oh look, another redpilled hater living out his fantasies of someone caring what he says because he's so desperate for attention irl. Pathetic.
>
> ### @osterionprincess1
> DECEASED
>
> ### @osterionprincess2
> there are not enough skull emojis in the world to emphasize how funny this was

@awitchcalledwanda
Omg stop how many Kai fics does she have??? This is so sad. She must've been stalking him FOREVER. (Kinda wish it was me though lol)

> ### @gildedgladegal
> looool mood

@crowndisqueen
This is so creepy. Hope he reports her and gets a restraining order!!

> ### @therunestar
> Lmao have you seen how many Kai fics I'VE posted? That doesn't mean I'm stalking him. Get a life.

@eldritchlad_again
Idk how real/fake all this drama is but new fave fanfic author alert, hello! LOVE the way she portrays Kai in the other stuff I've read so far, and she really captures the whole neurospicy side of his character too. If Callum Denver is dating her, I don't blame him, she obvs totally GETS what he's doing!

@themagickinme
And THIS is exactly why I don't engage with this fandom. This is going way too far, leave the poor guy alone. Just because you're soooo into his character does NOT mean you're entitled to him irl! Does Callum even KNOW how obsessed she is? It's disgusting

@writingwizardry_eldritchstyle
There's no way a teenager wrote this. Sorry, this is absolutely all fake for the clout. Callum's team are def behind this whole charade.

@kingroachtheorist1
You're kidding me. THIS is her? The writing's not even that good what

> **@therunestar**
> your taste in fics isn't even that good what

@rubytherapscallion
SAY IT LOUDER FOR THE PEOPLE IN THE BACK @therunestar!

GIRLIE POPS 2.0! ✨

Nikita from college (Daphne's friend)
Has anyone heard from Anissa this evening???

@Anissa ???????????

Cerys
I know she was walking the dog. She might still be out!

Chloe with the Twitch channel
Everything okay?

Nikita from college (Daphne's friend)
@Anissa ??

Nikita from college (Daphne's friend)

Missed call (18:03)

Missed call (18:03)

Missed call (18:04)

Missed call (18:11)

Missed call (18:19)

> Hey so I guess you're busy rn or walking the dog or whatever but this TikTok came up on my feed like the one from last week and they had pictures of you and that Callum guy? And they shared your handle for some fanfiction website

> They've like, doxed you

> Anyway idk if you've seen already but if you haven't I didn't want to cause a whole drama in the group chat before you had chance to know. I hope you're okay. I reported the video, people were being real dicks in the comments

You shouldn't go look obvs but I know you'll be dying to ask 'what did they say' and basically it was a lot of 'what's she got that I don't/oh she's an obsessed stalker fangirl who tricked him into liking her/I could've done that' etc

I checked your socials and they're all private so you should be okay on that front. Maybe you could speak to someone on the show or this guy though, they might know what to do? Some of these fans are INTENSE...

Missed call (18:32)

Missed call (18:50)

Missed call (22:04)

I can see the blue ticks and I know you're online

I'll see you in the morning, pick you up for college as usual

You know where I am if you need anything x

Your Direct Messages

> **Callum Denver** *@callumdenver_owar*
> Hi Anissa. It was good to see you earlier. I think on reflection we're better off keeping our distance. Sure you can understand. Best – C.

This person cannot receive messages from your Instagram account.

CHAPTER 33

I sit on the foot of my bed with my school bag open on my knee. I think I was double-checking I have everything. My toothbrush is hanging out of my mouth, forgotten. I've put my shoes on, but got distracted before I could lace them up. I have no idea where I left my phone.

That last part might be for the best.

I was up all night frantically refreshing comment sections and flipping between apps. In the scheme of viral infamy, it's really not that bad. The latest whiteboard conspiracy video uploaded last night only has half a million views, and a good chunk of the comments are my friends from Discord arguing with people or shutting them down for being mean about me. It's a miracle nobody tracked down my personal accounts; I've been terrified all night that would happen.

I haven't told my family. Mum and Dad have gone to a yoga retreat for a few days anyway with no access to their mobiles, and I made the executive decision that this isn't enough of an 'emergency' to interrupt them with. I didn't even respond to anyone on Discord. Cerys, Jake and Max were radio silent last night, and I convinced myself they must have a whole separate group chat without me to talk about what a freak I am. They probably think I've been lying to them and secretly dating Callum all along and have decided I'm a horrible person they should just cut out of their lives.

I didn't even reply to Nikita, who was unnervingly *nice* after she discovered the whole thing. But replying would've made it too real. It would've meant I'd have to face it and do something about it.

All I wanted to do when I got home last night was message my friends and tell them every last detail about my 'date' with Callum. But even if the new whiteboard video hadn't dropped, I'd barely gotten off the bus home before Callum blocked me, *again*, and I found *that* message on my Insta. So I guess we're not going out after all.

And I'm a prize fool for ever believing otherwise.

How am I supposed to just ... *carry on*? Like we didn't kiss, like my life hasn't been ridiculed mercilessly, like the one thing I love most in this world – this fandom – hasn't been torn to shreds and set on fire? How am I supposed to go back to set knowing he must be laughing at me, that they all must be? How do I tell my parents or my friends any of this? How am I supposed to just get up and go to college and sit in class like *everything is normal*?

Tears flood my eyes and I blink them away furiously. I press my clammy palms into my thighs, my chest and throat suddenly so tight I think I've forgotten how to breathe.

And the worst part is – I really thought he liked me.

I really thought . . . when he kissed me . . . when he said those things . . .

. . . that he meant it.

That finally, *finally*, I got to have something of my own, the way everyone else seemed to.

That I got to feel normal, for once.

Was it just a game to him? A joke?

I know we've had a petty rivalry going on for weeks now, but . . . why would he go to all that trouble?

Does he really hate me *this* much? Enough to dox me, spread gossip about me, even arrange for someone to come and take a PHOTO of us together in the park last night to send to this whiteboard conspiracy theorist?

OWAR has a dedicated, worldwide fandom, but this is barely a drop in the ocean in terms of celebrity internet dramas. It'll blow over in a couple of days. I've seen it before.

I've not been *part* of it before, but still.

Still.

All the rationalizing in the world doesn't shake the fact that those comments are about *me*; they are tearing *me* apart. The photos in the video are taken from behind, and even in the one where Callum and I are clearly kissing, my face is at least obscured by his hand on my cheek. But that hasn't stopped people bullying the way I dress or look. Like how my hair's scraggly (duh, I'd just been knocked over by the dog), or the roll of fat above my hips. People even pick at my shoulders for being wonky.

New insecurity unlocked: do I have wonky shoulders???

I push myself off the bed so I can go scrutinize them in the mirror – which is when I trip over my shoelaces and almost drop my toothbrush.

Okay. New plan: finish getting dressed. Finish cleaning my teeth. Small steps. No big-picture stuff. Just one thing at a time.

I force myself through each task, talking to myself to make sure I stay on track, and by some miracle, it works. I manage to get myself ready for college. I even find my phone, buried in a pile of plushies next to my bed, and I steel myself before I turn it over to check my notifications.

The group chat with Jake, Cerys and Max has 173 messages. I have five missed calls from Cerys and another three from Max. Jake's sent me a voice note outside of the group chat, so I open that.

'Anissa! Bloody hell, this is a plot twist, isn't it? When did this happen?! Anyway that doesn't really matter, because this is so bloody cool! You're basically famous! Everyone's reading your fics and talking about you! You're practically a celebrity! Can't believe you kept this a secret . . .'

It doesn't *feel* very cool.

Not at all.

A quick skim through the group chat shows that Cerys thinks more or less the same as Jake – they're swept up by the glamour of it, seeing the shine not the scandal. She begs for details about how it all happened and if me and Callum are official now, wondering if we'd had to keep our relationship secret on set and if that's why I was so quiet on our drives home sometimes.

How do I explain I wish I'd never met him?

My phone buzzes in my hand and I almost hurl it straight out the window.

But it's just Nikita, letting me know she's outside and threatening to come in and drag me out if I'm not down in the next five minutes.

Message received . . . At least *she* recognized the nasty reality of all this when she texted me about it last night. The fact that Cerys and Jake *don't* feels like a betrayal – the rug pulled out from under my feet, like maybe they aren't my people after all and I've been kidding myself this whole time.

I know that's not actually true, but it doesn't stop it *feeling* that way.

I call goodbye to Nan and give Harley a quick pat on the head, then hurry outside where Nikita gets out of the car – and *hugs me*.

'Are you okay?'

'Not really.'

She nods, and we both get into the car. 'I reported as many of those shitheads in the comments as I could. I checked again this morning, but it looks like it's already dying down. And you had some people defending you on your fanfics.'

The bottom of my stomach falls away. 'You looked at my fanfics?'

'I didn't read them,' Nikita says, as if she couldn't care less she found these secret, too-honest parts of my soul laid bare. 'I don't get any of that fandom stuff. I only went to see the comment section.'

'Oh. Um, thank you. Yeah, some internet friends were, um, helping out.'

Nikita nods. 'Cerys messaged in the group this morning, too, but I don't think you've seen it.'

'I haven't.'

There's a pause, and unlike the normal stretches of silence between me and Nikita – a sort of mutual 'We don't really have anything to say to each other, so let's not pretend otherwise' – this time it feels suffocating. Until I cave and blurt, 'We aren't dating. Or – we weren't. Still aren't, now, I think. He blocked me on Instagram last night, and that's the only place we message. But we weren't dating before that, although I did kiss him yesterday evening . . .'

Nikita's mouth falls open, and we idle at the end of a junction for a little too long. Someone behind us beeps, jolting her back into action.

'I know you don't think anybody would fancy me. But –'

'What? I don't think that.'

'Yes you do. I saw the texts you deleted in the group chat when that first whiteboard conspiracy video came out. You said there was no way I could be dating him. *Have we all met Anissa?* That's what you said.'

She flushes pink from the tips of her ears all the way down her neck. 'I didn't think you noticed. That's not what I meant, though.'

'Isn't it?' I scoff, turning away. 'It's fine. I'm used to it. You're not the first person to say stuff like that about me.'

'You're just never interested in *anyone*! Any time we gossip about a fit celebrity or someone at school, you never seem bothered. Dating seems like the absolute *last* thing you care about. Not because people wouldn't fancy you.'

I bite the inside of my cheek, not sure if I believe that's the whole truth. I mean, she's not wrong . . .

She carries on, 'I guess I'm just . . . surprised you wouldn't say anything about him to us? Maybe not me, but at least to Cerys and Chloe. Dating the actor who plays your favourite character on a show you're so obsessed with sounds like exactly the sort of thing you'd never want to shut up about. No offence.'

'None taken.' Again, she makes a fair point. 'There really *wasn't* anything going on between us to tell.'

'Until yesterday?'

'I guess . . .'

And that's all it takes for the dam to break, and it all to come spilling out. It feels *so good* to finally talk about it. I even tell her every embarrassing detail of my speech at the park he overheard, which makes Nikita throw her head back with a big belly laugh. I crack a smile, too.

'So I thought we were, I don't know . . . *a thing*. It's not like he asked me out, and we didn't label anything, but I thought at least we were on the same page about being, you know, *together*. And then this whole online drama kicked off, and he blocked me. Again.'

We're parked up at college by now. We've already missed first bell, but Nikita doesn't make a move to go inside. She frowns, tapping the steering wheel thoughtfully, which surprises me – she's always so quick to dismiss boys at the first hint of a red flag. I would've thought she'd be champing at the bit to tear Callum to pieces.

'It is *weird* that someone was there to get a photo,' she says eventually. 'Don't you think? And that video last night, the girl with the whiteboard – she said she'd already filmed most of it *before* she got the photo of you guys kissing, so that "source" she apparently has on set had to have known you'd be there. Did Callum tell someone he was meeting you?'

I shrug. 'I guess he could've done. But he's said everyone on set is like one big family. I don't know who'd want to do that to him.' Or me. I didn't realize I'd been racking up enemies. 'He still sent me that message, though. Even if he had nothing to do with the video, he clearly doesn't want anything to do with *me*.'

'Shitbag,' Nikita mutters. She sighs, leaning back in the driver's seat, and we watch a few stragglers hurry in through the gates to make it to their first class. We should join them, really. Both of us have French this morning.

I pull my bag up on to my lap, ready to go. 'Thanks for letting me word-vomit at you.'

Nikita cocks her head to one side. 'Of course. That's what friends do.'

'Are we friends?'

She considers it for a second. 'I mean, yeah? You're weird as hell and I don't get half the things you say sometimes, but you're chill. And you're smart, so it's handy having you to sit next to in French and history.'

'Valid.'

'I know I come off a bit . . . bitchy, sometimes. Daphne usually calls me out for it. I'm trying to work on it.'

'That's okay. I probably come off really intense sometimes.'

'A little.' She smiles. 'You know, it was . . .' She sucks in a sharp breath. 'This summer *sucked* for me. The others were gone, and you and Cerys were in this little bubble with work experience and your game thingy that I got totally left out of. Which, you know, fine, whatever. It's not my thing anyway. But . . . I guess what I'm trying to say is, I got stuck being the outsider for once, and it sucked. So I'm sorry if I make you feel like that sometimes. I guess it's kind of a defence mechanism.'

Nikita shrugs, like none of that is a big deal. It's a *huge* deal. It's the most open she's ever been with me.

I suddenly feel so horrible for flaking on plans this summer. I can't believe I was so in my own head about how awkward it might be to hang out that I ended up alienating her, just like I used to feel. Talk about selfish . . .

As if she can sense the 'I'm sorry' on my lips, Nikita cuts me a stern look and holds up a hand. '*Anyway.* Point is, we're friends. And that means I've got your back. Why else would I come pick you up for college?'

'Um. Because the others told you to?'

'I mean – yeah, alright, kind of. But also because everyone likes having you around. Like, Daphne's a bit scared you might actually be a bit of a witch because your nan does some psychic stuff or whatever, but she loves your whole vibe. Evie's always saying how clever you are, and Chloe thinks you're hilarious. And you're just – really *nice*.'

'Probably because I've conditioned myself to be as likeable as possible when someone *does* give me the chance to be their friend,' I deadpan, and Nikita snorts.

Then she says, 'Do you still want to dye your hair?'

CHAPTER 34

I've never bunked off school before.

It's thrilling and terrifying all at once. Sixth form college is different: we're treated more like adults, but we're still expected to *show up*. We can still get in trouble.

My heart is thundering as Nikita pulls up at a big Tesco, but it's totally exhilarating; I can't stop grinning. The sheer recklessness feels like the perfect remedy for the horrible rollercoaster the last twelve hours have been. It feels good to be in control of *something*, at least.

We grab boxes of dye and some sweets, then head back to Nikita's house. It's huge, with a neat front lawn, fresh flowers in a posh vase in the porch, and an entry hall so big that the armchair and lamp under the stairs look like they're there just for decoration.

While I'm busy gawking, Nikita strides straight on upstairs without even taking her shoes off.

'Are your parents at work?'

She nods. 'They're *always* working.'

Something in her tone keeps me from prying too much; I figure after I've spilled my guts to her, she knows there's an open invitation for her to do the same if she wants to. I've always been so close with my parents, I can't imagine how awful it must be for Nikita not having hers around. I'd be missing mine a *lot* more lately if I hadn't had so much going on with work experience and Callum that I hadn't been able to put into words over the phone.

We set up in a bathroom that's as big as my whole bedroom. There's a separate bathtub and shower. Nikita disappears to find a stool upholstered in velvet and gets me to sit on it near the sink while she puts a white towel around my shoulders.

'Won't it stain?'

She shrugs.

'Cerys said you help your mum dye her hair.'

Nikita snorts. 'Yeah, sometimes she forgets to book an appointment – or forgets to tell her assistant to book it for her – and she'll lose her mind if she's got a few greys showing before a conference, or whatever.' She opens the first box of dye and lays it out expertly, then says quietly, 'If they weren't so "university or bust", I would've loved to be a hairdresser.'

'Your hair does always look brilliant. Couldn't you just do it anyway, though?'

She winces, and that's all we say about it.

By the time I'm sat waiting for the dye to take, the constant low level of anxiety that I've been battling since last night has finally disappeared, a crushing weight finally lifted off my lungs.

This *will* blow over. I *can* deal with the fallout. It'll be *okay*. I genuinely believe that, in this moment.

My phone buzzes with a call and I reach for it – it's probably Jake calling during a free, or Cerys wanting to see if I'm still going to Red Wings Studios with her this afternoon . . .

It's a random number.

My traitorous heart skips a beat.

'Don't answer it!' Nikita tells me, looking ready to slap the phone out of my hand. 'It might be some internet creep who's tracked you down or a journalist or something.'

'But what if it's Callum? He at least owes me *some* explanation for all this,' I say, and she can't argue with that. Instead, she hovers close as I answer. 'Hello?'

The voice that booms through the phone is familiar – but it's not Callum, and it takes me a second to place it. 'Hello there! Is this Anissa O'Shea? I think I've got the right number . . .'

I pull back in surprise, my gaze flickering to Nikita before I put the call on speaker. '*Richie?*'

'Yes! Hello! We haven't formally met, but I imagine you know all about me. As I know all about you! Although, of course, so do a lot of people at the moment . . .'

Nikita pulls a disgusted face at the phone, mouthing at me, '*The agent?*'

He answers for us: 'So, Anissa – is it alright if I call you Anissa? – as you know, I'm Callum's manager, and it's my job to look out for his best interests . . . And Anissa, I've got to be honest with you, this is a sticky situation. You've got some of the OWAR fandom really up in arms about this little fling; it's not exactly looking good for you, is it? Not with all those fanfics you've written about Callum's character . . .'

As if I need the reminder. I cringe, and Nikita motions for me to scoot over and make space for her on the stool. She squashes in next to me, the coolness of her arm pressed against mine. It's grounding, comforting.

'I'm not sure how much he's told you,' Richie blathers on, 'but Callum's got a *lot* happening for him right now. As soon as filming wraps for this season he's going to be back-to-back! We've got him on location in Canada for a YA drama adaptation, and then he's due in LA for a *huge* dystopian action movie . . .'

'He – he is?' What happened to all that stuff he said about not liking who he'd become and hating acting? Was it just another way to mess with my head? Or was the promise of fame too tantalizing to give up in the end? It shouldn't hurt as much as it does; I feel it like a knife twisting in my stomach.

'So, really, he's not got time to date – well, anyone, really, but especially someone . . . normal.'

My laugh catches me off guard, a loud snort I barely manage to turn into a cough. I have to press a hand over my mouth before the hysteria bubbles over and I end up in a full-on fit of the giggles.

That's the first time anybody's ever called me *normal* and made it sound like an insult, not an aspiration.

Next to me, Nikita is visibly seething. Her hands ball into fists in her lap and she looks ready to reach right through the phone and throttle Richie. (I bet she'd love playing Dungeons and Dragons or *Of Wrath and Roll*, if she gave it a chance. A good, murdery adventure game might be right up her alley.)

Richie clears his throat and his voice takes on a more soothing tone. 'Now I know this isn't ideal for *either* of you. Really not fair. Terrible stuff. So here's what I'm thinking – I'll cut you a cheque, you take a step back from your little job on OWAR, and that's the end of this. Sound good?'

'S-sorry, *what*?'

My *little job*? Is he serious? He's going to ... what, *pay me off*, to stay away from Callum?

'Does Callum know about this?' I blurt.

'We were thinking ten thousand. How does that sound? It'd really help set you up for university. Or a trip to France, maybe? You could take a proper gap year and flex those language skills of yours! And, of course, we'll have an NDA sent over, too. You'll be familiar with that already from set, I would've thought.'

'I –'

My blood runs cold. *We* were thinking. *We*. As in, him and Callum. Because Callum wanted space, and blocked me, and even though he kissed me, he doesn't want to date me. I'd be ruining his life – so he had to get in and ruin mine first.

'So, Anissa? What do you say? All good?'

'Er ...' I'm so shocked – so appalled – that all I can do is blurt out, 'Do people even write cheques anymore?'

Richie laughs, and I can't explain it, but it sounds like money. It sounds like *arrogance*.

'If you'd prefer, you can drop me a text with your bank details, and I'll transfer it straight over. Glad we see eye to eye on this, Anissa! Callum and I really appreciate you being so understanding. Ciao for now!'

He hangs up.

Nikita erupts, 'THAT SCUMBAG! I'm going to rip him to pieces!'

'Callum or Richie?'

'Both,' she snarls, then gets up to push my head back over the sink. 'Right after I finish your hair.'

And I say, 'How does Richie know I study French?'

nerds unite ⚔

Me
Hey guys, figured it was easier to drop you all a message here

Consider this your FAQ!

1) no, Callum and I have not been dating, at all
2) yes, I did kiss him
3) the viral infamy is not cool, at all. A lot of it was actually really hurtful and horrible and stressful. I've had to make my fanfic account private, and Nikita went on to mass-delete the comments for me so I didn't have to see them
4) Callum isn't talking to me, and I don't really have a way to talk to him, so I guess that's that. I'll tell the studio I can't work there anymore, and in a couple of years I'm sure this will all be a funny story instead of weirdly traumatic?
5) moral of the story: never meet your heroes lol

Jake
I'm sorry but YOU SNOGGED A GENUINE CELEBRITY!! How is that not cool?! I'd die to be in your shoes

Cerys
So would most of those commenters from the sound of it lol

I'm sorry this was all such a mess but how could you not tell us this was happening??

Max
Guys, come on

Not cool Jake

Jake
Beauty is pain fame is the game I know it must be super bizarre rn Anissa but like!!! YOU'RE DATING LITERAL PRINCE KAI FROM OWAR!! Even you've got to admit that's pretty awesome!

Me
Thank you for your contribution, I will not be taking further questions at this time

(I love you guys, but I just can't right now. I'm sorry. This has all been a lot, and 'but it's so cool!' is just making me feel even more alone and horrible. My head is a mess. I don't need anyone making me feel worse, even if you don't mean to.)

Cerys
I'm sorry Anissa, really didn't mean to. We're here if you need us! Love you xxx

Jake has been removed from the group chat

Max
That was me lol

I'll add him back when he learns to behave ☺

OWAR Discord Kai-rry On My Wayward Son
General

@osterionprincess3
Hope you don't mind me temporarily stealing your handle 1 and 2, I need to fly under the radar for a little while. PS. This is Anissa!

@osterionprincess1
You're alive!!! You're okay! Are you okay?!

@wrathfulqueen93
ANISSA! Are you alright????

@therunestar
What happened?! This has been wild

@rubytherapscallion
hope you're doing alright babe xx

@osterionprincess3
So I didn't tell any of you bc NDAs but basically I've been doing work experience on s6 of OWAR (the new production studios are local, me and my friend got lucky bluffing our way into the art department) and it's been really fun! And obvs I made a total fool of myself fangirling over Callum at first! (He was in his Kai costume and everything, can you blame me lol!) Then we sort of hung out a bit and then I guess this all happened, but it really got blown out of proportion . . .

@osterionprincess3
I'd also like it to be known (among us) that he definitely has a sock puppet account or something to lurk. He is FAMILIAR with OWAR forums in a way only a true fan could be, and he read my fanfics. So he was well aware Kai's my fave. There was no actual stalking or secret romance or anything lol

@therunestar
We didn't think for a minute that there was!

@osterionprincess2
SCREAMING OMG I MUST FIND CALLUM'S SECRET LURKER ACCOUNT THIS IS WILD I LOVE IT

@osterionprincess2
also hope ur okay Anissa and pls tell us everything about what it was like working on set

@wrathfulqueen93
When you're ready, ofc. But please! Was it as magical as we think?!

@osterionprincess3
Honestly? Yes.

@osterionprincess3
I'm really going to miss it ☹

CHAPTER 35

I've officially gone rogue.

The girl looking back at me in the mirror looks self-assured and bold as brass. I swipe on some eyeliner and it feels like warpaint. My favourite snake-cuff earring glints at my ear, and Nikita's dye job makes me feel transformed: the deep violet shade is subtle but shines through my shoulder-length waves. It's perfect.

I put on my favourite pair of dungarees and my usual Converse, aware that I look a bit like a lilac Crayola and maybe it's a little bit childish, but it's all the stuff that makes me feel most comfortable – most *me*.

And if I'm going to do this, I want to do it right.

I've been mulling it over for days, playing out different scenarios in my head the way I would for a TTRPG battle. What spell slots do I want to use up, what weapons do I have that I can wield, what defensive tactics have I got at my disposal? What am I going to say, how do I phrase it, who do I speak to first, how righteously angry is it worth being?

I even pop my lucky D20 in my pocket on the way out. *Roll for courage* . . .

College has, mercifully, been pretty normal. People there aren't really into the OWAR fandom enough to have caught on to the niche internet maelstrom I found myself in. It feels surreal to have all of this going on and nobody know, like it's not quite real life – intangible, a fever dream. Mum and Dad finish their yoga retreat and call from Auntie Neha's, but the FaceTime is so full of chatter from distant relations wanting to say hello and tell me I should visit soon that, lucky for me, I'm spared having to explain everything that's been going on. I will when they're home, but right now, it feels too big. Maybe when they're back next week, this will all be like some distant memory and I'll be able to actually face it.

The online furore dies down, too. I think mostly because I've made everything private and changed my screennames, but even when I go and refresh the comment section on the whiteboard conspiracy video or peek at some of the other forums, there's no new content, which is a relief.

I know Nan suspects something's up, but so far I've

managed to pretend I've been so keyed up because I finally dyed my hair and I'm excited about properly looking at some university courses (which isn't *really* a lie . . . I think after the party last weekend I've finally been inspired as to what I'd like to study).

Nan insists on doing another tarot reading though, and she lays out the Death card with a satisfied bark of laughter. (She explained to me ages ago it doesn't *literally* signify dying – more like rebirth and new beginnings.)

'Well, that seems about right for this new attitude of yours, doesn't it? You seem like a different person these last few days.'

And I don't think that's exactly a bad thing.

My phone buzzes: Cerys, letting me know she's outside. I grab my stuff, shout goodbye to Nan and dash out the door.

Cerys is shaking, her cheeks flushed bright pink. She looks way more nervous than I feel. 'Ready?'

'Absolutely.'

She insisted on coming for moral support. So, instead of going to college this morning, we're going straight to Red Wings Studios. It's Friday and they're meant to be filming a huge scene with lots of the main characters; Cerys and I were gutted to miss it originally, but it's guaranteed that Callum will be there. I want to have a face-to-face conversation with him – I think I deserve the closure, after everything. It might spoil things for him filming today, but so what? He didn't seem to care when he was leaving my whole LIFE in flames. (Never mind the imaginary Mida, this is exactly what *Nikita* would do in my shoes.)

He'll get over it, just like he apparently got over me.

Plus, it feels like the mature thing to do to speak to Lisa in person and resign, instead of just ghosting the studio.

During the drive, Cerys tells me softly, 'I know we haven't spoken properly about it all yet, but . . . I'm really sorry me and Jake jumped on the bandwagon about you and Callum. It wasn't fair. You *were* dealing with a lot. We should've been there for you.'

'It's okay.'

'It's not okay. We were crap friends. I'm sorry.'

'Well . . . thank you.' I smile at her. 'You're forgiven.'

She exhales, looking a bit teary-eyed, but smiles back at me and nods. 'So . . . *was* it Callum you fancied, or was it just because he plays Kai?'

'I told you, I don't fancy *Kai*. He's just my favourite character. My comfort character, like I explained to you before.'

'Well it does make sense. What with the whole . . . you know, all the neurodivergent coding.' She smiles, hesitant, like she's worried about offending me, but it takes me a second to process why.

'No, no, wait, back up. *What* makes sense?'

'I mean, Kai's visions are meant to be like ...' She pauses. 'People think they represent autistic meltdowns, right? Like, they're a symptom of him being overstimulated and stuff ...'

'Right ... but I'm not autistic, Cerys.'

'No, but you're ADHD, aren't you? Like Jake?'

'I – what?!'

Her cheeks are turning pink, and she starts to stutter a little. 'Jake said it, um, presents differently in girls, though, like they tend to mask a lot more? A-and that's probably why you haven't had a formal diagnosis, like he has ...'

All those times Jake's cracked 'neurospicy' jokes, I don't think I ever really took him seriously. I never realized he *meant* it – and he must not have realized he hadn't ever told me about his official diagnosis. Although he *is* so scattered sometimes, I'm not surprised he'd forget to tell me something like that, but ...

'I don't have ADHD?' It comes out like a question, though.

'Oh! Okay. Wait. Don't you?'

'I ... *do I*? Hang on, have you guys *talked* about this? About me?'

'Not like that!' Cerys looks aghast. 'We talked about *him*, and it sort of – came up, that's all. I'm sorry! I didn't mean to ... God, I'm *so*, so sorry. I think I thought you knew? Not like, a *secret*, more ... it's just part of you? Like your hair, or how tall you are. It's why you're always rushing around last minute when we have to go somewhere, like Jake does, or have a million and one things going on in your head at once and sometimes you need a second to refocus!'

It catches me off guard that she's noticed I do that – but I guess she *is* one of my best friends. She does know me better than almost anyone.

And, apparently, better than I know myself.

'I ... guess it would make sense why I got so attached to Kai ...' I muse.

'I might have got it all wrong! Why – why don't you ask Google? Just to see?' Cerys suggests gently. I can feel her anxiety, almost taste it on my tongue like lead. I'm too dazed to do anything but nod and follow her suggestion.

Which is how I discover some 'common traits' that make me feel a little *too* seen: hyperfixation (does everyone not get that?) and something called time blindness (hang on, do people just *know* how much time is passing when they're doing stuff?); forgetfulness;

sensitivity to certain fabrics and low self-esteem (who, me? Never . . .); and even creating 'doom piles' (I just thought that was something everyone did! I *knew* I wasn't just being messy and lazy!).

I do three online quizzes that each tell me it's 'highly likely' and encourage me to seek a 'professional diagnosis'. I'm so mind-blown that I don't even notice we've already arrived at the studio car park.

It's like being in a dark room, then realizing you've been wearing sunglasses and finally taking them off. Something shifting into place, clearer and sharper than before. A little anchor settling in my chest to ground me; something to finally make sense of *me*.

'Well,' I say at last. 'Okay then.'

Cerys is chewing on her lip, eyes wide. 'I really thought you knew! I'm SO sorry, I didn't mean to out you – or dump this on you when you're about to have your big showdown moment with Callum! I'm so sorry, Nis.'

'You will be, when I have to explain to my parents that not only have I been sneaking around snogging a sort-of famous actor, but I also think we've finally figured out why I am the way I am.'

Cerys smiles warmly, and nudges me with her elbow. 'We wouldn't have you any other way.'

*

Cerys is the one who knows the drill for filming today since I called in 'sick' earlier this week (for obvious reasons) and she leads the way. Today's scene involves the rebels being ambushed at the tavern by Oscar, Kai and a swarm of palace guards, all led there after one of Kai's visions.

It's going to be a big, dramatic bust-up scene and part of the season six finale, and I can't wait to watch it unfold properly when the episode finally airs. There have even been rumours about a main character death that everyone on set is keeping tightly under wraps.

Walking to the tavern, I'm prepared for a fight – on all fronts.

Obviously, I'm not going to barge in and interrupt filming and scream in Callum's face about how he broke my heart and betrayed me, how dare he, etc., etc., but I'll corner him once the cameras are off – even if it's just to get him to agree to talk to me properly later.

He owes me that much.

I *deserve* that much.

Cerys grabs my hand as we get nearer, squeezing it tight. I file away our conversation in the car to deal with later; compartmentalizing like that is one of my strengths after all. There's the sound of shouting and raised voices – too muffled to make out the words – but I can hear Brayden Brown; Daxys must really be gunning for his former brothers-in-arms he used to fight alongside when he was in the palace guard during the early seasons . . .

But when we get inside, it's not the brawl we're expecting to see.

Callum's stood in the middle of the room, ignoring the cameras. He's tearful and shouting, 'I'M SO SICK OF THIS! I'm so sick of you always insisting you know what's best for me!'

Cerys gasps; I'm busy gawping. What is happening right now?

'Listen, kid –' Richie approaches him, hand outstretched, and Brayden Brown gets in between them, rebuffing Callum's manager with his sheer size and bulk. With his arms crossed over his barrel chest, his full leather armour costume, and the massive Greater Fae wings he wears as Daxys, he looks *terrifying*.

'How many times has he got to tell you to back off, huh? And *stop* talking down to him like that. Calling him "kid" like he's five years old. He's old enough to speak for himself, Richie.'

Cerys tugs on my hand, drawing me further into the room, closer to the unfolding drama. The crew have formed a wide circle around the scene, and the director and chief make-up artist look at each other, unsure if they should intervene.

A muscle twitches in Richie's jaw, before he says, 'This doesn't involve you, Brayden, as I've told *you* before. I'm responsible for Callum –'

The woman who plays Lady Adanna lets out a scoff of disbelief that's half a shriek. 'Oh yeah, *so* bloody responsible, leaving him to fend for himself most of the time! His parents trust you to look after him, and you're never there! Too busy rubbing your hands together trying to make more gold appear!'

'Stay out of this, Sienna,' Richie barks, all semblance of charm vanishing now as he scowls at her. 'Callum is *my* nephew –'

'Exactly! But you treat him like he's only your *client*,' she snaps. 'If you cared about him at all, you'd actually *be* there for him.'

'Oh my God,' Cerys breathes, and my jaw's on the floor, too. The resemblance is suddenly obvious: they have the same stocky build, the same facial structure. No wonder Callum said it was so complicated. He even *said*, before, Richie was family – I just assumed he meant it in the same way he called the cast his family.

Prince Oscar moves forward, then, too. He's got a fake cut on his cheek and a blood spatter artfully painted across his face, like he's beheaded someone. He claps a gloved hand on Callum's shoulder. 'We've all had to put up with your bullshit for months, Richie.

Everyone can see the toll it's taking on Cal, and the pressure you're putting him under. It's not on.'

Callum, in the midst of it, looks pale even beneath his Kai make-up, but he squares his shoulders and sets his jaw as he stares Richie down, bolstered by the support. I've seen all the actors joking between takes or hanging out together near their trailers, but this is the first time I've realized how true it is: they *are* family.

Richie scoffs, turning in a half-circle back and forth like this is all a huge joke and the cast are going to surrender with awkward smiles any second. But, with nobody to back him up, his grin looks a bit frayed around the edges and there's sweat visible at his hairline.

Callum takes a step forward. 'Maybe we should roll the cameras for posterity, so you can be sure of *exactly what I say*. I don't *want* to keep acting. I don't *want* these auditions you're finding for me or the roles you keep pushing me towards. You even manipulated everything I said in that Deadline interview to try and make the fans hate me so much I'd get kicked off this show!'

'Well, that's not –'

'Don't lie to me! I *want* to stay here on OWAR and *then* I want to go to university. I want to be a normal fucking kid, Richie! I want to get drunk on bad cider at a house party and have to decide between video games or homework and I want to *write*! I want to learn how to make something like this!' He gestures around him. 'I don't want to *be* this person you're turning me into! And I want to date a cute, funny girl and for it not to all blow up in my face because *you* think it's a bad look for my career!'

(Wait, am *I* the cute, funny girl? This is too much.)

Richie laughs, but it's a nervous sound. He runs a hand over his hair, the agitated action weirdly Callum-esque, and then smiles and holds his palms out in a very *non*-Callum-esque way. It makes him look every bit the slimeball they're accusing him of being. Brayden cracks his neck ominously and Lady Adanna – Sienna – glowers at Richie furiously enough that she might actually turn him to dust right where he stands.

'I know what you did,' Callum presses on, shouting to talk over whatever paltry defence Richie is cooking up. 'Anissa's friend told me all about the DM you sent her from my account, and that phone call you made. Trying to pay her off to leave the show. To leave *me* alone. Because *you* think she's not good enough. Nobody asked you, Richie! Nobody!'

Brayden drops his arms slightly, looking back at Callum before turning a glare on Richie. 'Sorry. You tried to bribe Anissa? Are you kidding me? You *scumbag*.'

'She's just some kid!' Richie protests.

'Just another reason that's so messed up!' Sienna explodes. 'Do you even hear yourself right now?'

Sweat pools around Richie's temples. 'It's not like she does anything *important* here, is it? She's not an actress! She's just set design –'

'Oh, that's charming that is,' Lisa pipes up. 'Did you hear that, Danielle? *Just set design*. Glad to know we're so valued.'

Danielle Poulter, lead set designer, steps out from the other side of the crowd and looks at Richie like he's an annoying bit of Blu Tack stuck on a velvet curtain. 'That girl's got more talent in her little finger than you've ever shown in your life, Richie. Next time you try to bribe my staff – *don't*!'

Cerys squeals quietly at my ear, 'Ohmigod, Danielle Poulter *knows who you are*. She thinks you're talented!'

'I should hope she knows who we are – we've been here long enough,' I whisper back. Still, it *is* nice to hear that the crew have *my* back as well as Callum's.

My face is warm, and my stomach feels fizzy. It's weird hearing people talk about me when they don't know I'm there – and it being *good*. I'm not even sure how to process it. It sort of makes me want to run away, but I also want to bottle it up to remember forever.

'Richie,' Callum says at last, 'I don't know how else to say this: you're fired.'

Richie's laugh echoes through the set. 'You can't fire me, kid. Your parents signed a contract. Look, I'm sorry, you're right. Maybe I didn't handle this in the *best* way, but you're overreacting. We can sort this out, yeah? And then –'

'Did he stutter?' Brayden says.

Sienna says in a sweet voice, 'Don't worry, Richie. We're *more* than happy to talk to Callum's parents and make sure they understand the situation.'

The director comes forward then, clearing his throat, and a sound behind us makes me and Cerys look over to see a few of the security guards approaching the fray.

'You've disturbed my set for long enough, Richie; it's time you were on your way. I'll be speaking to Callum's parents, too, and letting security know you're no longer welcome. Can't have disgruntled ex-staff harassing my actors, can I? So I suggest you run along, before I have to call the police.'

It all happens in slow motion, like a movie scene. The blood draining from Richie's face, leaving him looking sickly and small under all the heavy-duty lighting. The way he slopes away, and the way Callum is swarmed with hugs and claps on the back and people telling him how proud they are of him.

And the way the crowd seems to part, just for a second, in exactly the right place, so that Callum's eyes can meet mine.

CHAPTER 36

The director heaves a long sigh, kneading his knuckles between his bushy eyebrows. He shares a look with Callum, who nods once, looking smaller – younger – than usual. Only a teenager, not some sort-of famous actor.

'Alright, everyone,' the director shouts to the room. 'Why don't we take ten? And then I want you *back* on your marks!'

The crowd disperses all at once, while some of the core group cluster a bit closer around Callum. Several people notice me as they leave, nudging their colleagues. But for once, I don't mind if they are talking about me.

Danielle and Lisa are chatting away together as they leave, but Danielle catches sight of me and stops, changing direction to lead the pair of them towards us instead.

Cerys goes rigid. 'Oh my God. If I start to fangirl, please just knock me out before I humiliate myself.'

'Anissa, there you are,' Danielle says. She has a broad Yorkshire accent and projects her voice loudly. Her all-black outfit looks incredibly chic – if you ignore the paint stains and stray threads all over it. 'Lisa said you'd been off all week. I hope that arsehole hasn't put you off working here?'

'Um, I mean . . .' I pull the resignation letter I wrote using a Google template out of my tote bag. The envelope is all crinkled. 'I was going to resign . . .'

Lisa's face falls. 'Obviously we can't stop you, if that's what you want, but I hope you know Richie's views don't reflect the rest of the team's. We've loved having you on set design. You've done such a brilliant job.'

'You really have.' Danielle smiles at me. It feels a bit like my favourite teacher putting a sticker in my homework planner; I don't hate it. 'It's been wonderful to have someone on the team who truly understands the spirit of what we're trying to do here, the story we're telling and the world we're building.'

'Th-thank you! Yeah, I . . . I mean, I do really love it.'

'Excellent! Well, then, if you don't mind . . .' Danielle gently takes the envelope off me, rips it neatly in two, then hands it back with a wink. 'We'll carry on seeing you around, in that case. Oh, and it's Cerys, isn't it? The make-up department have been trying to steal you away from us, haven't they?'

'Yes!' Cerys squeaks. She clears her throat, then adds in a very low, deep voice, '*Yes.*'

I snicker, ducking my head to hide the laugh.

'Can't say I blame them. Your work is *wonderful.*' Danielle grins. 'If you're ever looking for a more permanent job, just say the word. And if you're ever in need of references, either of you, please do feel free to use me.'

She leaves and Cerys yells, 'We will! I – thank you!' then practically melts in a puddle next to me.

I laugh, taking Cerys's arm to keep her upright. 'You okay there?'

'I think I just had an out-of-body experience.' She bites her lip. 'Was I as embarrassing as you were when we met Callum?'

'Oh, *no*, nowhere near it . . .'

Cerys rolls her eyes, smiling. 'Alright, then, come on. Time to go get your man.'

This time, the crowd surrounding Callum is a lot smaller and tighter. There are a few of his fellow cast members, one of the executive producers and the director, all of whom seem concerned about him, and half of whom are tapping away on their phones with angry, focused scowls. Presumably to blacklist Richie or contact Callum's parents, or something.

Brayden notices us coming over and peels away from the group. 'Alright, ladies? How are we doing? Anissa, you all good? Right bloody mess that scumbag got you in.'

'Er – yeah, I'm . . . um . . .'

'Listen, I've got a really good PR team. Sienna uses them, too. If you like, I can talk to them about this, get them to do something to clear it all up? Say Richie was just inventing the relationship to get Callum some clout, and you had nothing to do with it, or something.'

'They can do that?'

'It's hardly stretching the truth, is it? I'll give you their number, and let them know to keep an eye out for you. And if any journalists come knocking, you give them a call, okay? They'll help.'

Sienna comes over then, smiling broadly. 'I'll let them know, too. This really isn't fair on you or Callum – it's disgusting Richie dragged you into it at all. I'm so sorry.'

Oh my God, Lady Adanna di Silver is talking to me. Looking out for me! Being nice and friendly and lovely! To me!

I swallow a small scream. 'Thank you. That really means a lot.'

'Course!' Brayden exclaims. 'We look out for our own here.'

Sienna winks at me, and I almost pass out entirely. 'Until the end.'

Then Brayden shouts, 'Come on you lot – what about that coffee break? Let's give these lovebirds a minute, yeah?'

'*Four* of them, to be exact,' the director mutters, none too quietly, with a pointed look at his watch. But he gives me a polite enough smile as he walks out, and I notice Cerys getting swept up with Sienna and Brayden, looking giddy as they include her in their conversation.

Jake and Max will have a field day when they hear about this.

And then it's just me and Callum, surrounded by cameras and lighting rigs and boom mics and a bunch of people trying hard not to eavesdrop as they carry on with their jobs.

I swallow, hard.

Callum clears his throat.

'I didn't –'

'I had no idea –'

'Sorry, you go.'

'No, you first.'

'I only wanted to say –'

'It's just that –'

We both falter and exchange awkward smiles. Callum gestures for me to go first, and I realize that all the stuff I wanted to say to him to get closure, to tell him off and stand up for myself, is useless now.

So I end up blurting out, 'I only came here to tell them I was resigning.'

He baulks. 'Did you ... did you take Richie's money?'

'What? No! After your Instagram message, I just thought it'd be best if –'

'I didn't send it,' he tells me, the words tripping off his tongue so fast they almost merge into one. He steps closer. 'Richie has ... *had* access to all my socials. That's how he knew I was meeting up with you. He leaked everything to that TikToker, even the photo of us at the park – he took it. He leaked my exam results, too, assuming I'd blame it on you. He thought there was something going on between us and wanted to shut it down. You weren't a "good look for my career".'

Callum looks irate, spitting the words as he repeats them. '*He* sent you that message and blocked you. But then I couldn't find our messages and assumed *you'd* blocked me because of the whole video thing ... I'm so sorry, Anissa. I never should have ... I'm so sorry.'

I'm too stunned to speak, the explanation making sense of so many of our arguments. It makes sense of *everything*, even his sanitized Instagram posts.

'Then your friend Nikita started spamming me with comments to get my attention. She DM'd me to say he phoned you and tried to bribe you to stay away – and how he acted like it was my idea, too . . .'

'Nikita?'

Callum smirks. 'She's kind of terrifying. I can see why you're friends. She seems like a great person to have in your corner.'

I feel a rush of affection towards Nikita that's new, and lovely. I'd so misjudged her. 'Yeah, she really is, actually.'

'I'm sorry everything got so out of hand. I saw some of the comments people left on your fanfics. It was out of line. I didn't know how to shut it down without making things worse for you, and –'

'No! No – it's alright, honestly. I get it.' And I really do. If he'd waded in, he probably would've only stoked the fire and made it a thousand times worse. 'But you . . . didn't send that message, after . . . after we kissed in the park?'

'Of course I didn't! I thought we were ... that you . . .' He blushes, and scrubs a hand along the back of his neck.

'I thought so too,' I say softly.

'Yeah?'

'Yeah.'

'We could . . . I mean, we could, er . . .' He's blushing. Blushing! Over me! I could scream. 'We could go on a proper date somewhere, if you like? Something normal. The cinema, or bowling?'

I grin. 'I'd like that.'

Callum beams, his whole face lighting up, and the breath he exhales seems to release so much tension; I can see his body visibly relax.

The room starts filling back up. Our time's almost up.

'You know, I meant all those things I said, even if I didn't exactly say them *to* you. I do really like you,' I blurt. I barely hear the words over the cacophony of noise as people take their marks back on set, my heartbeat roaring in my ears.

Callum laughs. 'How unfortunate for you. You want to be careful, Anissa. A guy could fall for you with lines like that.'

I blush, and he darts in close to kiss my cheek, near the corner of my mouth. My eyes close, and for a split second that stretches on for eons, we just stand there, holding hands, his body against mine. When he finally moves back, our pinkie fingers stay linked.

'Will you stick around? So we can talk after this scene? Maybe we can arrange that second date?'

'Careful,' I warn him, jokingly. 'A girl could fall for you with lines like that.'

As the director calls everyone back to their marks, Callum Denver winks at me. 'Here's hoping.'

EPILOGUE

Birds chirp overhead and golden sunlight falls in dappled patches on the long, thick grass. I pick a nearby dandelion and blow on it, making a wish and watching the fluffy white seeds drift lazily away.

I smile to myself. I'm surrounded by friends, with a long and glorious summer stretching out ahead of us, and I feel more certain of myself than ever. The greatest adventure of our lives is behind us; we can finally let go of the stress and worry we've been carrying for the last several months and enjoy this next chapter, whatever it brings.

I recline back in the grass, my head pillowed on a strong thigh while a hand cards tenderly through my hair. The sound of my friends chatting washes over me pleasantly.

Suddenly there's an almighty *CRASH!* of wood

splintering, horses neighing, someone swearing loudly, and a small explosion.

I sit up abruptly and Prince Kai leaps to his feet, sword drawn. 'What in the blazes was *that*?'

Across our clearing in the Gilded Glade, the Moonwalker sighs before standing, drawing his own blade in readiness. 'Nothing good I'd wager, Mida.'

I take it back: the greatest adventure of our lives might be only just beginning . . .

Jake sniffles loudly and Cerys leans against him, wiping a stray tear from her eye. Max gives a shaky exhale as he closes his faithful notebook he uses during all our TTRPG sessions, and he lays his hand flat over the cover, staring blankly ahead for a moment.

'Shit, Anissa, how do you *do* that?' Nikita says, leaning back in her chair to blink furiously at the ceiling and clear the tears from her eyes. 'You've even got me going.'

I laugh, but it's wobbly; I'm feeling just as affected as the rest of them – it was *so* hard to keep it together for this final session of our campaign. None of us want it to end, of course, and I've got plenty of ideas for our next storyline using some pre-existing villains from the official *Of Wrath and Roll* handbook, but we're not under any illusions.

In only a few weeks, we'll all be scattered across the country and focusing on what's next; devoting ourselves to weekly meet-ups – even virtual ones – to play our TTRPG won't be so easy as it is now.

It's hard, letting go.

It's exhilarating, knowing there's still so much to come.

Beside me, Callum captures my hand in his and lifts it to his mouth, brushing a kiss across my knuckles. 'That was a really beautiful last session, Nis. Thank you.'

'It's bloody alright for you,' Jake exclaims, his voice thick. 'You don't have to let go of *your* character! You've still got years to play Prince Kai before you have to say goodbye!'

'This isn't goodbye, though,' I say. 'It's just . . . *see you later*.'

'Don't,' Cerys cries with half a wail and half a laugh. 'I really can't bear to think about saying bye to you guys properly.'

It didn't feel quite so real until a couple of days ago, when we all got our final A-level results and official uni decisions. (Which, funnily enough, coincided with my official ADHD diagnosis. Dad put it on the fridge alongside my results; Mum made a really lopsided cake and some virgin 'neuro-spicy margaritas' to celebrate.)

Cerys is staying in Cardiff; Danielle's helped her get a proper job at Red Wings Studios and, even though filming on OWAR has wrapped for a little while, she's decided to pursue some qualifications to help her get a leg up in the industry instead of going to uni.

Max is going furthest away, to Manchester for an engineering degree, but he and Cerys have such a solid relationship, I'm not the least bit worried about them. Even if they do argue every now and then.

Nikita, Daphne and Jake will all be at Exeter Uni, and Evie's taking a gap year before heading to Bristol. Chloe's own gap year is a lot more indefinite: she's moving to London properly with her auntie to pursue her flourishing career as a streamer and influencer.

And I'll be starting a creative writing course at Swansea Uni in a few weeks. I've never been particularly *excited* about school before, but I am excited about this. Plus, it's not too far from home or Cerys that I can't visit often. My parents are equal parts proud and devastated – you'd think I was moving to the other side of the world, but I've promised to still make time to watch *MAFS Australia* with them. Nan's already making plans to come back from Ireland to visit, too.

And I won't be too far from Callum, either, who's staying in Cardiff but taking a part-time online course in screenwriting and film production. It's ideal for him to carry on filming OWAR while also pursuing what he *actually* wants to do with his life.

They've even let him into the OWAR writers' room on set in a more official capacity as sort of work experience, now they know he's not just meddling with their scripts for the sake of it. And Callum's well rid of his horrible agent, too: Uncle Richie moved to LA, where he's apparently having zero success. Callum's dad got a job here to be around for Callum, and his mum's been visiting more often on weekends.

On other weekends he spends a lot of time with me and my family, and he even started playing with Jake and Max on their football team. Brayden Brown took it upon himself to become their assistant coach.

(Jake's never simultaneously played worse *and* scored more goals in any given match in his life. It's kind of hilarious to watch, and his now-official boyfriend, Teddy, thinks his crush on the actor is totally 'adorkable'.)

We all linger at the table in the cafe for a little while, nobody quite ready to officially wrap up our adventure. But eventually we do, bit by bit. Dice rattle as they're packed away, papers rustle as character sheets are tucked neatly, lovingly, back into bags, and chairs scrape as we leave the table one by one.

Nikita goes first, off to meet up with the other girls for a bit. Then Jake, whose parents are taking him shopping for some bits and bobs for uni. The rest of us walk outside together, Cerys hand in hand with Max, and me and Callum side by side.

'We'll see you guys tomorrow,' Cerys says, pausing near the door. 'Still on for bowling?'

'Wouldn't miss it,' I promise, and we hug tightly. It's so silly, how fragile these final few weeks of summer feel, but really, I think, it just proves how important we've all become to each other. And even though it's bittersweet, I know that this is what true friendship is – and I wouldn't change it for anything in the world.

We wave Max and Cerys off, then turn in the opposite direction to get the bus back to mine.

Callum slings his arm around my shoulders as we walk and it settles there, an easy, comfortable weight that I sink into.

It's just like all the books promised; every cliché I've ever read in fanfiction. It makes me truly appreciate every domestic fluff piece I've ever read. Because it *is* beautiful, knowing that I have this person who sees all of me, who understands me so completely and who knows all the messy parts and helps bring out all the good ones, too. It's not so much like finding half of my soul, or like he completes some part of me, it's more like this absolute sense of comfort and peace when he is there.

And the reality is *so* much better than the fantasy.

I tug Callum to a stop, and draw him in for a kiss.

His mouth curves into a smile against mine, and my heart skips a beat.

It is, still, incandescent.

ACKNOWLEDGEMENTS

One for the chronically online, the fandom-obsessed, and the resident weird kids ... This book is such a big part of me, and was such a joy to write!

Of course, we've got to kick off the acknowledgements with an ode to my very own TTRPG group: the hivE (née Gobble Gals), with our wildly irregular D&D sessions filled with bartender Svens, accidentally adopted dragons, and a very murderous turkey. Hugest of thank yous for always rooting for me and my stories, whatever shape they take!

To Lauren – fellow fanfic devotee and forever my sounding board, I owe you my sanity some days. (Most days.) To Aimee – the *Doctor Who* references are specially for you, thank you for always being a fellow fangirl! To Amy, my fellow lover of chronically online nonsense. To George – this will make a FABULOUS edition to your Beth shrine (I mean, shelf) among your crafting goodies. For the Physics gang and the Cluster – my fellow nerds, always and forever. I love you guys wherever in the world we are! Roll for initiative! And to IJ, for the regular supplies of tea during edits, thanks for keeping me smiling through the deadline stress cycles!

Thanks as always to my family for all your support – and K, if you like this one as much as DYSI, we might make a fangirl of you yet!

And no acknowledgements section is complete without a truly MASSIVE thank you to the entire team behind the scenes! Katie – thank you SO much for believing in my fangirls! They wouldn't exist without you! Thanks also to Awo, Jess, Katy, my fantastic agent, Clare, and the rest of the team at PRH.

IF YOU ENJOYED

FOR REAL THIS TIME

WHY NOT READ MORE ROMANCE BY BETH REEKLES?

THE KISSING BOOTH

When Elle decides to run a kissing booth for the school carnival, she never imagines she'll sit in it – or that her first ever kiss would be with bad boy Noah.

From that moment, her life is turned upside down – but is this a romance destined for happiness or heartbreak?

THE BEACH HOUSE

Elle is now officially dating hotter-than-hot Noah – it's amazing, but with Noah leaving for Harvard at the end of the summer their future is unknown.

Meanwhile Elle and Lee have always been BFFs, but can everything stay the same with Lee's new girlfriend, Rachel, on the scene – and with Elle now dating Lee's big brother?

Can Elle have one last perfect summer with her two favourite boys?

GOING THE DISTANCE

Elle seems to have finally tamed hotter-than-hot bad boy Noah Flynn, but now they're facing a new challenge. Noah's three thousand miles away at Harvard, and they're officially a long-distance couple.

Then she sees Noah getting friendly with another girl online, and a new cute boy at school shows interest in Elle.

With her heart on the line, what's a girl to do?

ONE LAST TIME

It's the summer before college and Elle needs to make a difficult decision: go to Harvard to be with boyfriend, Noah, or Berkeley as originally planned with best friend, Lee.

Back at the beach house, Elle and Lee find a bucket list they wrote as kids, and it's a great distraction. She's determined to make this the best summer ever, before everything has to change.

But in the end will she choose love or friendship?

THE SUMMER SWITCH-OFF

Loved The Kissing Booth? Why not try *The Summer Switch-Off*, a hilarious summer must-read from Beth Reekles.

Solo travellers Luna, Rory and Jodie arrive at Casa Dorada in desperate need of a relaxing holiday.

Luna's relationship just ended, and it feels like her old school friends are ghosting her . . .

Rory lives for posting her art on social media, something her sensible family just don't get . . .

And **Jodie's** life is great on paper, but she's exhausted from trying to keep up with her friends.

When the idyllic resort turns out to be a digital detox retreat – no phones, no internet – no one knows what to do. But with zero distractions, maybe this will be a summer the girls won't forget . . .

SINCERELY YOURS, ANNA SHERWOOD

Romance was not supposed to be on the agenda . . .

Annalise Sherwood has worked hard to get a place on a prestigious internship programme, and nothing is going to stop her now. She figures one night letting her hair down won't hurt, though – especially when it ends with the best kiss of her life.

But to Anna's horror, the owner of the mystery kiss turns out to be Lloyd, the company CEO's son. And from the moment they meet again, he rubs Anna up the wrong way.

But when a lot of late-night working brings them unexpectedly closer, she begins to wonder if there's more to him than she originally thought . . .

DO YOU SHIP IT?

Shipping: the desire by followers of a fandom for two people (either in real-life or fiction) to be in a romantic relationship

When Cerys's best friend and secret crush Jake moves to a new college, she realizes she's running out of time to take their relationship from platonic to romantic. She'll do anything to get out of Jake's friendzone, even if that means diving into the huge fantasy fandom he loves so much.

But when Jake introduces Cerys to his shiny new friend Max, who goes to all the conventions and loves a costume, she realizes she'll need to do a lot more to grab Jake's attention than just read a few fanfics.

Can Cerys convince Jake they should become the new couple to ship? Or will he see straight through her cosplay?